GW00459103

LIMBO GIRL

JUNE BURNETT

Blond & Briggs

First published in Great Britain 1980 by
Blond & Briggs Limited, London NW2 6LE

British Library Cataloguing in Publication Data

Burnett, June
Limbo girl.
I. Title
823'.9'1F PR6052.U65/

ISBN 0-85634-102-9

Typeset by Texet, Leighton Buzzard, Bedfordshire
Printed in Great Britain by
Biddles Ltd., Guildford, Surrey

To
Philip Burnett

Acknowledgments and thanks to
Jean Drumer
Sheila Thompson
Anthony Blond
Desmond Briggs

ONE

Connie Marlowe arrived on the spine-chilling doorstep of her aunts' house in Hesketh Street. In that rundown area, the house, from the outside, was impeccable. Fussy George Washington style curtains flounced at the windows and the brickwork had recently been cleaned with red tile polish. There was no sign of life in the street. The other houses, neatly terraced to the crown of the dusky hill, stared balefully back at her. Connie peered through the narrow, mock-leaded light that decorated the middle of the front door and knocked on it gently with a small, clenched fist.

She heard noises for some time before anyone came. Pink and dull red shapes moved behind the mottled glass. At last the door opened like a bright red mouth exhaling the warm breath of the interior.

Aunt Beatrice stood in the frame of the door, and welcomed Connie with cold hands attached to arms that disappeared into the short sleeves of a pink angora jumper like the twisted roots of an arthritic tree.

'Hello, Auntie,' said Connie lightly, shifting her chewing gum into a convenient position for speaking. 'It's O.K., isn't it? Mum told you I was coming, didn't she?' Connie rushed out the words as she squeezed past the thickened body of her aunt in the narrow hallway.

'Of course it is, my love, you know you are always welcome,' Beatrice told her, pausing to poke an unruly wisp of hair back into her carefully arranged nest of ginger curls with a finger reminiscent of a gryphon's claw. Aunt Beatrice followed Connie into the living-room saying, 'Your Auntie Rachel should be back soon. She had to go out for a few moments to see someone. She won't be long really.' Beatrice spoke past the stump of a dead cigarette in the corner of her uncompromisingly large mouth which, at one stage in the day, had been painted a livid shade of violet. Now the colour had been smudged on to the dark pancake make-up of a hairy upper lip.

Connie liked Beatrice the less of her two unmarried aunts. Beatrice was sixty and the elder by ten years, and her many trials and illnesses could be charted in the lines under her eyes, which looked like the powdered underside of a gecko. However, Connie had always felt sympathetic towards her and was amazed at the quiet way she moved around the house in spite of her large, ungainly body. Beatrice's eyes had, in her youth, been her most striking feature. Now they were looking back at her niece, pale, large and grey-violet. Connie had often remarked, much to Rachel's chagrin, that Aunt Beatrice must have been beautiful when she was a girl. Now there was nothing left but the large eyes to indicate the one-time marble beauty and smooth-cheeked poise that lay trapped inside the fading photograph album on the window shelf.

Beatrice removed the defunct cigarette from her dried lips and said, 'Rachel will be pleased to see you, dear.' Then, putting the stained, fibrous butt into a glass ashtray on the brass table at her side, she rose and went into the small kitchen to make tea. Connie snuggled into the big armchair and looked at the crimson caverns in the banked-up fire.

Connie knew this house well. It was where she had been dumped by her mother in times of stress since early childhood. There was a frightening finality about this particular occasion. Connie had not wanted to renew her acquaintance with her two middle-aged aunts, but she had been summarily dispatched by her mother and her new young husband. There had been no place for Connie in their vision of a new future filled with G-plan furniture and little glass knick-knacks on the teak veneer shelves of their fitted bedroom. She had seen her mother in the yard, bent over the dustbin, stirring the remains of burning photographs of her father. The half-consumed pictures sank and rippled into fine pale ash. She had watched her mother's final act of separation with restrained bitterness. She could shed no tears. She watched, purposefully trying to imprint the memory of him. It was important to her to be able to conjure him protected in her mind.

Connie knew that her father and mother had loved each other as much as most ordinary couples, at least in the beginning. However, the last few years had proved too much for their already fragile marriage. Her mother had bravely suffered the sneers of fringe relatives and the occasional mad local shopkeeper who, with barely suppressed rudeness, would serve the young couple truculently and without speaking. When Connie had arrived and been pushed forth proudly in her coach-built pram, neighbours would sometimes whisper behind-hand remarks such as 'They're born white, but they go black when they grow up, you know' or, 'Isn't it disgusting, a nice white girl like that. She must have been hard up.' Remarks like these, made just within earshot, had, over the years, picked away at the cement of her parents' bonding. The locusts had stripped away their love, and her father had killed himself. He had been found hanging by his belt in the boiler-room of the tannery where he worked. Connie tried to imagine him hanging from the disconnected pipe like a ripe brown fruit, his calm, delicate features inherited from a Scots mother, and the hooded dark eyes, and skin like clear cast bronze from his black, West Indian father. He had not survived the ordeal of his life.

Connie had been brought up by her maternal grandmother, and, as far as the old lady was concerned, had been blessed with a fair skin and light eyes. Only her hair, which grew glossy and abundant, had the nerve, in spite of her grandmother's constant training, plaiting and pomading with de-kinking creams, to proclaim the fact the she had a 'touch of the tar brush'. Connie smiled as she remembered her grandmother's insistence on trying to obliterate her father's memory, and her attempts to make Connie believe that her existence was a mistake due to her mother's foolish failing that was shrouded in a mystery as defensive as parthenogenesis.

Connie could hear Beatrice moving slowly in the kitchen making Argentinian tea. There were strange smells in this house that existed nowhere else Connie had ever been — not just the slightly stale smell of old-fashioned perfume on middle-aged bodies, but something she could not put her finger on. Something lay festering sweetly somewhere in a glass-stoppered jar sealed with pink wax.

She recalled the last time she had stayed with Rachel and Beatrice seeing the door of the large Victorian wardrobe which stood on the landing swing noiselessly open, just as she had been about to close her bedroom door. It was an invitation she could not resist. Both her aunts were out and would never know. The wardrobe had been for years forbidden territory, and the prospect of exploring it excited her. Inside were eight exquisitely made rosewood drawers, each with its own individual, countersunk brass handle. Connie remembered putting out felon's fingers to grasp the sunken lip of the first handle to pull it slowly and smoothly towards her. She had had no idea of what she might find, perhaps some old lavender bags between layers of yellowing tissue paper where her aunts' winter clothes lived. No, that was the first time she had noticed the peculiar smell. The drawer had widened to show a smooth white cloth. She had peeled this back to reveal yet another piece of white linen that she could see had narrow sections sewn into it with different coloured cottons. Inside these many pockets were rows of surgical instruments. Fine, needle-pointed scalpels of many sizes, and syringes. All had glittered in the dull light of the fly-spotted Tiffany lampshade. Once she had trespassed into the wardrobe it had become easier to open the other drawers. The next had been full of rubber tubing and glass funnels. In the remaining drawers she had seen small glass bottles of clear fluid sealed with plastic-covered cork, more syringes and a few chipped kidney dishes. Each item had been individually wrapped in tissue paper and covered with a clean, starched cloth. Her imagination had strained to allocate a possible function to each new discovery as she examined it. Eventually she had replaced them all exactly as she had found them, covered them with the white cloths and slid the drawers back to their waxed security. If her aunts ever did discover her evening's voyaging into wardrobe country, it was never mentioned. Like her reasons for staying with them, it was a topic that was avoided.

Aunt Beatrice emerged from the kitchen holding a bowl of hot, sickly-sweet brew and sucking it noisily through a silver straw inserted through a hole in the side. She sat down in an armchair opposite Connie. Her dyed ginger hair, appearing more unkempt by the minute, stood out from her head in small thin curls, as more clips and pins shook loose. Connie thought she looked like a satiric Statue of Liberty, and buried her nose into the crook of her arm to prevent a giggle escaping.

'Want some tea, love?' said Beatrice, proffering the tannin-stained silver straw and smiling just enough to show a smear of lipstick on her otherwise surprisingly white teeth.

Connie smiled back, shook her head in mock distaste and said, 'No thanks, Auntie. It's not my time to die.' They both laughed.

Connie was more amused at her aunt's high-pitched giggle, which, as now, she often appeared to produce from a hat in response to the most unfunny jokes. Beatrice's large, unfettered breasts jiggled around underneath the pink angora jumper like two eggs in a hankie. Every now and again, between bursts of laughter, she would clutch at one with her hand as if to restrain it in its mad dancing. Her knees jerked upwards, straining the good, thick green tweed of her skirt.

'Oh, it is good to have you here with us again, dear, you always manage to make us laugh.' Beatrice, gasping, stopped her performance to speak. She went on, this time more quietly and with a hint of amusement still in her voice, her lips pursed in small, fluted creases. 'I do wish Rachel would come home. It's late now and I think you're as tired as me, aren't you?'

Connie nodded, as Beatrice extended her large hands towards her. Understanding the request, Connie pulled her aunt up from the jaws of her easy chair. Beatrice stood on her thin shaky legs that looked as though they had been built from an erector set. Beatrice confided, 'It isn't always easy with your Aunt Rachel, you know, dear. Sometimes she gets very cross with me, almost for nothing.' She stared down at her shoes like a suddenly regressed eight-year-old, twisting the corner of her pale blue hankie. She went on, 'She doesn't trust me you know, and she positively hates Mr. McKenna.'

'Who's Mr. McKenna, Auntie?' asked Connie, suppressing a wave of laughter, and, at the same time, attempting to look at Beatrice's face underneath the cloud of red hair.

Beatrice looked up at her niece and said proudly, 'Mr. McKenna, dear, is the gardener at the Conservative Club. We play bridge at his house in Sefton Park every other Sunday evening. Sometimes we persuade him to play the piano too. He's a lovely touch and can play anything you ask.'

Connie said wickedly, 'You want to get him to give you a number from the Sex Pistols, Auntie,' and then stopped short, realising that perhaps she had gone too far.

Beatrice scowled but not too fiercely. 'Now dear, don't be dirty. It doesn't suit you.' Then, with a kindlier frown, she picked up her empty tea-bowl and walked soundlessly out of the living-room and its dying fire. Connie could hear her washing the dishes and putting things away with her awkward hands.

Connie called through to Beatrice, 'Shall we go to bed soon, Auntie? I don't think Auntie Rachel will be back tonight somehow, do you?' Beatrice came to the door of the kitchen, stretched up an arm like an orang-utan and pulled the light cord.

'Yes, dear, we may as well go now. I suppose she is making a night of it,' she said, her purple lips easing into a tired smile. She wiped her long spatulate fingers on a clean dish-cloth and patted it out on the Dimplex radiator behind the door. 'I do wish we had a telephone, they're so useful at times like these, aren't they, Connie? Especially when Rachel decides to stay out on the tiles all night. She does it quite often now, you know.'

Connie pushed the shape back into an ancient cushion and hit the crumpled newspaper behind it out of the way. 'Anyway, Auntie,' Connie said, 'I'm dead beat, so if you don't mind,' she yawned, 'I'll go up now. Same bedroom is it?'

'Yes, dear,' her aunt lazily said, affected by Connie's yawn. 'You remember where everything is, don't you? There are plenty of clean towels in the big cupboard in your room.'

Connie was already on her way out of the room. 'Good-night, Auntie,' she slurred over her shoulder. Somewhere at the back of her head she could hear her aunt's voice drain away in the peculiar quiet that surrounded her, from lips already handicapped by yet another cigarette.

Connie entered the small, pink-painted bedroom and looked around. Nothing had changed. There was the same old-fashioned, pink and gold wallpaper. The same pale pink, sun-bleached, damask curtains with the fleur-de-lis design. The dove-grey dressing-table which had passed its prime in 1940 sat in the same corner sporting the same pink duchess set. On this lay the familiar, silver-backed hairbrush and its companion mirror. The hand mirror was cracked but Connie had always been fascinated by the strangely wrought designs on its back, in thinly beaten silver. The centre was polished until the wood had worn right through in the highest places. Round the sides were exotic fruits and flowers which undulated on the flat surface to which they were forever bound. She had often sat before the mirror and brushed out her long hair, pretending to be some great lady or other. She kept her eyes closed as if she were blind, trying to memorise the pattern. Satisfying herself with the touch of these familiar things, she opened her eyes and began to take off her old school cardigan. The sleeves, which were meant to fit snugly at the wrists, were, as she had grown so much in her last term at school, halfway between her wrists and her elbows. Her mother had not seen fit to get her a new one, or to help her let out the grey pinafore dress that she had worn in her last year at Colclough Street Secondary Modern School.

Connie had always wanted a bust that stuck out in front like other girls', but the pinafore dress had successfully flattened her generous breasts. So, almost no one who knew her had any idea that there was a young woman underneath it all. Connie had always been what was unkindly termed 'a skinny kid' but, in the last few months, she had joyfully watched her body take on the smooth roundness of a proper woman.

Everything in the room was orderly, inspiring her to place her clothes neatly on the silver-painted basket chair. The pink and russet Art Deco design on the threadbare rug at the side of the bed made her feel comfortable, and the rosy glow from reflected street lights shining in the big, tilted dressing-table mirror reinforced the feeling. Connie got into the narrow bed and lay flat on her back with her arms underneath her head watching the searchlight beams of passing cars lick over the polished surfaces of the furniture and slide down the rose pink wallpaper like radioactive snail trails. She stretched out her toes like tendrils to the far corners of the cool sheets. Everything that possibly could be was starched at her aunts' house. The beds were changed every day during the week. They were both fanatics about clean linen. Connie had always been amused by their constant complaints about dust and spotted lunch-time tablecloths, which in any other household would still be usable. She slept.

She woke suddenly to the noise of a thrumming car engine in the street below her window. Connie threw her legs out of the bed and, going over to the window, looked over the top of the net curtain. She recognised Rachel immediately in her silver fox jacket and large, black, floppy hat. She was paying the taxi driver while another figure was emerging from the offside door. It was a man, Connie could see that; but it was his sudden burst of high-pitched laughter at something Rachel had said as they walked towards the door that made Connie take a step back from the window, not wishing to be seen.

The taxi went off into the Liverpool night like a clockwork toy.

The laughter had come from a man Connie had hoped never to set eyes on again. The family had, for as long as she could remember, called him 'three-fingered Frank', because of an injury he had received as a running-boy for a gang in the West Indies. He had been caught by the opposition and they had punished him by forcing his hand in the jamb of a car door and slamming it shut. He had lost the thumb and first finger of his right hand. After this, he had come to England and worked as a waiter until Connie's aunts had taken him under their wings. Frank was now a reformed character, according to Beatrice, who liked to give people a chance to redeem themselves. She always tried to give Rachel's boys the benefit of the doubt, even when they were picked up and questioned by the police, which happened from time to time.

Connie threw the sheet over her head as if to blot out the memory of Frank. He seemed to her everything wicked in the world, and she remembered her grandmother telling her that Chinese half-castes were not to be trusted as they were the worst of all possible combinations. When Connie had been small she had played games with Frank and he had let her ride on his back round Rachel's living-room and she had not been afraid of him them. Her misgivings had been triggered by a single incident and bolstered by her grandmother's prejudice. Connie had had a streaming cold and Aunt Rachel had given Frank instructions to rub her chest with camphorated oil. Connie had been about eleven at the time, and she recalled vividly the sense of revulsion at the strange delight Frank seemed to take in his task. She had sat before the fire holding her vest before the small buds of her breasts, and looked directly at him as if challenging him to make her remove it. Frank had enjoyed his work, and had loaded the oil on to her bare, fire-warmed back with his three good fingers, working it in, around her neck and the upper part of her chest. Connie remembered the feeling of the maimed hand stroking her body and she shuddered at the thought of his ever touching her again.

She lay back in bed and listened to Frank laughing and talking to Rachel in the kitchen. Outside, the sky of the clear night covered the sprawl of the city with washes of quiet indigo. Turning on her side Connie went to sleep half listening to a complaining midnight dog.

The next morning it was dark and threatening rain. Connie could hear the paper boy mashing the sordid Sundays through the narrow letter-box, and the rhythmic snoring of Beatrice through the wall that separated them. Connie took a towel from the big cupboard and, opening the door, stepped out on to the only new carpet in the house. She crept along to the bathroom past the open door of Beatrice's room in case the old lady should wake and see her in her underclothes. She washed hastily and, running back across the landing, caught sight of her aunt's large body turning with the tell-tale signals of waking. Beatrice's head was encrusted with small pin curls like a sea bottom crustacean. She thrust her face clear of the earthquake of sheets, and appeared more flushed than usual. The small broken veins on her cheeks looked like hysterical spiders. Connie could just see

Beatrice's false eyelashes stuck to their velvet pad on the corner of her dressing-table, and the battery of oils and unguents to feed, nourish and stimulate the amphibian skin which hung from her throat like the dewlap of a great Brahma bull.

Rachel was still asleep in the room opposite her own. There was no sound from there. Connie knew that Frank would be asleep downstairs on the couch in the living-room, his black leather gloves still clutching the lapels of his coat.

Connie hated quiet and felt threatened by it. As a rule Sundays were very quiet and lazy. Their traditional entombment still flourished at her aunts' house. She dressed and went down the red-carpeted stairs, stopping at the front door to lever the remains of the tattered newspapers from the letter-box. The end of the newspaper that had been exposed to the street had the consistency of blotting paper. She took it into the living-room and opened it out on the table by the window. Frank was still mercifully asleep, his arms now folded. He had turned over on to his right side, his knees folded towards the back of the couch in a thin foetal shape. Connie pressed her hair to the back of her ears and gazed at the soggy newspapers. The first heading she noticed ran, 'Bald-headed man found in back of caravan with fourteen-year-old tattooed schoolgirl'. Others were written in the same titillating style. Connie turned over the pages until she found the Goods for Sale notices, which advertised latex body stockings and other strange delights, to be sent in the strictest confidence.

She opened the curtains on the day and poked the fire, which was still alight, and put on some of the anthracite which her aunts kept in a brass coal-scuttle by the fireplace, finishing the job by cleaning the fender and mock marble tiles of the grate with a dampened cloth. She took the dirty cloth to the kitchen, half-filled the yellow plastic bowl with hot water and busily washed out the stains of coal dust, finally pegging it out on the line in the small backyard conservatory. As Connie put on the kettle to make her aunts' tea she was aware of Frank moving around in the living-room.

'Frank, is that you?' she called quietly.

'Well, honey, if it isn't, you sure are in a lot of trouble,'

Frank said, laughing in his familiar high-pitched tone. 'Come here, I haven't seen you for a long time, sugar girl,' he giggled. Connie turned from the stove and stood in the doorway of the kitchen. Frank was standing before the fire, his long legs astride.

'Jesus, I'm cold!' he said, rubbing his cramped arms, first one, then the other, with his black leather hands.

'That's because you slept in your clothes, Frank,' said Connie, matter-of-factly. 'You get chilled because you've got nothing in reserve to warm you when you wake. Anyway don't do it again, it's stupid, and, in any case, just look at your overcoat, it's creased to hell and back.' After this gentle tirade she folded her arms and added, 'You know it's O.K. if you sleep in your skin, and you're more than safe under that down quilt.'

Frank's pale, brown lips split open in a grin. 'Connie,' he said, 'you are the only woman I know who can tell me off like that without me getting all mad, you know, but I think Rachel would have something to say about me skin-sleeping around here.' Frank replaced his shades and stretched his head, appreciating the fire's warmth. They both smiled and laughed at the idea. Frank was right about Rachel who, from time to time felt it her duty to set a pretended moral tone to the proceedings in her house and would not take kindly to the idea of a full frontal Frank in her living-room. Connie made tea for them all.

'Connie,' Frank said, 'you sure are a female woman now,' and, throwing back his head, he giggled shrilly, displaying his fine, white, narrow teeth. Connie pretended to be too busy to afford the luxury of blushing and rattled the tea things around in feigned annoyance.

She carried in the wooden tray, trying to avoid Frank's eyes which she knew were concentrating on her from underneath his dark glasses. She gave him his tea and took the tray up to Aunt Beatrice's room. Beatrice was already up and busy pulling out the pin curls from her head. 'I hear Frank's up, dear,' she said as Connie put down the tray and poured her tea. Removing a dozen or so hairclips from her mouth Beatrice said seriously, 'He's always laughing, that boy, it must be glands or something.'

Connie smiled as she sweetened Beatrice's tea with the

maple syrup she liked so much. Beatrice sighed and struggled with the last few pins in her mad coiffure. 'You are a good girl, Connie, you think of everything.' Putting down her tortoiseshell comb, she took the teacup and sank her upper lip into the dark mixture right up to the coarse hairs that stood out in a thin moustache. Connie left her sitting drinking her tea with one elbow on the corner of her dressing-table. She still had on her candlewick dressing-gown over her dress.

Connie took the tray and knocked on Rachel's door, before opening it with one hand. Rachel was sitting up in her pale, blue-quilted bed nursing a lace pillow in the shape of a heart. She looked to Connie like a fading forties movie queen. 'Come in, Connie love.' Rachel smiled encouragingly and leaned forward to draw the pink Japanese kimono around her, tying it at the back more firmly.

Connie could see Rachel's large breasts flowing around under the thin material, so that the white embroidered dragons seemed to be endowed with a life all of their own.

'Come and sit beside me, love,' Rachel said, almost girlishly, patting the plump eiderdown to her right. 'Let me look at you,' she said, taking Connie's arms firmly in her two large hands. Connie felt Rachel's long, hard, lacquered fingernails test the skin of her shoulders as she was drawn towards her aunt for the kiss reserved for blood relatives.

At fifty, Aunt Rachel had managed, perhaps because of the luck of the gene draw, to preserve her raw-boned handsomeness. Although she had never had the beauty of Beatrice, Rachel's high cheekbones and superb feline carriage had made her the most attractive of the three sisters. Connie was sure Rachel would for ever retain the image of a precocious sixth former even if she managed to live until her eighties. Rachel was the tallest of the three sisters, and in her youth had had a wealth of hair the colour of summer corn. Since it had begun to fade she had doctored it occasionally with peroxide. Even so it had kept the silken fineness Connie had admired so much. Today it was done up in a high chignon on the crown of her head.

'It's nice to have you with us again, Connie sweetheart,' Rachel said, speaking to Connie as if she were a pet marmoset that had escaped and just been returned to her.

'We must get you to a hairdresser and see what they can do with your hair. I think it would suit you short and fluffy, don't you?' She asked Connie without expecting a reply.

Rachel took the cup and saucer from the tray and rested back on her pillow looking at Connie over the top of the fluted bone china with her quick, grey-green eyes. Connie wanted to mention that Frank was awake downstairs but thought better of it as Rachel did not like to mention Frank unless it was entirely necessary. Aunt Rachel put down the cup on the bedside table, stretched, and slid a pair of long legs out from the sheets and on to the pale blue carpet. She searched blindly for her mules with big painted toes but they were just out of reach under the bed. Connie sprang up and retrieved the fluffy mules from their hiding place and placed them in front of Rachel. She watched as her aunt pressed and wriggled her toes into the narrow bands. Putting a finger into the band across her left foot to ease its entry, Rachel said to Connie, 'Listen, pet, we'll have to get you some new clothes as well.' Then, straightening up, she went on, 'You really do need a bit of looking after, don't you?' Connie was pleased with the idea of having some new clothes and with the way Rachel appeared to care what happened to her.

'I'll go now, Auntie,' Connie said, picking up the tray and placing the cup on it, anxious not to displease Rachel while her aunt was still thinking in terms of her rehabilitation.

Rachel answered her carelessly. 'O.K., hon, I'll be down soon, just going to have a bath to wake myself up, and then we'll see about some food, unless Beatie's done it.'

Connie held the tray with one hand and backed out of the room, serf style. She stopped at Beatrice's room and collected her cup — a cigarette end swam in an inch of maple syrup at the bottom like a capsized U-boat. Connie found Beatrice in the kitchen making breakfast and trying to have a conversation with Frank who, by now, felt safe enough to remove his gloves and black overcoat. He wore a lilac shirt with ruffles down the front and a barman's blue velvet bow tie.

Beatrice told Connie, 'Sit down, dear, you've done enough. Frank's helping me with things here,' and then, 'Is Rachel up yet?'

Connie thought she could detect a note of irony in her

aunt's voice but she chose to ignore it. 'Yes Auntie, she's in the bath. She said she wouldn't be long.' Connie sat before the now fierce fire, watching the warmth make patterns on her long, slim, golden legs. When the fire got too much for her, she swung her legs over the arm of the well-padded easy chair and sat in a comfortable U-shape, flicking through the pages of the *T.V. Times*, looking at the advertisements for holidays in the sun. Beautiful brown bodies leaped out of every page; bodies oiled and sandblown, advertising everything from suntan oil to athletes' foot powder. Putting down the magazine she closed her eyes and dozed until Frank came and slid a plate of toast and marmalade under her nose.

'Wake up, little Connie bun,' Frank smoothed with his voice.

Connie opened her eyes wide, blinking to see Frank's face at the other end of her nose, distorted with its closeness to her.

'Frank, you have some very frightening habits,' she said, pushing the plate away violently.

Frank backed off, putting the toast on the arm of the chair and raising the pale palms of his hands in mock terror. Finally he smiled at her from a safe distance before the fire. 'O.K. Con, sweetheart, I promise I won't approach the presence nearer than three feet,' he told her, still smiling whitely and rocking to and fro on the balls of his slender feet.

At this point Rachel arrived in the living-room with all the confidence of a bejewelled lady arriving late at the theatre. 'Hello Beatrice!' she called out to her sister, who was still up to her armpits in toast crusts and marmalade, and then, 'Frank!' She nodded to him and Frank smiled, hideously polite, like a black Uriah Heep.

'Good morning, Rachel,' he said, standing up straight and pulling from the corner of his mouth the live match he had been chewing.

Connie got up and offered the plate of toast to Rachel, then sat and admiringly watched her aunt eat. Rachel had always fascinated her, but it was never the happy carefree fascination of the child, more the cold and fearful mesmerism associated with watching slow and gaudy reptiles behind glass at the zoo. Connie remembered the Keats poem they had done at school called *Lamia* with the same mixture of chill and romance with which she viewed her Aunt Rachel.

Rachel ate some of the toast and drank two cups of tea one after the other, occasionally looking at Frank over the top of the newspaper. Unlike Beatrice, Rachel's make-up was impeccable. Her mouth was glossy, and her eyes, steady, serpentlike, with their brown, shimmering lids were still those of a young woman. Connie's mother had often said that Rachel had sold her soul to the devil, but Connie had accepted this revelation only as sour grapes, as the sisters had, in her limited experience of family affairs, always been less than delicate in their descriptions of one another.

Rachel took her wallet from her handbag and, looking into it, peeled back banknotes and credit cards with a set of long tangerine fingernails. Taking out a card, she waved it towards Frank without speaking. He took the card from her, looked at it and smiled at Rachel knowingly. Frank reached for his velvet jacket which lay on the back of the couch. Finally, he put on the big black overcoat which had been hanging on the back of the living-room door, and, winking at Connie, said, 'See you, Connie bun.'

She waved idly as Beatrice got up and opened the front door saying to him as he slid past her, 'Keep your chest covered, Frank, it's raining, dear.' She spoke to him as warmly and convincingly as if she had been his mother.

Rachel stuffed her wallet and other bits of paper back into her handbag while Beatrice closed the front door. Coming back into the living-room she picked up the tray with the remains of their breakfast things on it and wobbled into the kitchen saying, 'Rachel, it's so cold today, did Frank really have to go out? He's not very strong in the chest you know, dear.'

Turning in her chair, Rachel looked hard at Beatrice and said grittily, 'Don't be stupid, Beatrice. Frank knows as well as you do the collections have got to be made, whether it's bloody raining or he's got swine fever.' Then, annoyed even further by a crease in the paper, she shouted, 'You make me bloody sick sometimes, swanning round the house like you're the Queen Mother and pretending it all isn't happening. For God's sake, where do you think the bloody money comes from, you soft get?'

Beatrice put down the tray on the draining board, and shuffled back into the living-room making placating little humming noises.

'I'm sorry, dear,' Beatrice cooed, looking stupidly at her younger sister. Her overpowdered face hung over her dark dress like a burst blister.

Connie listened silently. She knew Frank would be on his way to lean on someone. It was all part of the business. Rachel had begun to lend money on a small scale several years ago and, since then, things had snowballed into a thriving business. There was no security needed, as most of her customers preferred to pay up than receive a visit from her friends. Frank was the talker; he tried to persuade people to pay their debts before the two heavies went in to deal with the debtor — nothing serious, just a finger or two would be placed on a convenient chair arm and broken with a poker or anything that came to hand. It was very seldom that this had to happen. Connie knew that Frank's fierce loyalty to Rachel had made the sisters very comfortable indeed. Most of the money was kept under Rachel's bed in a large suitcase or in the big wardrobe on the landing. Rachel was very hard about the business and teased Beatrice, who would often retire in tears from her vitriolic attacks. Poor, slow, tongue-tied Beatrice, Connie thought, who tried hard to imagine that the money in the suitcase had come from God, who had thoughtfully counted it all into hundreds and wound elastic bands round it.

Connie pretended to be asleep. She did not want to come between these two experienced flesh-eaters.

TWO

Rachel was as good as her word and took Connie to a hair-dresser where she gave instructions to cut her hair short. Connie sat in the clammy black vinyl chair and watched in the mirror as her black locks fell about her shoulders. Rachel sat in the opposite corner of the salon having a manicure and reading *Harper's* as if she were contemplating buying the business. Later, they went to shops in the city centre where Rachel bought Connie the sort of clothes she thought she ought to have. Connie did not mind. She enjoyed being at the centre of someone's attention. Connie wore one of the new dresses to go back home in.

'Beatrice will like this one, won't she, Auntie?' she asked Rachel excitedly. 'It's her favourite shade of pink.'

Rachel re-tied the blue silk scarf at her neck and smiled delightedly at Connie, amused by her show of childish enthusiasm and gratitude.

As Rachel never travelled on buses 'because of the smell of unwashed humanity', they sped back to the house, through large tracts of demolition, in a taxi. The route took them through parts of Liverpool that had been excavated and set alight by pygmies of ten or twelve. Connie could see them scurrying through broken window-frames in the empty houses. She was herself removed from these kids by four years and a new pink dress, but somehow felt at one with the loping figure she could still make out on the skyline, of a girl in a ragged red dress sniffing the smoky air like a free, wild thing.

Connie enjoyed the weeks that followed. When Rachel

was not taking her out buying her things, Frank took her to the cinemas in the city centre where he sat behind her, a black duenna, watching in the dark. Connie became more adept at avoiding his shadow-like presence. After being subjected to three separate houses of *Airport 78*, Frank gave in and went out for a beer.

Leaving the cinema, Connie walked the fifty or so yards down to the coffee shop on the corner where she bought a cup of froth and sat by the soiled window watching people go by. A youngish man sat down on the seat beside her. Connie leaned on one elbow and took surreptitious looks at him. He wore a dusty bomber jacket with a broken zip and a hat crocheted in green, purple and bright chicken yellow. In front of him on the table he had both hands wrapped around a large open sandwich which, from time to time, he lunged at savagely. When he finished he wiped both hands on his bleached denims, and looked at her appraisingly for a moment and said, 'Have another coffee with me, love.'

Connie, amused by his impudence, said, 'O.K., then, but it will have to be a quickie. I've got to go home soon.'

The young man, picking the bits of food from between a set of none too clean teeth, said, 'Oh Christ, that's what they all say. I'm not going to give you the kiss of death or anything, you know. Go on, be a devil and take a chance.' He grinned at her. She smiled back at him, scanning his friendly but inane face for the tell-tale sign of the 'bastard'. There was none she could detect.

He waved the waitress over. 'Two more coffees please, love, and this time could you put some hot water on.' Turning to her he asked, 'Seriously though, kid, have you got to go home? We could go to a picture or for a drink if you like.' He looked at her pleadingly, but Connie had had enough of cinemas for one day and shook her head. She could see Frank outside the café leaning against the glass.

'Sorry, I've got to go now,' she said brusquely.

He got to his feet and let her pass, watching her go as if he had dropped a five pound note down a drain. Frank was reading the racing news and did not speak to her. Connie pretended surprise at seeing him.

'Oh, hello Frank, fancy seeing you here!'

Frank did not speak, but folded the paper and eased it into his pocket. She looked away, but he got hold of her arm in a grip that made her feel as if she had been bitten by a steel grab, and hurried her into the taxi he had hailed while he had been waiting. Inside he turned on her like an enraged woolly monkey. 'Look girl, don't you ever fuck me up like that again, otherwise I'll have to get nasty. Rachel says you've got to be back at four and what she says goes. Understand?'

Connie nodded, her eyes filling with tears at Frank's departure from his usual, smiling, Uncle Tom image, and the pulsing grip he had on her arm. Connie knew Frank meant what he said; it did not take much imagination to work out the pleasure it would give Frank to hurt her just enough to make sure of her continuing obedience. She slid back into the protective anonymity of the darkened cab and Frank relaxed his grip on her arm and folded his hands on the lap of his overcoat. Neither spoke for the rest of the journey.

It was late one Sunday afternoon. Mr McKenna had arrived for a bout of cards in the rival camp and had lost. Connie was looking at the photograph album to stave off the boredom that reared over her shoulder. She looked at the first picture of Beatrice, who gazed at her out of the frame of the picture like a hoopoe. Her crown of orange hair stood up from her forehead as if in fright, and above her long straight nose there arched dark brown eyebrows over deeply hooded eyes. She, like the hoopoe, always wore her black banded feathers off the shoulders. When Beatrice had been a girl it was felt by well-meaning relatives that her small delicate frame could not possibly stand up to the rigors of the smog-laden Liverpool winters so, as often as they could afford, they had sent her to the seaside at Southport for enforced strolls on the promenade to imbibe liberal doses of ozone-laden air. There were photos labelled *Southport* and *Bridlington 1936* which helped to explain to Connie the swimming costumes that made the girls look like used toothpaste tubes, and why the youth of the period formed strange pyramids of laughing people in order to have a photograph taken. As Connie turned the pages, Beatrice's strange beauty winnowed into air.

Subsequent pictures showed her ageing until the last one seemed the most cruel — her thick body mounted on spindly legs caught by Rachel's Russian camera in the act of striding a grassy tussock on their last holiday together. The sun had gone down on Beatrice's beauty, and there were no more visits to the country with bicycles and baskets of food.

Connie saw her mother's father seated proudly on his ancient motorcycle combination in an obvious pose for the benefit of his three daughters intent behind a box Brownie. Grandfather sat astride his machine, arms folded firmly in his old black flying-jacket and leather skull cap, looking out from the picture from beneath isinglass goggles. Connie thought him an imposing figure and remembered Grandmother telling her that Grandfather had flown the Dragonfly airplanes that seemed to Connie to have been made from balsa wood and piano wires. After the war he had developed a genius at failing every enterprise. Eventually he had become a reluctant insurance salesman. He had just about given in to this less exciting life when he had died. His daughters had had opportunities to marry, but neither Beatrice nor Rachel had felt grateful enough for the offers from retinues of pallid clerks from shipping offices or salesmen of women's underwear who seemed to come their way. Grandfather had brought up his daughters to believe in themselves. He had been wildly disappointed in his only, sickly boy who had had the temerity to die of scarlet fever at fourteen. After that, the old man had made sure his daughters developed the self-reliance of Amazons. Connie closed the photograph album and adjusted her mind to the year.

Mr McKenna got up and made going-home noises. Connie looked over her shoulder at the aunts and their visitor and, glad it had all come to an end, said, 'Have they cleaned you out, Mr McKenna?' Mr McKenna placed his newspaper under his arm, grunted and smiled over to her, indulgently saying, 'They always win on home ground, Connie, but this dog will live to bite again, I think.' Rachel was sitting bolt upright and gathering in the cards from the smooth dark green chenille tablecloth on which they had been playing. Beatrice gave Mr McKenna his stick and his hairy tweed hat with the feather at the side. He took it with a reddened hand that looked like a ham bone. Connie got up and went over to the door, placing her hand on the lock, ready to open it as Mr McKenna approached. 'Thanks ladies,' he said, 'I'll see you next week then, shall I?' Then, placing the hat on his shiningly clean pink head, he backed out of the small hall and into the frame of the front door, waving at Connie as he went. Rachel, getting up from the table, shouted, 'Don't worry, Fred, we'll let you get your own back next week, won't we, Beatie?' Beatrice looked up, hurt by the deliberate shortening of her name. She hated it when Rachel called her 'Beatie'. It seemed a cruel diminishing of her, and of what little status she could still lay claim to. Connie closed the door on Mr McKenna, flicking the lock down with her thumb.

The two aunts were in the kitchen preparing their tea. Connie got out a clean cloth from the drawer under the table, and spread it over the green turf of the chenille cloth in preparation for the offerings the two aging augurs would bring to it. Rachel shouted from the kitchen in response to a gentle knocking at the front door. 'Connie, would you go, love, see who's there.'

'Yes, Auntie,' said Connie, putting out the flaking chromium cake-stand the aunts always liked to have on the table. She went to the front door and carefully undid the lock. Opening the door she found herself face to face with a taxi driver.

He pushed his suet face towards hers and asked in a hoarse whisper, 'Excuse me, luv, but does a fella called Frank Baxter live 'ere?' He went on confidingly, 'Ye see, I gorr'im in the cab but he looks as if somebody's banged 'im up or summ'at. I don't mind bringin' 'im in but, if yer understands me, all I want is me muny and ter gerrof. I don't want ter ger involved with anythin'.' Connie felt afraid. Why hadn't Frank got out of the taxi? Rachel was behind her now. She could feel her aunt's hands on her shoulders.

'What's the matter, love,' Rachel said, looking straight over Connie's head and at the diminutive taxi driver. Connie thought her very cool.

The taxi driver was getting more and more distraught by the minute. 'Look 'ere, missus, all I want is me muny and I'll be off,' he said. Rachel gave him his money. 'Thanks missus,' he said. The note of relief in his voice spread out like the climax of the Hallelujah chorus. 'I'll help yer ger 'im out,' he volunteered. ''Es thin but 'es 'evy an' 'e hasn't said a werd since I took him on. 'E must be bad.' The driver bent inside the cab and none too carefully, humped Frank out. Rachel helped him carry Frank inside. There was no one in the street but Connie felt the curtains twitching in an agony of suspicion. They put Frank into one of the easy chairs where his head, which was swathed in his black silk scarf, leaned ominously to one side like a broken doll.

Rachel told the taxi driver Frank was epileptic and that he must have had a fall. The taxi driver was grateful for the good tip and the false information. Coming back into the living-room, the door locked and bolted behind her, Rachel was more than annoyed to find both Beatrice and Connie transfixed, watching the dark red liquid oozing from the end of the scarf, making a small, swiftly coagulating pool on the carpet at the side of the chair.

'Beatrice,' she snarled, 'for God's sake, get galvanised. He's in a hell of a mess. Connie, love, put the kettle on and make sure it boils.'

Connie did as she was told and returned in time to see Rachel begin to unwind the scarf which was already stiffening with drying blood. The last layer was difficult. Beatrice stood beside Rachel, holding a bowl of warm water and a roll of cotton wool with which Rachel soaked the scarf to release it from Frank's skin. Connie could see Frank's hands clutching and straightening in a pain she found hard to imagine. She felt overpowered by the intense feeling of mute agony Frank transmitted to her. Beatrice baulked and turned her head, tears in her red-rimmed eyes.

'Don't you go and faint or anything, Beatie, you daft get. I need all the help I can get,' Rachel said, examining Frank's mangled face. 'We will have to stitch him ourselves. If the busies get to know about it we'll all be in trouble. Now get a grip on yourself, for God's sake. If you want to feel sorry for anyone feel sorry for Frank, poor sod,' she said, pulling at the last of the sticky blood-laced scarf. Rachel spat out orders like offending bits of gristle. 'Con, get the plastic clothes-line from the conservatory and tie his hands as far as you can behind the chair, oh, and his feet as well. Tie them together and Beatrice will stand on them while I stitch him.' Connie thought her wonderful; she was not afraid of anything. Rachel looked at Connie sternly willing her to be sensible. 'I'm afraid you are going to have to hold his head, Connie. He'll fight you but you must not let him move. O.K.?' Connie nodded and bit into her lower lip.

After they had secured Frank, Connie put his head back in preparation and whispered to him, 'It's going to be all right, Frankie. I'm sorry, it's got to hurt, though, there's nothing to take the pain away, but I will stay here with you.' She had tried to sound confident for Frank's sake although her stomach was churning with anxiety and her mouth was sour and dry.

Rachel had returned with her 'equipment', some of the instruments which Connie had seen in the drawers in the wardrobe on the landing. Frank's eyes rolled around in his head like a man preparing for a death stroke. Rachel placed all the things in one of the chipped kidney dishes and poured boiling water over them, replacing the dish on a low light on the stove until everything was seething hot. She then washed and dried her hands and carried the kidney dish with its contents into the living-room and placed it on the small brass table beside Frank's chair. Beatrice stood on the toes of Frank's shoes, and Connie held his head in her hands as gently as she thought advisable. Rachel looked carefully at the wound that had bitten a hole into the side of Frank's face. She asked slowly as she dabbed at it with her cotton wool, 'Was it a bottle, Frank?' His eyes closed briefly in acknowledgement. It was impossible for him to speak. His upper lip had been torn and some of his teeth showed through whitely, penetrating the wound's rich plumpness.

Taking the curved needle from the bowl, Rachel threaded it with button thread that had been stroked with surgical spirit. She pressed the sharp needle through the skin, making the first stitch. In the breath-halted quiet Connie heard Frank's skin pop like a taut sausage stabbed by a fork. Frank bucked and hissed, sending a stream of bright red bubbles through his teeth as Rachel worked on his face. His body arched in pain as she lifted the flap of loose skin on his cheek to join it with her needlework. The wound closed slowly.

Frank groaned, giving himself up to the crude anaesthetic of agony. Connie wept over his restrained head with a mixture of fear and pity.

Rachel finished dressing the wound and Beatrice took the scarf and other blood-soaked cotton wool out into the yard and burnt it all in the dustbin. Connie stayed, holding Frank's head as though her life and not his depended on it, until Rachel took her arm, raising her to her feet, and persuaded her to sit on the couch by the fire. Connie felt cold and numbed by the experience.

'Frank's going to be all right,' Rachel told her. 'He's asleep now. When he wakes, Beatie and I will take him up and put him in your bed. You will have to sleep on the couch for a few days, Con.' Rachel stroked Connie's head until, by experience, she could feel the girl's body begin to shake off the tensions of the hour. Connie looked up at her aunt and thought she read kindness in her face. Rachel continued to sit by Connie until she knew the girl had gone to sleep. Then she and Beatrice began to work at cleaning the carpet and wiping the blood-spattered legs of the chair Frank was sitting in.

Connie woke, her head pierced by aching. She fetched some aspirin and a tumbler from the kitchen, swallowed hard and watched Beatrice flowing round the house. Beatrice had changed into pale blue chiffon that made her look like a Reg Butler dragonfly as she busied about some trivia or other on the mantelpiece. Soon Beatrice sat down and turned on the television programme *Stars on Sunday*, sitting back in the mock piety of the blue-rinse-brigade.

Connie looked around her. The room looked undisturbed. There was no evidence of Frank's torment. She deduced that the sisters must have carried Frank upstairs and that he was now asleep in her bed. Connie watched the television screen blankly as the professional virgins, all of them looking for a break, sang *All in an April Evening* in nuns' habits with sickly, glossy faces. Beatrice got up and made tea for everybody. Connie could not help feeling there was something ghoulish about the way they tucked into the boiled eggs and bread and butter without once mentioning Frank whom she could imagine upstairs in her room, looking at his shredded face in the cracked mirror.

After the tea things had been cleared away, some sort of normality returned. Rachel asked Connie to go upstairs and feed Frank some sugar and warm water from a hospital feeder that had been discovered in a cupboard in the kitchen. Connie took the cup up and into the silent room. The curtains were drawn but light was filtering through softly. Looking in the direction of the bed she could see that Frank was lying on his back, his arms folded under his head on the pillow. 'Frank,' she called, 'are you awake? I've brought you something to drink. It's not rum so don't get excited!'

She saw his bandaged head move towards her and he raised his arm to show her that he understood, then let it drop and fall back towards his slim body in the bed. Connie went over to the bedside and, holding his head, slipped the spout of the feeding cup into the side of his mouth furthest away from the wound. He drank in short, choking gulps, finally pushing away the spout of the cup with his tongue.

'Frank, I'll stay with you if you like,' said Connie, wiping his sweat-beaded head with a cold, water-soaked cloth. Frank took her hand with his good one and held it gently, his thin fingers moist and needful. Connie sang snatches of *Sweet Chariot*, which she thought might please him until his fingers relaxed and he drifted off to sleep. His eyes closed in the curtain-drawn twilight.

Connie took it upon herself to nurse Frank. Soon he was able to sit and get out of bed when it was necessary to visit the lavatory, but he was still sucking up liquid food specially prepared by Beatrice from a mixture of Complan malt extract and selected baby foods. Rachel had taken off the dressing and appeared satisfied at the granulation that had taken place on the wound. After a week, Rachel took out the stitches, and Connie, ceaselessly amazed at her aunt's abilities, marvelled at the way everything stayed together. Rachel went out as usual in the afternoons, leaving Beatrice to shout at the washing-machine, and make the tea.

It was in the afternoons that Connie read aloud to Frank from *Wind in the Willows*, the only book she could find in the house that would not be an embarrassment to read. Frank proved a keen listener and soon he would get out the book from the bedside table when Connie appeared in the room. He watched her with his teddy bear eyes wherever she went in the room, but she did not mind anymore. He held no more terror for her. Connie put Frank's pillow against his back to make him as comfortable as she could. Unable to do anything but mumble at her through his still swollen upper lip, he reached for her hand, and then touched her hair as if trying to share with her the deep grief he still felt. Connie took his hand and brought out the maimed one from underneath the sheets where he kept it hidden from her. She saw tears momentarily stand in his eyes before bouncing down the velvet of his skin and over the assault course of the wound.

'Oh Frank,' Connie said through the sadness that she feared would engulf her. 'It doesn't matter anymore, honest. I just want you to get better again,' and then, as if she had to feed him information for his soul's sake, she said, 'Rachel's got the bastard that did it to you. She sent Dan and Toby, you know. I wouldn't like to be him right now anyway,' she said joyously. 'They say his face looks as if someone's had a game of noughts and crosses on it.' She laughed as he took her by the arms and drew her to him. As she lay on top of the bed beside him, her cheek against his springy hair, revenge in this instance was sweet for both of them.

THREE

The following Sunday Connie packed her duffle bag, carefully including a couple of the dresses Rachel had bought for her and some other goodies which she thought would come in handy. She had never intended to get near to Frank and had been more than surprised to find herself lovingly attracted to him. She had enjoyed the role she had taken as sacrificing nurse when Frank had been a wounded animal needing care, and unable to indulge himself in his usual pastimes. Connie had just begun to understand Frank and she was not prepared for the change in him that would inevitably take place once he had begun to make sufficient recovery to be able to take up his specialised work.

Connie was enough of a naïve optimist to believe that fate created shelves for people to leap up on to when hard-pressed by life. Everything pushed her forward to the next stage. She chose to ignore the grim fact that her father's death had been brought about by a society that had applauded when he missed his footing. She believed that staying with her aunts would seriously limit her choices, and that she might even end up becoming a victim of an attack, to be attended to by the Frankenstein sisters. She shuddered at the possibility, all too real, of ending like Frank with a face that looked as if someone short-sighted had attacked him with a cheese grater.

Before opening the door on to the street, Connie looked around at the room in which she had been entombed, then up the steep stairs where she knew Beatrice would be still asleep wrapped in her plum red, crocheted shawl, and easing her head full of bobby pins from one discomfort to another. Rachel, too, would be sleeping soundly, her long, white, gold-freckled arms out of the covers, her fine hair lying stroked across her face guarding the mystery of her eyes. Connie closed the door behind her as if on some great secret.

Out at last, unsupervised, on the early morning streets there was the last of the summer to enjoy. Connie held her coat over her arm, the duffle bag hung from her shoulder with the small amount of cash she had managed to secure nestling inside it. Connie was delighted with the freedom from her aunts' claustrophobic way of life. She skipped along the cracked flags of the pavement surprising herself with an agility she thought she had lost, leaping and swirling around lamp-posts supported by one slender arm. She made a celebratory progress down to the bus stop on the main road.

The bus lurched past Northumberland Street with its open spaces blackened and concrete-rimmed, like the craters of giant duodenal ulcers, and then forged on towards the centre of the yet unawakened city. A small block of flats lay in ruins against a pretty, pink sky. The balconies were burst open and sagging with threatening lumps of concrete. Hunks of concrete swung ominously overhead, suspended like discarded chip-baskets. The iron-meshed skeleton of the building, red with rust, stood a testament to oblivion.

Soon the bus had travelled through the town centre and had picked up considerable speed. Five stops later, Connie decided she had gone far enough. She got off the bus and walked for what felt like a long time, until she came to a corner shop-cum-Post Office. She bought two bars of chocolate, one of which she began to eat greedily while she read the advertisements pinned to the door. She stood on one leg for as long as she could, counting how long she could stay in the position without tottering over. Among the advertised chests of drawers and bitch whippets for sale, she saw a card that read: 'Room for rent, furnished, £5.50 per week, apply Mrs. Oldshaw, 35 Kirkby Street.' Connie, still on one leg, with the chocolate bar resting in the corner of her mouth, considered this seriously. It was cheap and she knew she would have to go to ground soon, for Frank would be sent out to track her when it was discovered she had gone with money and clothes.

The woman proprietor who had been watching Connie out of the corner of one narrow, sleep-filled eye, out of habit, said, 'Are you interested in anything there, lovey?' She smiled over the top of a cold-looking, pinched nose that reminded Connie of her Aunty Beatrice. The woman wore her thin, straw-blonde hair wound tightly round twenty or so turquoise rollers over which she had tied a black georgette scarf, flock-printed with acanthus leaves. The woman still had on her quilted nylon housecoat which she held close against her throat as if caught in imaginary gusts of wind.

Connie found an old envelope and a stub of crayon in one of her pockets and held them in readiness. 'Yes, I'd like to know if this room's gone yet?'

'No, lovey, it's been on the door all week. Nobody's been round as far as I know.' The woman unfurled a roll of newspapers and shoved them into a silently watching newsboy's bag.

'Thanks,' said Connie, hastily bringing her crayon into operation. 'But is it far? I've no idea where I am in this district.'

The woman put up a nervous hand to the side of her thin throat in concentration. 'No, love. It's first right, then right again, cross at the lights, and it's the first street on your left.'

Connie smiled broadly at the woman, lifted the duffle bag on to her shoulder and left the shop, crunching her way through the last of the melting chocolate bar.

35 Kirkby Street was a clean-looking, terraced house, one of many that stood soldier-like all the way down to the main road. There were no curtains up at the front bay, but a notice said clearly in bright yellow paint: 'Oldshaws, Fish and Chip Shop'. Below this notice was a black and white cardboard clock the hands of which showed the next time of opening. Connie could see the big fish fryer inside and the empty, white plastic trays neatly stacked in the tiled window bay. Part of the high counter was also visible from the street, and there on the top Connie could see the large vinegar bottles and giant aluminium salt cellars. Outside, the frame of the bay window was painted cream and brown. She noticed that the paintwork had been washed recently. Whoever it

was must have been up at the crack of dawn, she thought to herself, and stared with disbelief at the dark, moist circles that suggested the places where the bucket had stood. She looked behind her and saw the remains of the soapy gush of steamy water that had flowed into the gutter and swilled down the grid just opposite the door.

Connie knocked on the clean, cream-painted door and waited. Before long, the door opened, and Connie found herself face to face with a short, lumpy-looking woman of about fifty-five. The woman looked out suspiciously from dark eyes under eyebrows that met across the bridge of a high, aquiline nose. The woman's mouth was a tight, small line above a narrow chin shattered by small creases like a broken pane of glass.

'Yes, what is it?' the woman enquired, drying her vein-knotted hands on the apron she wore tied around her middle.

'It's about the room. Has it been taken yet? If it hasn't, I'd like it please, that's if you're still letting.' Connie spoke as politely as she knew how, but her voice faltered as her newly acquired confidence seeped slowly away.

The woman's eyes never left Connie's face for a moment and her impudent stare made Connie feel very uncomfortable. 'I'm Mrs Oldshaw,' the woman said unblinkingly, adopting a curious, hen-like pose, her head cocked to one side as if waiting to ward off some sudden, unexpected movement.

Connie spoke louder this time. 'It's about the room. Has it been taken yet?'

Mrs Oldshaw moved her head and viewed Connie from another angle. 'You look a bit on the young side to be wanting a room on your own, don't you?' She rolled her cardigan sleeves down muscular-looking arms, and then folded them across her formless breasts which somehow had managed to get tucked into her belt.

'I'm eighteen,' Connie lied brightly, her eyes opening wide with the thrill of the experience. 'I can pay two weeks in advance, and I'm very quiet,' she added, bolstering up her claim with a final word-garnishing which she knew would be acceptable to the old lady.

In the small silence between the two people, Mrs Oldshaw moved to one side of the door and said rather sharply, 'Well, you'd better come in then, but mind the step. I've just done it with the stone and I don't want to have to do it over again, so be careful!'

Connie stepped over the yellow stoned step as if it were a dead body.

Once in the shop, the old woman closed the door and slid across the top bolt. 'Can't be too careful these days. We've been broken into twice this year, and I know the boys that done it, an' all. I just wish I could lay my hands on them, that's all.' So, grumbling, Mrs Oldshaw bent down to shoot the bolt at the bottom of the door as well.

Connie looked at the bent shape of Mrs Oldshaw. The ridges of an old-fashioned corset stood out in a fan shape through her dark skirt like the ribs of an umbrella, framing a wide, flat backside. Underneath the skirt could be seen a pair of directoire silk knickers, gathered with elastic at the knees over lisle-stockinged legs ending in varicosed feet pushed flatly into a pair of bright tartan slippers. Mrs Oldshaw's thin hair had been drawn aggressively back into a small bun at the nape of her neck, which was the colour of old parchment. The parting showed snow-white, and the hair, greasy and taut, looked as if it had been painted across her narrow skull. Connie smiled as she followed her into the small back room behind the chip shop. Lifting aside the dark green velvet curtain that served to exclude draughts, Mrs Oldshaw nodded Connie into the room.

It was extraordinarily hot. The fire in the imitation marble grate looked ready to tumble like boiling lava out on to the home-made rug that lay in front of it. Over the mantlepiece hung a large mirror with a painted wooden frame. On either side of the mantlepiece stood a pair of Staffordshire flatback dogs with ginger moustaches. The dogs looked out blankly to the wall opposite. In the centre of the crowded room there was a round table covered with a dark blue velveteen cloth. Next to the table, and a little set back in the only alcove in the room, stood an ancient harmonium with a little carved stool set just underneath the keyboard.

'Mr Oldshaw,' the wife said, pretending to be cross, 'we've got a young lady for the room.'

Connie looked in the direction of the divan that was sticking out from the wall under the window. The sheet moved from what Connie had taken to be a rolled-up mattress to expose the huge, florid face of Mr Oldshaw. Connie was more amazed than shocked by the sight of him. Mr Oldshaw lay in bed covered only by a sheet. His body was a monstrous travesty of swollen flesh. One huge arm, already bursting from the striped, home-made pyjamas, signalled her to sit down with a hand the colour of a fungal growth she had once seen under a hedge.

She sat, quietly viewing the enormous body that lay in the bed before her like a drowned ship, anchored by feet that stood out stiffly from the bottom of the bed, it was still rippling with the undercurrent of life. The skin was firm and lined with tiny, silver-scaled stretch marks, the heels red with lying. His toes stood away from one another like a cluster of bottle tops, each one erect with an unhealthy plumpness. Mr Oldshaw was bald except for a few hairs which were combed neatly over the pink Kalahari of his head. His eyes were remarkably lively in spite of being buried in a face resembling raw smoked ham. His eyebrows, like those of his wife, met in the middle of his forehead. His nose, swollen and distorted, was host to three warts and peppered with large blackheads which gave it the appearance of a purple, lunar landscape. Under this remarkable nose, that hung like a saiga's retractable trunk over his pink pout of a mouth, was a moustache, cut scrubbing-brush style straight across his upper lip.

'Would you like a cup of tea, love? I'm just going to make one, so it's no trouble.' Mrs Oldshaw pushed past Connie's knees and the round table between her and Mr Oldshaw's bed.

'Yes, thanks.' Connie looked up at Mrs Oldshaw as she passed, and then round again at the strange ornaments and knick-knacks that were festooned above the mantlepiece and almost covered the wall by the side of the harmonium.

By this time, Mr Oldshaw had heaved his enormous bulk up into a sitting position, and leaned against the bank of pillows at the wall, one great hand lying red and flaking like an exploded sausage on top of the sheet. 'E, lass, yer look fair dun up,' he boomed from underneath his moustache. 'Cum near t' fire and get thee warm.' He shifted uneasily on his pillows, observing her.

Connie was glad of the warmth and friendship that seemed to radiate from the Oldshaws. She looked steadily at the fire's blaze in an attempt to hide her embarrassment. She had the uncomfortable feeling that Mr Oldshaw was probing her piercingly with his eyes, so she avoided any further conversation or visual contact with him.

Mrs Oldshaw came into the room bearing a tea tray that had the scratched images of two pups and a budgie printed on it. She put out the tea things and poured some thick, dark tea into three mugs with Snoopy designs on the sides. She passed one of these mugs to Mr Oldshaw and tucked under his chin a large muslin napkin saying, 'There you are Daddy, you'll enjoy that. It's got plenty of sugar in it.' Smilingly, she watched Mr Oldshaw's face sink down towards the mug, his nose disappearing as he drank.

Mrs Oldshaw cocked her head to one side and asked, 'Anyway, love, what's your name?'

Connie, reaching for her mug on the tray, answered, 'Connie — Connie Marlowe.' She held the mug in her two hands to feel the warmth flowing through the earthenware.

'I'll show you your room as soon as we've had our tea. Here's the key and I'll see about a rent book later, too.'

Connie had already begun to accept the overpowering heat and the lingering smell of ammonia from small over-spills of urine. She remembered poor Uncle Jesse, being nursed at home where he'd been sent to gain some comfort from the remains of his family. Uncle Jesse had been her father's elder brother and had died in unspeakably damp and dirty conditions in a basement in Canning Street. It pained Connie to recall Uncle Jesse with his gentleness and undeserved illness.

Mrs Oldshaw led the way up the stairs, her body heaving gently from side to side like an inebriated sailor. 'Can't go any faster — ' stopping to take on another cargo of twice-used air — 'It's my legs, you know. Mind you, it's been better since the nurse suggested I kept Daddy down-stairs where he could see what was going on. Keeps them interested when they're ill like he is.' Connie made suitable noises as they both trod the black-painted staircase up to the landing that seemed only inches above their heads.

At the top of the stairs Connie could see into the box room.

The room appeared to be so full of bits of broken furniture and towers of yellowing newspapers that the door could not be closed properly, and was held to by a piece of string fastened between doorknob and lintel.

'The room right at the end there is mine, Connie.' Mrs Oldshaw volunteered the information like an invitation to Sunday tea. Connie could see that the door to her room had been locked with a small shed lock that hung brightly from a loop of metal-threaded green plastic. Mrs Oldshaw placed a heavy arm on the bannister. 'This one's yours, love. It gets all the light from the back. We have to have the light on most of the time, even though it's summer.'

Connie avoided looking at Mrs Oldshaw as she felt herself dangerously near to tears.

'I've put new curtains up in your room. Hope you like it, love.' Mrs Oldshaw shoved past Connie and stumped down the stairs. Connie saw her face illuminated by the naked light bulb on the corner of the stairs. Her narrow, solemn face appeared to be making a silent assessment of her, but a second or two later it slid out of sight.

Connie went into the bed-sitting-room with some trepidation. It was dark in this house. The vague unease Connie felt was not due to the Oldshaws. They seemed to her exuberantly odd. Connie thought them no worse than her aunts. Connie had lived most of her solitary childhood in the company of one or more elderly or middle-aged relatives. In some ways she had never felt as awkward with older people as she sometimes did with people of her own age. She looked around. The walls rose from the darkly varnished skirting-board in an unpleasant, throat-retching yellow. There was a rag rug before the grate, and a wood-framed bed and an easy chair. The easy chair looked comfortable, so she sat down for a while wondering what the time was and trying to disguise the sense of loneliness she had begun to feel.

Suddenly Mr Oldshaw's deep voice rasped out, 'Shut bloody up, Adolphe, or I'll come out t' ye!' There was a dog barking somewhere but she could not tell if it was inside the house. She heard someone bang firmly on a wall. 'It's all right, Daddy.' Mrs Oldshaw came in from the kitchen — Connie could track her voice through the floorboards. ''E's after that bitch down the road, poor thing, 'e might as well not have an 'article' as all the use it is to him, tied up there in t' yard. You having him in for Christmas doesn't count, Daddy.' She could hear Mr Oldshaw chuckle. 'I don't care, Mother, 'e's for guarding the 'ouse, and, what's more, me and Adolphe have an understanding — we hates each other.'

Connie went to the window and looked out over the rows of terraced back-to-back houses, each one with its own crowded back yard. The houses swam out to a blue middle-distance. Next door to the Oldshaws the hopeful occupant had reinforced the roof of the outside lavatory and had lugged up half a ton of soil, spreading it lovingly over the roof. This miniature Garden of Babylon was planted with geraniums of every possible variety. Round the outside was a neat border of ever-lasting lobelias. The flowers had kept their fine mist of early dew. Two large dustbins formed a centrepiece. The cleaner of the two had a healthy white rose growing out of it whilst the other, once profuse with begonias, stood waterlogged and slowly rotting. Tiny drops of water bejewelled the chicken wire that protected the garden, and the whitewashed wall that separated the Oldshaws from their neighbours had been sprinkled with broken glass set in cement. It reminded Connie of one of the stories in her Grimm's fairy tale book, that had been left behind in her quick getaway from her aunts' house.

Down in the Oldshaws' back yard Connie could just see the corner of the animal that Mr Oldshaw disparagingly called 'Adolphe', sitting on the potato sacks opposite the lavatory. It was difficult to see what sort of dog it was, except that it was black and white and appeared to have no legs. Close by the ramshackle back door there stood a chip machine that looked like an instrument of torture devised by the Inquisition. Caught underneath the tripod legs was a deep plastic bucket to hold the chipped potatoes as they were squeezed through the decorative iron fretwork on which they were spiked. An old, cast-iron bath stood against the longest side of the wall. It was full to the brim with washed potatoes covered with cold water which she could see was directed into the bath by a piece of black hosepipe that disappeared into the kitchen window. With her exclusive view directly over the bath of creamy white potatoes, Connie imagined that the Oldshaws had been visited in the night by a giant toad, who, after depositing its eggs in the old bath in the yard, had gone its merry way, skipping over the broken glass deterrents of the back yard walls, and off into the smouldering sunrise of the Liverpool dawn. The six glass panes of her window were spotless, marred only by her breath as she struggled to catch a glimpse of the dog.

Connie, who had fallen asleep in her comfortable easy chair, woke to the voice of Mrs Oldshaw calling up the stairs, 'Connie, Connie, you all right, love?'

She stumbled from the orange velveteen chair, still dazed with sleep. 'Yes, Mrs Oldshaw, I'm fine. Must have fallen asleep. Do you know what the time is? I've not got a watch.'

There was a shuffling at the bottom of the stairs. 'Do you know, it's half past seven. I've been reading to Daddy. I just haven't noticed the time.'

Connie put some of her money into the small leather purse that hung from her neck by a thong and, going to the top of the stairs, shouted, 'I'm going to go out for a bit of a walk. Perhaps I'll drop in at the local pub as well.' She grabbed her jacket from the rail where it had found a temporary home and clattered down the stairs on her sensible heels. Composing herself at the green curtain she knocked politely on the door jamb.

'Come in, love, no need to knock, now we know who you are.' Mrs Oldshaw was sitting before the fire, her legs splayed, grotesquely out of proportion with the rest of her body. She held in her hand a toasting-fork with a piece of bread speared on the end of it. Mr Oldshaw sat semi-upright on the bed. His eyes closed, the fire's reflections danced in his steel-rimmed spectacles. His ruddy mouth parted, taking in air like thin soup, jerking it, wheezing and bubbling, into his chest. 'Are you going out right away, Connie? If you like, I'll make you some toast and tea. Daddy's asleep now. He likes a bit of a sleep in the afternoons. Which pub were you thinking of going in? The Black Horse is nice but my friends like the Grapes better. They're more friendly there and the glasses are clean.'

Connie smiled at this last remark and sat down at the table. 'Thanks, Mrs Oldshaw, but I really don't feel like anything at the moment. I think I'll trot down to the Grapes. It's the one near the main road, isn't it?' She put her arms into the black leather bomber jacket, zipped it up and plunged her hands into the two side pockets. Standing up, she took out of her pocket the front door key she had been given earlier and threaded it on to the leather thong round her neck so that it hung side by side with her purse. She smoothed out the creases from the front of her pretty, blue-tiered skirt and, bending towards the old lady, whispered, 'I'll try not to be too late. I've got my key safe, look, it's round my neck.' She pushed a fresh stick of gum between her wine-red painted lips, then pressed them together again out of habit. She posted the silver wrapper in the fire. 'Bye now, see you later.'

At the bottom of Kirkby Street there was a sweet and tobacco shop, its dismal exterior shuttered against attack. Connie did not feel at all uncomfortable going into the Grapes on her own. Standing outside only heightened the depressing feeling of being alone. She had been in pubs before but never on her own. She was a lively girl but, for all that, she was not half so confident as most girls of her age. Connie's Gran had prided herself that she had brought the girl up 'respectable' and not 'hard-faced'. What she really meant was that she had successfully suppressed the child's natural gaiety and curiosity. Connie had often quaked under her grandmother's rigid discipline, never daring to mention its extent at school, where she knew the other girls would be only too ready to enjoy the information. Concealing her nervousness, she walked calmly to the bar and ordered a drink from a young lad who, it seemed to her, was only a year or two her senior. She sat with the half pint of bitter on the table in front of her.

As it was still early in the evening there were only a few customers in the bar. Two men engaged in a game of darts at the far end of the room gave her a passing glance before sinking their darts into the soft surround of strawboard. She smiled a half-smile as the men, embarrassed, agreed to begin to score again. On the bench opposite there sat an old man with a Yorkshire terrier beside him, its head covered in several small bows of pink ribbon. She watched as the old man smoothed the steel-grey silk of the dog's coat with a gnarled hand. He fed it peanuts and a bowl of Black Velvet. The old man took off his flat cap and placed it upside down on the table. The tiny dog promptly jumped into it, turned round twice and settled down.

'By God, mate, yer've gorr'im trained.' One of the darts players had come across and sat looking wonderingly at the animal in the old man's cap. 'If I could only get the owl girl t' do that, I'd be quids in, we'd never go short and that's a fact.' Everyone laughed and an elderly woman bought a drink for the old man. The darts player leaned over the old man's shoulder and said confidentially, 'Cum on, tell us the secret of yer animal magnetism, Dad. Go on, we won't ler on will we, kids?' The old man signalled him to come closer and mumbled toothlessly in his ear. The young darts player exploded with the bombshell of the shared secret. 'You dirty old bugger, I bet you didn't tell yer owl lady, yer a dog, honest you are.' Then, still laughing intermittently, he went back to his partner to pursue the game.

Connie watched, laughing with the other drinkers, as the now fragmented game collapsed in utter confusion, the two men made helpless by breathless giggles. The young barman turned to face the mirror-tiled back wall and adjusted his large bow tie, vainly trying to avoid laughing.

Connie smiled at the old man and put out her hand to stroke the dog's head. She was warned by a throaty growl as the little animal curled its upper lip over small threatening teeth. The old man smiled indulgently at her and said through a stump mouth, 'Yew'd better not touch 'im love, 'e's a bugger when the drink's in 'im. Sumtimes 'e's all right and then sumtimes 'e's a liability. Cum on, love, 'ave a drink wid me and Lil 'ere.' The old man pointed to a woman in an orange dayglo headsquare who was about his own age. Nudging Connie, he said coyly, 'She's me Judy.' Connie liked them. Nodding to the barman, the old man took out his packet of Park Drive from an inside pocket and offered the old lady a cigarette.

'No thanks, Alf, me chest's a bit thick tonight.'

The barman came over with a drink for Connie and set it down in front of her on the table. 'Thanks,' said Connie, raising the glass in a silent toast to the old couple seated in front of her.

'New round 'ere are yer?' The old man scooped the dog out of the cap and replaced it on his head. 'Not seen yer round 'ere before.'

Connie took a sip from her glass and drew a sun pattern from the wet ring left on the table. 'I've got the room over the chippy in Kirkby Street. Perhaps you know them — the Oldshaws.'

The old man's face became suddenly animated with recognition. 'Ernie Oldshaw! Yes, I used to know 'im before 'e got took sick with the dropsy. 'E used to be a good dancer, although yer wouldn't know it now, lovely and light on 'is feet. Must be all of twenty-eight stone now, though, poor divil.'

The old woman craned her neck forward, 'I know 'is wife too. She's a good woman. It can't be much fun for 'er, poor soul. They say the nurse 'as t'cum and tap the fluid from 'is legs, otherwise they'd burst open like sausages in the pan.'

'They're Spiritualists.' The old man interrupted her flow and Connie was grateful. 'Mrs, she 'as séances every month or thereabouts. There's a lot round 'ere has cause t' be grateful to Lizzy Oldshaw.' He sucked in his beer between iron-hard gums, his pale translucent eyes static over the bony ridge of his nose. Once again he lapsed with his companion into the catatonic symptoms of old age.

Connie relaxed in the friendly atmosphere of the pub and chewed her way through the bag of nuts Lil had given her. She was drowsy with the events of the day, secure in the knowledge that Frank would be safely searching the south side of the city, and that before long he would be called to heel by Rachel, in favour of other, more lucrative duties. The pub filled up. People came and sat by Connie. Some of them were just curious about her but others were willing to speak at great length on the subject of Spiritualism and the Oldshaws. Living with Ernest and Lizzie Oldshaw had suddenly become more exciting and attractive than the afternoon had promised. Draining her glass Connie rose from the table, tossing goodnights around her as though she were scattering largesse from the roof of the Julian basilica.

It was still only just ten o'clock when she arrived back at 35 Kirkby Street. Letting herself in to the shop she remembered to shoot the bolts before going upstairs to spend her first independent night on the Anglepoise mattress.

FOUR

Connie struggled with the dough vat until her arms ached with the unaccustomed activity. The huge aluminium drum lay on its side, the machinery stilled as she manoeuvred the white dough from the sides with a huge plastic spatula, pushing it into a chute where it lay white and flaccid. She wrung her hands to rid them of the bits that hung from her wrists and fingers like decaying bonds, and wiped her fingers on the stiff, white apron that was tied in front of her.

The summer had long since disappeared and thin drizzles of cold rain had taken its place without her even noticing. She had hardly spoken to anyone in all the time she had been working at the meat factory. She stood by the drum waiting for the machine to be re-filled and thought how lucky she had been to get even this temporary job. She noticed a window set high up in the clean wall opposite her machine. She could just see the thin, black branches of a young tree outside the meat-canning factory. Connie watched it for a while before her mind returned to the prison of the metal drum. She stuck another piece of gum in the corner of her mouth, chewing it in bit by bit until it lay in her cheek tasting like a lump of soggy cardboard.

Suddenly Connie was aware of a small giggle somewhere to the side of her. Then a bubbly voice asked, 'Ay gurl, what does this remind yer of?' The voice came from the direction of another dough vat only a few yards away. Connie looked up and saw two girls of about the same age as herself. They were talking and laughing together. One of the girls held up a yeasty piece of the dough, which had been roughly shaped to resemble the male generative organ. The girl waggled it obscenely in the air in front of her. Connie smiled half-heartedly. She was not shocked but puzzled by the crude introduction.

The two girls fell about in paroxysms of helpless laughter and grabbed at each other's arms to accentuate their fun. Connie turned defensively but there was no need; the girls seemed not to be interested in her any more and were busying themselves in turning out the dough vat. One of the girls was slightly built and wore the regulation white net cap pulled firmly down over a barrage of foam rubber rollers in shades of cerise and pale blue. The hair that was rolled over them was the colour of wet sand and the small, pinched face that belonged to the massive superstructure above it looked tragically youthful. The other girl was black, and had proud, almond-shaped eyes that reminded Connie of a Benin bronze sculpture that she had seen in a television programme. Her large, well-shaped lips were slightly turned up at the corners as if she were in a state of perpetual amusement. Connie watched the black girl, inconspicuous behind her upturned tub. The black girl scraped out the dough with a few deft strokes of her spatula which appeared to Connie to be an extension of her thin sable arm. The skin of her cheeks glowed with a maroon blush that gave her face the velvet texture of a fabled black rose. Her short wiry hair reached out from her head, teased into a giant dark powder-puff which made her cap strain and swell in its attempts to contain it. Connie thought her beautifully exotic and admired the confidence she seemed to radiate.

Later, the two girls sat opposite Connie in the canteen, staring at her and giggling. Connie's poor brand of self-esteem began to crumble and in no time at all she began to feel as though she were sitting there wearing only her knickers. Drinking her coffee, she gazed hopefully over to the left-hand side of the canteen where the older women sat so that they could be nearest to the hot water pipes. They were almost all very large indeed. Connie was amazed at their size. Under their white overalls they wore stretchy crimplene skirts in pastel shades and bootees that had little heels and collars of imitation fur around the ankles. Their arms wobbled on the Formica-topped tables like swollen grubs searching for food.

The doors at the end of the canteen opened and then sealed themselves behind a bevy of middle-aged ladies. Connie sat still and watched them over the chipped rim of her coffee mug.

The women from the carcass department seemed a different breed. Their overalls, already far from clean, were bloodied from their work, and they had the manner and appearance of strutting warriors, sure of their position at the top of the heap. Connie turned back to her view of the two younger girls and tried to pretend they were no longer there.

The morning was inhospitably cold. Although the factory was kept regulation warm this was no defence against the handling of frozen meat chunks with red and blistered fingers. The meat was prepared in eight-ounce portions and a piece of kidney must be placed in every tin, said Connie to herself as she became automatic tin packer of the year. The shiny tins passed her at eye level giving her just enough time to take them off the line and stuff them full of ice-crystal steak and kidney. From there they journeyed on to a collection point at the end of the conveyor belt, where they were taken in giant wire baskets and placed in vast steamer ovens to be cooked.

In the dinner break, Connie sat quietly by a radiator attempting to re-introduce a spark of feeling into her cold skinned fingers, and reading her school book of poems. It was one of her favourite possessions and she had been sure of taking it with her in her flight from Hesketh Street.

She had been sitting there for a while before she became aware of small drips of tea splashing on to the open page. Looking up she saw the black girl standing over her, grinning and flicking small drops of tea from her cup with two dampened fingers. Her friend stood behind her, arms folded, waiting. Connie tried not to look unnerved, for she knew that the two girls were longing for some sort of confrontation. Her mind searched for a way to back off without injury.

The thin, fair girl spoke slowly to her friend. 'She doesn't like us, Asunta. You can tell she doesn't like us.' The fair girl looked steadily at Connie, daring her to say something.

'Yeh,' said Asunta, and then, taking the book from Connie's grasp, 'you think you're a cut above us, don't yew, girl? You'd think yew wuz a college girl the way yew carry on. Gives herself airs and graces, doesn't she, Pat?' she said, turning to look at her friend who, by this time, was grinning widely, her chewing gum slugging from cheek to cheek like the contents of a washing-machine.

Connie looked at Asunta bravely and pleaded for her book. 'Please, Asunta, give it me back. It belongs to my Gran.' Connie held out a pleading hand.

'Oh, it's Asunta now, is it? Did you hear that, Pat? For God's sake, what a fuckin' wet cow you are, you make us all tired. What did you say yer name was? Little Miss Wet Knicks?' Most of the younger girls laughed out loud, watching with approval as Asunta strutted past Connie, holding the book, tantalisingly, just out of her reach.

Connie had lied about the book; she really did not want to acknowledge it was hers, and in the past such sentimental lies had often worked.

Asunta and Pat began hurling the book backwards and forwards to one another across the canteen. It was a pig-in-the-middle game with Connie as the pig. Realising she would not get the book back by any amount of pleading and chasing after the two girls, who were being egged on by some of the younger workers, Connie sat down dejectedly at one of the tables. The other women watched the entertainment, eager to see what would transpire. One woman, leaning on the counter by the tea urn, shouted weakly, 'Come on, Asunta, enough's enough!' but she was transfixed by a basilisk stare from the assembled company of women. Turning to the counter, she obliterated herself in consuming a cheese sandwich from the plastic tray and sat, without uttering another word, her mug cupped in her hands. Some of the younger girls began clapping slowly and repeating the ominous words, 'Fight, fight!' Connie felt cornered.

At that moment, the doors at the other end of the canteen opened and were held apart by a colossus of a woman accompanied by three of four others. The cries of 'Fight!' died away to a grumble of disappointed conversation as the seated women appeared suddenly to become interested in the colour of the salt cellars on the tables. The huge woman came over to the girls and stood between them, putting her blood-stained arms on her wide hips. A great roar came from her.

'That's enough, you lot!' She pushed Asunta firmly in the middle of the chest making her take a step backward. 'Well, girl,' she said, getting hold of Connie's arm and turning to face her. 'You'll soon get used to these. After a bit they just dry up and roll away. Anyhow, in future, just remember, if anyone says anything to you, just you refer them to Big Mary.' Big Mary released Connie's arm and pushed her down on to the seat beside her. 'Sit there, no one'll touch you now, and don't look so scared.' Big Mary moved over to the now silent but still disdainful Asunta. 'No more messing from you, m'lady. I've had to talk to you before about this kind of thing, remember?'

Asunta sucked in her left cheek and held her head high, saying nothing but looking at Mary from under finely sculpted eyelids.

'Pat, give this girl her book back.'

Pat crawled round the table and offered Connie the book. Connie looked at it sadly. The spine was broken in two places and the first few pages hung out like dead tongues, discoloured and wet with tea. But having the book back was all that mattered to her.

'We didn't mean anything by it, Mary,' Pat's voice soothed.

'Yeah, Mary, we was only 'avin her on. Just a bit of fun. Anybody would think she was made of gold or sommat. We was going to give her the rotten book back.' Asunta's head was proud, but her voice held notes of submission.

Connie basked in the protection of Big Mary. She sat by the enormous woman studying her more closely. Mary ate huge mouthfuls of cream bun from a bloodstained hand that more closely resembled a paw. There were stiff black hairs on the knuckle of each finger. Connie could see that washing was not one of Big Mary's strong points. There were still fragments of offal glued to the back of her hand, and on the apron that was pulled over her large stomach, which creased and bubbled as she shifted in her chair.

Mary wiped her forearm across her mouth, smearing the residue of cream and crumbs onto her thigh. 'Don't let them sods worry you, love,' she mumbled, spattering crumbs into her raised mug of tea. 'I'll see if I can get the supervisor to move you to where I can keep an eye on you for a bit, O.K.?'

Connie burbled her thanks, spilling some of her tea from unco-ordinated lips. The bell sounded for the end of the dinner break and the women got up in small groups to leave.

Mary said to Connie as she rose from her chair, 'Look, girl, you go back to the packing department and I'll have a word with Moira. She'll get you moved. She's a good skin.'

'O.K., Mary, and thanks. Asunta would have floored me. The last fight I had with anyone was at school.'

Mary, as good as her word, arranged for Connie to work opposite her that afternoon on an electric carcass saw. It was hard work, although learning to control the saw was not difficult. Occasionally, on looking up, she would see Big Mary watching her as if she were a pup she had saved from being drowned. Connie worked hard at her saw, halving and then quartering the frozen sheep and beef carcasses as if she had done it competently all her life. As she worked, her secret thoughts drifted through her head; shrouded and mystic, they came to her to give comfort. Connie wanted her life to produce some excitement. She was becoming tired of fighting for some small corner in which she could read her poems without ridicule, and even pretend that she had written them. She had written one or two poems herself in an old school book, but, somehow, even vague comparisons with Keats and Coleridge had forced her to abandon her scribblings to the anonymous flames of the Oldshaw's fire. Now she had to be careful, and grateful to Big Mary under whose protection she now found herself.

After the day's work was over, the women working in her section on the carcass saws fetched buckets of hot water from the canteen and brought the cloths which had been left to dry the previous night on the pipes leading to the massive steamers. Two women shared a bucket and everyone had a cloth of her own. Before the women could leave, every piece of machinery had to be washed down thoroughly. Connie plunged her cold hands with revulsion into the diluted, bloody water, which was greasy and smelled of warm meat. Because she had no suitable shoes, her feet were wet and squelched about inside her leather sandals. That morning, when she had set out for work, she had had no idea that she would, by the end of the afternoon, be standing in a quarter-inch of warm, fatty water.

After the cleaning process, the bell rang and they were all free to leave. Connie was very tired and cold as she walked through the enormous yard on her way to the bus stop. She held her knitted scarf close over her mouth and nose so that she would not smell the truckloads of massive thigh bones that stood in tubs against the outer wall of the factory. The wall, like all the others of the indistinguishable factories on the estate, reared up in bright, new, red brick behind the tubs. Connie watched numbly as the buildings disappeared and the bus moved swiftly away out of the desolation of the factory estate and on towards the city.

Connie was glad to get back to the Oldshaws. They had become her anchor in the time she had lived with them. The customers who came regularly to the chippy had got to know her, and the Oldshaws treated her more like a niece than a lodger. Developing this friendship eased her path and made life at the meat factory a little more bearable. She hated the job, but was glad of it. She knew that having a job was not something that was debatable; it was entirely necessary, and certainly not a thing she could afford to be choosey about.

The night was cold and frost-laden as she broke through the line of customers waiting patiently in a small queue across the counter of the chip shop. Mrs Oldshaw was busy battering the cube-like sections of coley in the big bowl of yellow batter in the corner by the window. Connie half expected them to scream as Mrs Oldshaw plunged them into the bubbling fat in the flat wire baskets.

'Hello, Connie love,' Mrs Oldshaw said, looking up as Connie hung back a little, waiting to be noticed. 'Good Lord, girl, you look fair frozen! Go in and say hello to Daddy. The tea's made. I'll bring your chips in later, O.K.?'

Connie nodded, bringing her nose out of her scarf for the first time since leaving the factory.

Inside the living-room, Mr Oldshaw was semi-upright, his napkin already tucked in at the neck of his pyjamas. He held his fork clumsily in a swollen fist and poised it carefully before striking at a portion of thick Cumberland sausage.

'Ello lass, cum, sit thee down 'ere beside me.' He motioned with an elbow for her to sit by him and shuffled on his half-acre of backside on the narrow bed. 'No, it's all right love, you sit you down there, and get thee warm, poor little soul. Have sum tea. Mother'll be in in a tick and you can 'ave your chips.'

Mr Oldshaw stuffed a huge piece of the sausage into his mouth; the hot juices burst out from between his plump lips and dripped on to the first of his several chins. Connie watched, trying hard not to show any sign of the distaste she felt crawling up her throat. Pouring out their tea, Connie smiled at Mr Oldshaw.

'How many sugars, Mr Oldshaw? Shall I put in the usual four?'

'Yes, lass, but for God's sake don't tell Mrs will ye, promise? That nurse as comes 'as an 'art like a swinging brick.'

Laughing as she passed the tea over to the sick man, Connie said, 'Of course not, Mr Oldshaw, it's none of my business to clat on you. Anyway I wouldn't.'

At that moment Mrs Oldshaw came in, carrying the familiar orange bucket. 'Connie will you get me some chips from the yard? The shop's full now and they all want serving at once and I've only got a handful of chips in the fryer.'

Connie jumped up from her seat by the fire. 'Right away ma'am,' she said, willingly taking the proffered chip bucket and squeezing between the end of Mr Oldshaw's bed and the round table. 'Won't be long.'

Opening the back kitchen door she braced herself for a dose of the great outdoors. She could see the gloomy outline of Adolphe seated on the potato sacks just above his kennel. She hated going past the dog even when desperation forced her to seek the comfort of the outside lavatory. Things were always worse when she came out for chips, as Adolphe seemed to think this act an infringement of his canine rights, and behaved accordingly. He had seen Connie advance and place the chip bucket under the legs of the machine. Standing up stiffly on the sacks he bristled with indignation at being disturbed.

'It's only me, Adolphe,' Connie said quietly through teeth held firmly together against the cold.

Adolphe stalked around her as far as his chain would allow, growling and shivering with the prospect of a bite. Connie felt about in the cold water for the cleaned potatoes. Lifting some out, she put them on the side of the chip machine. Balancing one of the larger ones on the metal grid, she took hold of the handle that was shaped like an old-fashioned beer pump, and brought it down hard on the waiting potato, shattering it through the mesh, the chips falling into the orange bucket like a rain of dragon teeth. Walking past Adolphe, her task complete, she held the bucket by her left side as a protective buffer against any attack he might decide to launch. She leaped the last two steps to the sanctuary of the kitchen door. She felt safe from Adolphe only when the latch of the wooden door dropped into place.

Connie basked in the warmth of the Oldshaws' fire in their living-room. She poured out the tea for Mr Oldshaw, and carefully passed him his mug. Mr Oldshaw listened to her telling him all the events of her small day at the factory, quietly sucking in great mouthfuls of his sugary tea.

'You be guided by me, lass. Don't let them get on to you. Fight back.' He rested against his mountain of pillows and closed his eyes as if in some pain. 'Oh, don't listen to me. I'm an old man. You must do what you must, and you're not like that, anyway, are you?'

Connie rubbed the warmth into her knees, like linament. 'No, Mr Oldshaw, sometimes I can't even *talk* to other people, never mind push them in the face. The trouble is I don't swear much, and I'm probably too quiet for them. They think I'm stuck up because I don't read their 'love books', and I know what things mean when sometimes they don't.'

Mr Oldshaw took off his steel-rimmed spectacles and rubbed them on the sheet. Then he wiped his eyes on the napkin that was still under his chin. 'What you need, Connie lass, is a nice young man to look after you. You haven't got a boyfriend, have you? Come on, you can tell me.' Mr Oldshaw leaned to one side confidentially.

Connie smiled at him. 'No, I haven't got a boyfriend. But I don't want one yet, anyway. I don't want to end up married with nine kids. There are plenty of boys around, anyway, Mr Oldshaw. There's bound to be one left for me when I want one.' Connie spoke bravely but, as usual, she kept her real feelings fiercely secret. She remembered how her mother had devoured her father, small pieces at a time so that for long periods he had hardly realised the erosion which left him finally helpless. Connie feared being a sexual captive, bound by drives she felt were better kept under control until she felt better able to cope with them. She disliked the pretence she had seen at the beginning of developing relationships to such an extent that she saw no possibility of forcing herself to join in the dance.

Mr Oldshaw was fumbling blindly for his napkin which he had let fall. Connie passed it to him but, finding his clumsy fingers could not manage, she got up to help him tie it loosely round his neck. Surprisingly, Mr Oldshaw placed a massive hand on her bottom, jiggling the cheek up and down before she could escape him.

'Eh, lass, you've a fair little bum on you, you know.'

Connie's skin warmed with the unexpected familiarity. 'Mr Oldshaw,' she said indulgently, 'you are an old devil. Somebody else might have got mad. You better be careful or I'll have to glue your hands to the pillow if you're not good,' she laughed. She did not really mind Mr Oldshaw's clumsy recognition of her, and felt sorry for the man, unable as he was to enjoy any consummation of such feelings, trapped in a gross body, a travesty of a human being, left only with remembrances of his youth when he had danced elegantly in northern ballrooms with the pick of the girls, courting them furtively on windy corners or shop doorways, like all the youth in his good old days.

FIVE

At half-past seven, trade was slackening off in the chip shop and Mrs Oldshaw came in and sat down heavily by the door, her mouth in a tight, straight line as if she were contemplating something of great importance. She sat without speaking, staring at the clock on the mantelpiece which pointed permanently to 4.15.

'Daddy, do you know it's four years today since we lost our Alice?'

Mr Oldshaw nodded and let his mouth crease into a flattened pink bow. Lizzie Oldshaw appeared to Connie to be tired and near to tears.

'It's the first time I've forgotten to say a prayer. I've been that pushed, I've not known whether I've been coming or going.' Her high voice cracked with emotion.

'There, there Lizzie, don't fret on so, lass. Alice knows, Alice knows.' Mr Oldshaw's voice stretched over and stroked his wife like a fur glove. Connie saw a tear stand jewel-like in the corner of Mrs Oldshaw's eye, before it was pushed over the rim by a blink.

'Must get on, anyway. This won't do at all. Crying like a baby at my age!' Lizzy Oldshaw, embarrassed at succumbing to weakness, got up and straightened her rough apron. Connie patted her landlady's shoulder gently and with as much affection as she could, but this caring gesture had a cataclysmic effect on Mrs Oldshaw. Turning away from Connie for the privacy of the dark green curtain, the old woman's body jerked out the necessary tears.

'You sit down, Mrs Oldshaw, I'll finish in the chippy for

you. Please don't cry any more. You'll make yourself ill. Then who'd look after Mr Oldshaw? Now sit here and have this cup of tea. There's plenty of sugar in it. It'll do you good.'

Mrs Oldshaw looked up at Connie, her usually waxen face flushed and damp with weeping, still juddering with unsuppressed emotion. 'I'm sorry, Connie love, but Alice was our only one. She was a lovely girl, only thirty-two when she died. I'll never forget it. I had to stay in the hospital all night. She had meningitis, so the specialist told us. She never woke up. Didn't even get a chance to say goodbye.' She smoothed down her patent hair with both hands and wiped her nose on the handkerchief Connie had passed to her. 'Sometimes we get in touch, don't we Daddy?'

After a little while Lizzie Oldshaw's eyes brightened considerably. Connie stood by the door of the living-room and watched how tenderly Mr Oldshaw comforted his wife without needing to touch her.

'I'm just going upstairs to change my sheets now. Can I take anything for you while I'm going, Mrs Oldshaw?'

'No, Connie, I can manage until the middle of next week.'

As Connie stumped down the stairs carrying a bulging, blue, shiny launderette bag, Mrs Oldshaw came out from behind the green curtain and stood at the bottom of the staircase.

'Connie love, will you come in for a moment, Daddy would like a word with you.' Smiling, she held up the curtain as Connie passed into the living-room, having left the launderette bag leaning backwards on the bottom stair as if it were about to faint.

Mr Oldshaw looked at her solemnly over the top of his glasses, his hands folded over the tundra of sheets wound about his stomach.

'Connie, Mother and me 'ave 'ad a chat about asking you to join in our meeting this coming Sunday. But there's one thing as bothers me a bit.'

'What's that, Mr Oldshaw?' Connie was puzzled.

'Well, I'll put it to you bluntly. You believe in life after death, don't you? And in our Lord and Saviour, Jesus?'

Connie tried hard not to look as amazed as she felt.

'Yes, Mr Oldshaw, I believe in God. Of course I do. But,

to tell the truth, I've never been to a séance before. Does it matter much?'

'No girl, it don't matter a tap, as long as you're not a hostile.' Mr Oldshaw had come to life, sitting almost upright, his huge knees swung over the side of his bed, his paddle-like feet just touching the edge of the rag rug.

'What's a hostile, Mr Oldshaw?' said Connie, trying to stifle her amusement at his choice of words. She knew very well what he meant but sometimes she could not resist drawing him out.

'Oh, it's somebody who don't believe. A scoffer, you know. But we're always very careful who we pick to join our little band, aren't we Mother?'

Mrs Oldshaw nodded, still sniffling into her hankie, and then, hearing someone come into the shop, she got up and shuffled out in her flat tartan slippers.

Connie called out to her, 'I'll help. It's no trouble. I'm not going anywhere tonight. There's nothing on the pictures, so I might as well keep occupied. As long as I get this washing done sometime.'

'That's all right, Connie, I'm fine now. You watch a bit of telly with Daddy. You'll be company for him.'

Adolphe barked in the back yard. 'Shut bloody up, you, you dirty dog. I'll come out there and kick you in the privates.' Connie listened to Ernest Oldshaw's tirade against the dog. She knew that he used Adolphe to rid himself of the fear of his illness, often promising to perpetrate atrocities on the animal. They'd hardly ever met; the dog was always chained to his kennel in the same way as Mr Oldshaw was chained by sickness to his bed.

Sunday afternoon shrouded Connie's room. She sat up in bed reading her Sunday paper and taking occasional sips from the glass of hot milk Mrs Oldshaw had brought up to her. She had been brewing a cold for several days, and now it had burst out from every corner of her head in a cacophony of snorts and wheezes. Whines in her middle ear sounded like an ancient organ being played for the first time in a hundred years by an over-enthusiastic amateur. Below her, Mr and Mrs Oldshaw were holding their usual service for two. She heard Mrs Oldshaw reading to her husband from the Old Testament and, later on, pumping the harmonium with her purple, knotted legs. Connie snuggled down in her landslide of a bed, pulling the warm blankets up around her so that only her eyes and nose were visible. For a long time she stared through the window at the cold, whitewashed sky, listening to the high-pitched wailing of Mrs Oldshaw's rendering of *Abide with Me* to the groans of the unwilling instrument.

She slept, and the sound died away, but before long she was awakened by Mrs Oldshaw intent on reviving the final flickers of Connie's fire. She wore her good, navy-blue dress with a polka-dot bodice and cream collar. Her hair was arranged with its usual gothic symmetry. Putting the remaining coal on the fire she got up awkwardly. 'You must keep warm, Connie. I'm sorry I've wakened you. Don't come down this afternoon if you don't feel up to it. You'd probably be better off in bed, anyway, with that cold. There are only three others coming. That will make six of us. There's no special fuss or anything.' Lizzie Oldshaw glowed at the prospect of Connie joining them, and Connie could see that a refusal at this point would hurt her needlessly.

'I'll be there, Mrs Oldshaw. I don't think I'm infectious any more, just a bit miserable.' Connie smiled out of her igloo of warmth.

'I don't wonder you've got a cold now. You shouldn't go back to that horrible cold place. I don't blame you a bit for wanting to leave. You could get a better job than that, I'm sure. A nice shop or something like that. Suit you much better than being with that lot.'

Connie wriggled in the bed. 'It's not so easy now, Mrs Oldshaw. If you haven't got any qualifications you can't expect much. There's too many of us. I should have listened to my Gran and stayed on for a bit. I only got Art C.S.E. The teacher hated us. Nobody wanted to take us for anything, we were terrible, but it was just a bit of a giggle then, you know what I mean?' Connie looked into the fire, her head aslant. 'You're right, Mrs Oldshaw, I've had enough of that place. I'll go on the club for a bit and see what turns up. They pay the rent, anyway, and I don't go out much, so I'll be O.K.'

Mrs Oldshaw left the room, closing the door behind her. Connie counted up to ten and hurled herself out of bed and stood on the rag rug in front of the fireplace rubbing her chilled arms. They felt like the skin of a defrosted chicken. Hurriedly, she put on her clothes, desperate to get back to that state of warmth she had enjoyed in bed. As she stood by the window brushing her hair, she heard Mrs Oldshaw's voice welcoming the visitors through the chip shop and the sound of the two bolts being shot across the door. Connie sneezed and held her breath while she searched for the box of paper handkerchiefs under the bed. She looked at herself in the mirror which hung over the mantelpiece. She was very pale and her nose blazed bright pink round the nostrils which were becoming sore and flaky with almost constant wiping. Under her eyes the skin was pale blue, and the lids looked heavy and darker than usual. Breathing on the mirror, she made two little holes in the condensation just big enough to look through.

'That's better,' she said to herself. 'Put a bit of powder on and hope for the best.'

Treading downstairs, taking the box of paper handkerchiefs with her, Connie lifted the veil of the dark green curtain that hid the Oldshaws' living-room from the chip shop and went inside. Mr Oldshaw was sitting smartly to attention in bed. Over his pyjamas he had on a huge black coat. His arms, like forcemeat, had been stuffed into the sleeves, and from her position in the room she could see that his coat had been slit right up the centre seam as far as the collar so that it could be fastened over his stomach. He wore a blue tie round the collar of his pyjamas but, because of his enormous neck, it hung down only as far as the second button, making him look like an imitation Oliver Hardy. His thickened fingers held a hymn book on the top of the sheet close to his chest. Mrs Oldshaw had hidden him with the bedspread, carefully tucking it in all round the bed. Motionless, and dressed so strangely, Connie thought him frighteningly sinsister. He appeared to be sleeping, and he made no sign as she looked at him.

Mrs Oldshaw took Connie by the arm. 'You sit here, Connie love, just by Daddy. That's right, by the table.' Connie let herself be pushed gently into the chair as Mrs

Oldshaw manoeuvred everyone into position. She called out to Connie, 'This lady is Kitty, and this lady on my left is Frances, and this is Mrs Atkins.'

Connie nodded politely in the direction of the three women. Mrs Oldshaw went on talking and fussing and putting things out on the oval table. There was a glass, a book that Connie presumed was a Bible and a copper trumpet about two feet high. It had been placed upright on its rim. As Mrs Oldshaw was busying herself arranging things and lighting the three candles which were standing on the mantelpiece over the fire, Connie inspected the devotees.

The one called Kitty she estimated to be about thirty-eight. Kitty was pinch-nosed and narrow in the head. Her eyes were like cigarette burns in a blanket and Connie took her to be a bit mad. She seemed to have little control over her pink, pointed tongue which flicked in and out of her small mouth at regular intervals. Connie began counting how many seconds between each flicking movement of Kitty's salamander-like tongue. Kitty wore her dark hair swept back from her small face in curls and rolls that ended in a crest that made her look like a hornbill. Her bright pink mouth was overhung by a nose that was surprisingly large, and was unfortunately accentuated by two carefully rouged spots on either cheek. She was thin to the point of emaciation and Connie noticed that the legs to which she seemed only vaguely attached under her skirts were encased in long leather boots which had no calf at all, seeming to be the same measurement all the way up.

She switched her attention to the other two women who seemed to know each other quite well. Frances was a big, wide woman wearing crimplene trousers which were far too tight and nauseatingly revealing. She held her hands thrust between her legs as she talked to her neighbour. Her hair was held flat with pins as far as her ears, from where it sprang, teased out like candy-floss on either side of her head. In the muddy pink lobes of her ears hung a pair of large, gold ear-rings. Her features, which Connie thought might have been quite pretty at one time, were lost in the puff pastry of flesh that surrounded them. Over her big, rigidly controlled bosom she wore a powder-blue polo-neck sweater into which, neckless, her face seemed to plunge as occasionally, in turning her head owl fashion, her hair would take over where her face had previously been.

Mrs Atkins, the third of the visitors, looked back at Connie across the room, her eyes lively and full of curiosity. Connie looked away from her deliberate stare, convinced that in some way unknown to her, she had offended her. Connie could, however, see into the mirror from her seat by the table and contrived in this manner to continue to examine Mrs Atkins. The woman looked remote from the proceedings. She was, Connie guessed, about forty-five, but was still very handsome and elegantly dressed in her suede suit and cream silk blouse. Her fine chestnut hair peeped out in shiny curls from under the knitted pull-on hat she was wearing, and had so far refused to part with, in spite of the sauna effect of the living-room. Mrs Atkins stroked the brown and orange scarf that lay on her lap with long, wax-white fingers. On each finger of her right hand there were several small silver rings.

The conversation between the ladies came to an abrupt halt as Mrs Oldshaw put out the electric light and lit the candles. Mrs Oldshaw sat at the table and, casting down her eyes, seemed to pray silently. Connie felt charged by the atmosphere. She could see that Frances and Kitty had followed Mrs Oldshaw's example but that Mrs Atkins, her eyes still open, was looking steadfastly across the small room. The firelight on her face made her look like a mad Ophelia. Connie was beginning to feel uncomfortable, and closed her eyes like the others. A very long time seemed to elapse in this quiet communion. Then Mr Oldshaw leaned forward slightly.

'What is it, Daddy?' Mrs Oldshaw asked, her voice soft and expectant.

Mr Oldshaw's face looked mask-like in the half-light. Raising one of his arms he pointed at Connie, his fingers shaking like a bunch of bananas in a tropical storm. 'Don't move, lass. 'E's here.'

Connie felt stiff and cold.

'Can't you see 'im, Mother? She's brought an Indian spirit guide. He's just behind her chair.' Mr Oldshaw fell back against his pillows, exhausted by the experience.

Then, Mrs Oldshaw suddenly said, 'Look, the trumpet's

moved! Praise be! They must be here! Be quiet! They might speak yet.'

Connie was enormously excited. She felt that the séance was approaching a climax and that she was to be involved in it. However, there was a fresh pause. Connie's tension mounted, but nothing further transpired. In part of her mind Connie felt, almost with anxiety, like an actor who has destroyed the illusion of a scene by forgetting the part. But, at the same time, a sudden mischievousness was filtering to the surface. Some part of her divined in this situation an opportunity to take a kind of disguised revenge on the adult world.

Standing up, she proceeded to let her body tremble and, pointing to Mrs Atkins, she spoke in a high-pitched voice. 'I'm Jean, remember baby Jean?'

Mrs Atkins showed little signs of turbulence, but sat quite still, holding her hands calmly in front of her. 'Jean.' She said it several times as if a glimmer of memory was coming slowly to the front of her head.

Connie went on, consumed with the thrill of the role she had begun to play, 'Yes, Jean. Don't say you've forgotten me, Mummy.'

Under her heavy, darkened lids, Connie's eyes sought for signs of doubt on the five faces. In the performance of her 'trance' she felt her whole body was in a state of metamorphosis that was, to her, fast becoming real. Here was her opportunity of rising from the ordinary to the extraordinary. If there were indeed spirits in that dark, surely it was their doing and not hers. Her state as a divine vessel had been brought about by some unknown Lord of Earth and Sky, binding her to him with invisible cords to do his bidding and produce his truth before the uninitiated. Her hands, now held above her head in an attitude somewhere between prayer and submission, were no longer fleshly and of this world, but instruments of instruction to benefit the chosen to whom she was now addressing the thoughts of the god. She was that age-old Oracle consulted by the fearful. Maddened and senseless with divine voices like the Argive women, her imaginings took her running in the white weeds of the insane, while humans, born to die, locked their doors as she passed.

Connie was no longer able to consign her feelings to a locked compartment. Turning slowly, she circled, touching each of them in the centre of their perspiring foreheads with an ice-cold index finger. She panted quickly and noisily at each touch. Then, going to the mantelpiece, she suddenly threw back her head and placed her hands over the lighted candles. She remained there, stock still, for several seconds, oblivious of any pain and exultant in her ability to make the heat feel like ice on her skin. The flames crackled and arced sending the hot wax spurting over the edges. Calmly, she removed her hands, her eyes wild with triumph, and held them in an attitude of ancient prayer, exposing the self-inflicted stigmata of carbon on her palms. Letting her hands drop to her sides, she stood in front of Mrs Atkins and, speaking again in the child-like high voice, said, 'Don't worry Mummy. Don't look so sad. There's plenty of people to play with. I'm very happy.' Connie's voice appeared to fade with the spirit's recall. 'Goodbye, Mummy, goodbye!'

Connie sat slumped in her chair, pretending to quiver with uncontrolled emotion.

'Don't touch her yet, Mother,' Mr Oldshaw said, convinced that he had witnessed the birth of a first-class medium. 'Put the light on now. That's enough for the moment. We'll exhaust her if we aren't careful.'

Mrs Oldshaw got up and shuffled over to the light switch. Kitty snuffed out the candles on the mantelpiece and returned to her seat without a word. Frances sat biting her lower lip and twisting a whisp of her fuzzy yellow hair, her other hand plunged between her round thighs. Mrs Oldshaw sat down beside Mrs Atkins who had collapsed unexpectedly in a froth of tears. Her command of the situation had completely crumbled with Connie's arbitrary revelation. Mrs Oldshaw comforted Mrs Atkins who, all the time, from under the shelter of her friend's arm wailed, 'My baby, my baby!'

Connie watched them all slyly behind half-closed eyes. She felt a mixture of delicious wickedness and shame for upsetting Mrs Atkins, but she felt powerful too. Was it possible that what she had thought of as sham had indeed become real? Perhaps she really had been guided to say those things. She began to half believe it.

Mrs Atkins, now reasonably recovered, sat talking to Frances while Mrs Oldshaw made them all tea and scones. Kitty came over to Connie and began to clear the paraphernalia off the table, putting it all on the top of the harmonium. 'Are you all right now?' Kitty said in a reverent voice.

'Yes, I'm all right. What's the matter? Is it all over?' Connie pasted across her lies to make them more firmly believed.

'Yes, Connie love, you came through for us,' Mrs Oldshaw shouted from the kitchen. 'I'll tell you later anyway. Daddy saw the guide. He was a lovely Indian brave.'

Connie smiled inside herself. It had all worked. They were ecstatic. Even Mrs Atkins smiled at her from the other side of the room and, like Kitty, Frances was now looking at her with an almost tangible respect.

Later, as the three women got to their feet to go, collecting scarves and gloves, Mrs Oldshaw spoke to Connie. 'Mrs Atkins wants a word with you, love.'

The woman was standing by the door easing her gloves on to her narrow fingers.

'I didn't believe it could be done. Jean was my baby girl, I lost her a bit after her fourth birthday.'

Connie saw that she had narrowed her eyes to stop her tears pushing over the edge. They stood shining in her eyes like suicides balancing on a ledge. She held her head tilted slightly backward on a long slender neck.

'Thank you. Thank you very much. Perhaps, another time, you would try again for me.' She faltered. 'Most of the time we don't get through to the people who have passed over but . . . well, anyway, thanks a lot.'

'I'm afraid I didn't have much to do with it all, Mrs Atkins. It just happened.' Connie gazed down at the rag rug, unable to look at the woman, knowing that everything that they had seen and heard she had deliberately manufactured. It had all been nothing but a game for her and she certainly had no idea they would all take it so seriously. She had not known why she had said 'Jean' or addressed herself to Mrs Atkins. It had been the first name that came to her mind. That part of the proceedings worried her slightly, but not enough to admit to it all now that everything had passed beyond return.

The women left, satisfied with the spectacle. Connie was beginning to see herself as an answer to the pubs and local bingo hall. Why not? she thought to herself, munching one of Mrs Oldshaw's scones. After all, if it made people happy even for a short while, it was as harmless as it was fun.

'Lass, you've got the power in you, and don't let anyone tell you different.' Taking her hand Mr Oldshaw squeezed it gently. She sat by his bed, letting him hold her hand in one of his, as he shielded his eyes with the other. Connie had seen him weep like this before when the nurse had been to attend to ulcers on his legs, and she was sorry. Soon Mrs Oldshaw came back in from the kitchen and Adolphe yelped in the yard.

'Bloody thing!' said Mr Oldshaw as he blew his nose violently on his dark blue handkerchief.

'Come on, Daddy, I'll take your coat off now.' He leaned forward to assist the operation while Mrs Oldshaw tugged at the back of the collar, eventually slipping it over his head like a split snake-skin. He leaned back on his bed as his wife took off his tie, loosening his collar to make him more comfortable.

'Shall I help you with the dishes, Mrs Oldshaw?'

'No, Connie, you sit there with Daddy. Do you want the telly on, Daddy?' She put her hand on the switch of the portable.

'No, Mother, but I'd like Connie to read to me if she will. There's a thriller on top of the harmonium.' He settled back on his pillows like an oriental potentate. Connie knew he was pleased with her by the way he lay grinning at her.

'By the left, Connie love, I'm that pleased with you I could hug you till you was breathless.' Still smiling, he took her hand and squeezed it gently and persuadingly.

'You will do some more sessions for us, won't you Connie, love, I've not felt the spirit world to be so close as it was to all of us tonight.' Although Connie felt sure that the old man believed in her little charade she regretted the extent to which she had become involved in order to worm her way into their affections.

'Come on, now, Mr Oldshaw, don't go on about it, please. It probably won't ever happen like that again, well, not as good, anyhow. In any case, I think everyone has strange things inside them that have to come out sooner or later. I don't think I'm anything special.'

Connie looked at the smoked marble candles that Mrs Oldshaw had put away in the box on the table.

'To tell you the truth, I don't think I fancy doing another session.' She saw the disappointment cloud his face, and, because she did not wish to be the cause of further damage, said, 'Well, perhaps once in a while when you've no one else to sit in.'

Connie hoped that what she had said would be enough to discourage them from relying on her as their main attraction at the Sunday gatherings. The old man nodded as though he understood, and closed his eyes while she was still speaking as if a great weariness had suddenly come upon him.

'Don't forget your medicine, now.'

Mr Oldshaw grimaced and stuck out a tongue that looked more dead than alive. Connie reached for the bottle and began pouring the yellow viscous liquid into the spoon. Mr Oldshaw dutifully opened his mouth and allowed her to tip the medicine inside. His lips closed over the spoon as she withdrew it, carefully holding the napkin underneath to catch the drips. She put the medicine bottle away on the shelf and put the napkin in the linen basket behind the kitchen door. Taking the thriller from the top of the harmonium, she sat at the foot of the bed and began to read at the point where Mr Oldshaw had turned down the page.

SIX

Connie had grown heartily sick of her idleness since she had left her job at the meat factory. Even though she had the approval of the old couple, she wondered if she would get anything better to do than helping Mrs Oldshaw to clean out the chip buckets and work out schemes to avoid Adolphe's teeth. Although Mrs Oldshaw gave her supper and a little money for a weekend behind the chip bar, she was really only being kind as the business barely supported two. Sometimes this was supplemented by the luxury of the occasional séance at which grateful souls would press on her the odd pound or two. In the beginning she had adamantly refused to take their money, feeling that she would be prostituting her art, but these finer feelings were soon overcome by simple greed. Mrs Oldshaw, sensible to both their needs, would wink at her at the close of a particularly fine Sunday session and they would share the spoils in the back kitchen unknown to Ernest Oldshaw, lost in the throes of *From Sinking Sands* much to his joy and their convenience.

Hands sunk deep in the pockets of her coat she stood looking at the cards in the Job Centre window. She had seen them all before. There they were, the stalwarts. Jobs that only a double-dyed looney would want. 'Shift Workers Wanted. Abbey Road Brush Factory', and 'Floor Workers Required, Sack and Bag Warehouse, no experience necessary'. Apart from these two attractive prospects there was nothing for which she had either the experience or the qualifications. Walking in, she stood by the desk.

'Yes.' The young woman behind the desk looked up, all

sensible, and wearing fresh-as-a-daisy spectacles that darkened as she spoke.

'I'd like a punchy career in the Bagworks,' said Connie, trying to eliminate thoughts of Groucho Marx in *A Night at the Opera*. 'You know, something with style, suitable for a personable young lady such as myself.'

The young-fit-and-twenty-five looked at her from behind her double-glazed eyes, handing her the card without a word.

'Thanks,' said Connie. Trying hard not to crouch she walked slowly out of the carpeted room and into the street.

She went into a café and sat down at an imitation marble table. 'Coffee please, and one of those bun things, er, hamburgers,' she said to the girl of about her own age who leaned over the table to wipe it. She found an unopened packet of sugar at the side of a discarded cup on the table opposite and ate it like sherbet. Putting it under her tongue, she enjoyed the stolen treat immensely.

The day was full of new excitements. Buses jerked along with the eight o'clock workers. Papers were opened, most of them to page three where women with beautiful bodies lay naked and unattainable. Sleepy-eyed women nodded with tiredness, thinking about that second cup of tea and wishing there had been time. People anxious to get to work crammed on to the bus until it was packed to the point of indecency.

The large iron gate opened shyly to admit a truck that lumbered and swayed on the uneven road. Connie looked at the address on the card just to make sure it was the right place, and then up at the tall Dickensian buildings across the road. They ranged, naked against the chewing-gum-grey sky. It had begun to rain fitfully. The railings gradually spattered with rain; the collecting drops zig-zagged heavily down the thick black paint. She looked through the railings into the dismal scene beyond. Everything looked dirty and decrepit. Through a hole in the wall she watched a group of laughing girls running about in the cobbled yard. They wore faded blue overalls and had sacks tied around their waists. They looked as if they had always been hungry. Thin, unwomanly arms hung loosely about their bodies; bony immature hips stood out at odd angles, depending which thin leg bore the weight. Connie watched while they slapped each other around, sometimes pushing one another almost off balance, with accompanying giggles and bursting bubbles of gum from wide, magenta lips.

She was later to learn that this seeming violence was a form of punctuation to their conversations and not done with any intention to provoke. She felt a bit afraid of them, and more than a little apprehensive as she remembered the weeks at the meat factory and the one-sided battle with Asunta in the canteen.

Connie was one of six new girls at the factory who had reported to the office on the second floor. She could tell that they all felt the same as she did. They were issued cross-over denims that fitted where they touched, and a white headscarf. Coiffed like angels of mercy they filed quietly into the workroom to be supervised by one of the more experienced women.

The canteen exploded with voices. Thick tea slopped on the bench-topped tables. Girls crammed into their mouths an evil assortment of cream cakes and vile-looking biscuits. Connie was aware of somebody speaking to her through a wreath of wild Woodbine. She felt herself prodded in a friendly way by a young woman who had sat down beside her. 'Ay girl,' the woman prodded again, 'are yer listenin' t'me or are ye in a brown study?' Connie nodded and smiled a placating smile she had found had worked before. The woman took Connie's arm, rattling her slightly. 'Cum on, ger up, de won't stay der fer ever, will de?'

'Who do you mean?' said Connie, looking puzzled. The other girl put a set of knuckes on her hip and, looking heavenward as if in intense exasperation, said, 'That's for me t'know and yew t' find out, right? Anyway, yew just wait till yew gerra load of 'im, yew'l rip yer drawers off wid desire. I bet yer any muney.' Then, winking wickedly, her scarlet mouth aslant, she pulled Connie good-naturedly to her feet and, towing her along, dashed through the doors of the canteen and down the yard to the outside tea stall. They both fell into the cobbled yard screaming with laughter.

A girl called Marie had arrived first, and she turned on her broken heel to greet them. Her usually strident voice was quieter as she spoke to Connie. ''Ello gurl, doin all right, are ye?'

'Yes, everybody's very friendly.' Connie held her fingers crossed behind her back.

Marie tossed her auburn hair free of the confining head-gear. 'Sandra 'll tell you, won't you San,' pushing Connie's newfound companion gently in the rear.

'Ye, I wuz just telling 'er, there's sum luverly fellahs 'ere. Thee all go 'ere for the break. Only sumtimes you've gorra watch it because sum of the buggers say der single an' de aren't, de ye get me drift?'

Marie went on to explain the purpose of the tea stall in more detail. 'There's one, ooh, 'e's the gear, 'e's gorra face like the feller in *Grease*, an 'is air is all loveley, ye know, 'e's gorra real duck's arse at the back an' a bit that curls just over 'is left eye.' Pausing, she sighed, 'God, I'd throw meself off da Pier 'ed if 'e said.' Her eyes closed as the cavity of brain was visibly penetrated by a thought.

A voice from somewhere behind Connie said, 'Cum on, let's get out of it, them nigger lads are cummin'.'

Connie made a half-turn and saw three black youths advancing slowly on the tea stall. They walked as if they were deliberately delaying their arrival until the girls had gone back to the factory. She watched them unwrap their sand-wiches and sit on the low wall, laughing and talking together, their backs against the railings. One of the boys noticed Connie's quiet attention. He nudged his mate who looked at her appreciatively as he chewed his sandwich. Connie looked down at her scuffed shoes and then at the cobbled yard in front of her.

'Cum on, girl, give us a smile then!' the oldest of the three shouted across to her. The other two began laughing shyly and eventually turned their backs, standing with their heads resting between the bars of the factory cage which imprisoned them all. Although the boys were laughing, Connie felt no hostility. She smiled until she began to giggle herself.

'Connie, are yew cummin' or are you goin' to end up nigger bait? Don't let them black buggers get up yer nose.' Sandra began tugging at the coarse apron Connie had tied behind her, coaxing Connie up the yard. When Sandra felt they were both at a safe distance she turned and shouted to the black boys, her face twisted in gargoyle ferocity.

'Leave 'er alone, yew fuckin' black bastards!' Sandra's

spittle stood in hysterical peaks in her wide open mouth. One of the lads made an aggressive lunge towards them but stopped short and instead put up two lazily insolent fingers as he turned and walked back to his mates.

'Shut your fuckin' poxy face, honkey cow!' the elder youth said, slowly and deliberately erasing the remains of a discarded crust with his boot. Connie looked over Sandra's shoulder expecting that at any moment the boy who was still waving his fingers above his head would suddenly advance upon them and that they would have to run for it, but he did not.

Sandra turned and steered Connie back towards the open factory door. She did not shout any more but continued to mutter under her breath savagely, 'Don't worry Con, only yew've gorra watch it with that lot. One of them went out with a girl out of the packin' department, and knocked 'er about when she wudden do it. You should 'ave seen the state of 'er when 'er mam opened the door. Anyway 'er brother found out and put one on 'im. God, me Dad would go bloody mad if 'e caught me goin out wid one of them.'

Sandra rolled back her sleeve and showed Connie a small pink scar on her forearm.

'See that, Con?'

'Yes, how did it happen? Did you fall or something?'

Sandra laughed. 'No, me Dad said that if I cum in late again 'e'd mark me, an 'e did.'

Connie felt somehow threatened, although she knew they would probably never guess. No one here knew anything about her except what she told them and so her secret, although safe, lay like a bag of stones in her stomach. No one had known about her when she had appeared at Princess Street Secondary until one night her father had decided to go to meet her at the school gate. Then the pretending was over. The white kids had been upset because of the way she had taken them in and the black kids despised her for not being proud enough of being black. The inevitable had happened, and she had quickly become the victim of both factions, a victimisation which had lasted for three weeks, until it all became a bore, and someone else looked more promising. Eventually, in a last display of distaste for her, both parties had temporarily joined forces and, carrying her struggling to the outside lavatories, had pushed her long hair down the pan and flushed her head. She had been rescued by an indifferent teacher. Later she had sat outside the Head's office bellowing with wounded pride.

Connie tried hard not to recall her father except on dangerous occasions, as her longing for him as a source of comfort increased with each desperate conjuration. As a child she had taken for granted his strength and gentleness, but in her present situation it no longer meant anything. She wanted to belong and to start to make her own life work for her. She pushed further back her father's advice never to pretend and to stand up for both cultures. There was no time, she felt. She needed friends now, not in some glorious future. The people she knew were not liberated and she could not chance the mindless hostility that being coloured seemed to inspire in them. These thoughts carved through her mind until she faced a paranoid in the cracked piece of mirror in the women's lavatory. Did they already know she was half a nigger? Connie looked at her face in the glass, inspecting the individual features. Was the mouth over-large? Her lips a little too full? Her nose, hardly an aquiline Norman job, but then neither were those of the handful of scrawny girls she had met so far. Marie looked dark, too. Gypsy probably, Connie thought, tucking a small dark curl of hair back into the white scarf. She went back to her work as if she would bury herself in the sacks.

Connie, for the first time in several months, now considered herself an alien. When her father had been there to protect her, she had been his beloved lily of the field. She wept there in the factory, in all the dust, for the sad need of him.

In the afternoon there was a ten-minute break, and Connie followed the girls from her department, trying to keep her eye on the figure of Sandra, who had almost reached the door.

'Hi Sandra,' Connie said, taking the scarf from her head and smiling at the other girl.

'Hi ya kid, can you wait for us? I just want a drag before we go down to Big George's.'

'Who's big George, San?'

'The fella who 'as the tea stall, y've seen 'im, 'aven't ye?

'E's an offer nobody can refuse. One cup of 'is tea an' it's curtains.' Sandra laughed, showing her clean but very wobbly looking front teeth. 'Anyway, cummon, we better be smart about it or we won't get none. Marie's already down there, did yew see 'er go when that bell went? Like a rat up a pump.' Sandra lifted up a heavy-looking foot and held it, crossing her shin, while she pressed out her cigarette on the sole. Saving the last half-inch she blew on it and pushed it into the breast pocket of her overall. They walked toward the tea stall together. Connie felt glad to be included in Sandra's plans for the next five minutes. Marie was there as Sandra had foretold.

''Ello girls, glad yew could make it. 'Ere, I've saved yer a cuppa tea each. I thought yew'd get killed in the rush so I got 'ere first, any of yew gorra fag?'

Connie took her hands out of her pockets, showing them palm uppermost with a gentle shrug of her shoulders. 'Sorry, Marie, I don't smoke.'

Sandra leaned over to Marie, an open packet of tipped cigarettes on her hand. ''Ere, 'ave one of these, girl, yew can pay me back later.'

Marie took the offered cigarette with a grateful smile and stuck the tip of it in her carefully glossed mouth. Lighting the cigarette and taking in the smoke deeply, so that it reappeared magically streaming from her nostrils, she looked up at Connie amusedly. 'What's all this then, don't wear make-up, don't swear, don't smoke? My God, girl, aren't yew the little plaster saint now?'

Sandra put down her cup on a bench at the side of the stall. 'Come on Marie, leave the girl alone, she's all right, ye can see she's a good skin.'

Connie tried to look Marie straight in the eyes but found it difficult to take her impudently steady gaze. 'It's just that I never have done, I've never wanted to smoke.' She was apologetic about her deviations from Marie's norm.

'Don't yer do that either?' Marie's voice trembled on the brink of laughter.

'Do what?'

'Oh, my God, where 'ave yew been livin', Connie, on Planet X? Yew know what I mean, cum on, you've gorra fellah 'aven't yer?'

'Not now, we finished about a month ago.' She knew she had to be pretty clever at lying to Marie but it was the only way she could remove herself from the total ridicule that appeared to loom larger by the moment. She went on more confidently, 'I can't be bothered with fellahs at the moment. They get on my nerves.' Looking away from Marie and Sandra, who seemed so far to be satisfied, she affected an air of slight but bearable boredom.

The stall owner leered at them over his dirt-ingrained counter and, wiping his filthy hands on an even filthier cloth, he shouted to Marie, ''Ullo love, gorra new one wid yer terday, I see.' His eyes rolled over Connie's body and he stuck out his tongue suggestively at her.

Marie tossed her loosened hair and gave him a look fit to stop a clock. 'Shurrup George, will yer?'

During this exchange of mild hostilities the girls had been joined for their hurried tea by four youths, all of whom wore the same regulation grey dungarees. The boys stood talking to George and taking sips of hot tea, and seemed oblivious of the existence of the girls who stood just behind them, nervously popping their wads of gum and hoping to be distinguished from the rest by a furtive glance, or a meaningful insult. Connie reckoned this sortie unsuccessful, but Sandra rattled on, determined to get some response. Marie put out her fag in the remains of someone's rancid tea, and, so signalled, they all trooped back to the factory to endure the remainder of the day. Connie worked at a machine that stamped names on to sugar sacks, and at the end of the afternoon there was baling to do. Fourteen sacks stitched into a swaddled bundle. The coarse string made hundreds of minute cuts in the surface of the skin, giving the hands the texture of a pangolin. Connie accepted these small inconveniences almost with gratitude in return for the beginning of some new friendships, however temporary.

At half-past eight in the morning the girls were collecting the things they needed for the day's work. Most of the machines had been set and one or two girls were making minor adjustments while others were already waiting for their quota to be pushed down the chute from the floor above, when Marie screamed over to Connie, 'Yer going to the dungeon terday, gurl,' and laughed at the prospect that she herself was to be included in the count.

'Marie, take eight girls with you, that should be enough; there's not that much down there now the lorry's been.' The supervisor's low-pitched voice could be heard over the general mêlée. Connie thought it sounded very like Big Mary's.

The supervisor seemed to rely on Marie for cooperation from the other women. She had authority and was a natural leader. Marie savoured the agitation expressed in Connie's face, but there was no real malice attached to it.

All the girls hated working in the dungeon. The supervisor had told them with relish that it had been the place where the black slaves had been chained, prior to their appearance at the auction block.

The decaying brick tunnels intersected one another and dripped ooze from the Mersey, a few hundred yards away. The place was cold and rat-infested. The rats came from the sewers and found their way into the tunnels to breed in the sacks, attracted by the small deposits of sugar left encrusted in the corners of the bags. Sometimes Connie had seen large individuals running along the hot water pipes in the canteen where a man skilled in the art would impale them with his baling hook. Twice she had seen a man take a throw from as far as twelve feet to thunderous applause.

The supervisor gave Connie a storm lantern and told her to follow the other women, led by Marie, down the narrow staircase, made slippery by the sugar shaken from the sacks. She pushed past the other girls until she stood by Marie's side. The girls looked at each other in the yellow light of the lantern that made Marie's lips look like black cherries and, smiling at each other, they ventured on together through the maze of low-ceilinged cellars lit only by three or four dim bulbs. The air was stale and heavy with damp. Connie thought it had a strange animal scent. In order to count the stowed bundles which were stacked fourteen high as far as the roof, the girls had to climb up over the protruding ends of the bundles and over the tops. Up there it was quiet and eerie. All the girls worked in self-imposed silence for about an hour, doing their jobs with the minimum of movement. It was a dark forest, where it was understood by all that the slightest jarring movement would bring down upon their heads a host of predatory beasts. Common fear prevented the girls communicating. Each observed a natural shut-down for protection.

As Connie crawled gingerly over the tops of the sticky sacking, Marie, who was only three feet away from her, fell forward over the centre of the stow crying out in revulsion as her leg disappeared up to the knee in a seething nest of baby rats who, twittering blindly, squirmed head to tail in the depression of rotting sacks. With an effort born from fear, Marie extricated her self from the mess as quickly as she had fallen.

'Jesus, Joseph and Mary!' she said, crossing herself and visibly shuddering with distaste.

Placing an arm on Marie's shoulders to comfort her, Connie took in a deep breath as both girls forced themselves to look down at the turbulent animals. Most had been squashed to death but others were more determinedly alive. Remembering that they had been instructed to kill any they found, they took courage from each other and began to beat the survivors to death with the wooden handles of their baling hooks. Almost hysterical and unable to stop, the two girls smashed them to a pulp while the blood spurted hot up their arms from the plump, hairless bodies. Exultant, Marie and Connie hammered the remains of the vermin into the sacks. They thought the place alive with shadows. Each girl imagined the rats were coming to take revenge for the death of the young. The swinging storm lantern, moored to the rusted hook in the wall, distorted the shadows, making them appear to the adrenalin-fed girls like enraged, giant rats screaming out to one another, massing in revolt with burning yellow fangs. Rows of bright eyes followed the girls as they made their escape through the maze of bricked tunnels. There was an almost tangible hostility. The rats leaped, weaving, gnawing, scratching, coming from dark holes in the brickwork with quick ferocity, ready to take a life with one well-timed leap.

They sat on the top of the stairs. The other girls had long gone. Connie bent down to wipe the bloody mess of Marie's knee.

'Thanks, Connie, yew know who yer mates are when you're up to your neck in it.'

Connie smiled, her usually enigmatic expression temporarily supplanted by one of warmth and companionship. 'You'll be O.K. and, anyway, you would be surprised to find out how many people I've looked after in my life. I give Mr Oldshaw his yellow medicine, poor Mr Oldshaw.'

Marie's nose wrinkled in disbelief at the name. 'Who the hell's Mr bloody Oldshaw? It's not real, is it?'

'Mr Oldshaw and his Mrs own the chippy. I live over their living-room. They've been very good to me. Mrs Oldshaw gets me books on her library ticket, and I get free chips and, oh well, they're just nice people. Mr Oldshaw's going to die pretty soon. I don't know what the old woman will do. She only had one daughter and she died a long time back. She lives for the old man.'

'Sounds just like me Mam and Dad before they broke up, I don't think. They 'ad their moments when they were workin' and had plenty to go down the club wid, but when things get tight, that's what happens, doesn't it?'

Connie held the lantern in front of Marie and watched as she cleaned a mark from the sleeve of her sweater with a soiled Kleenex. Connie laughed out loud but stopped herself quickly before the echo it made reached back at her.

'What's the marrer, Connie? You on happy tablets or somethin'?'

'No, I was just thinking about how Mr Oldshaw treats his dog, almost like a human being. The two of them hate each other, but Mr Oldshaw talks about the dog as if he's got an evil sense of purpose.'

'Connie Marlowe, you do talk lovely, you know. I wish I talked nice sometimes, but then I wouldn't be me if I suddenly started talking posh, would I?'

'I'm not posh, Marie, I wouldn't be working here if I was, now, would I?' Connie felt near to the brink of apology again, but only for safety's sake, not because she really meant what she said. She was pleased that Marie had seen and been impressed by her noticeable lack of foul language and tarty make-up. She preened secretly.

'All the same, Marie, I'd give anything to have Adolphe here with us. He'd see to these things.' She spat out the word 'things', as if mentioning the actual word 'rat' would once more put them in jeopardy.

Marie sat on the stair above Connie, her head resting on a pair of spiky knees and her arms swathed comfortably round her legs. Then in a dreamy voice, without looking up, she said, 'Who the Christ is Adolphe?' and then, 'You're a funny kid, Connie, must be all these books yew read.'

'No, it's the Oldshaws' dog. Remember, I've just told you about him. He'd be a good ratter. He's nearly bitten me more than once, and he plays hell with the chip bucket if he can get at it.'

Marie listened like a child in an infants' class being told a story before the afternoon rest. She had moved her thin hands until they were under her smooth pointed chin. Connie thought she looked exactly like a picture book gypsy with her wild, dark reddish hair bouncing in rich ringlets of solid colour about her pale narrow face. Connie itched to ask Marie questions about her family, questions that could perhaps lead to a natural exchange of secrets. In the end her curiosity was swamped by her fear of rejection.

'Ay, Con?'

'Yes?'

'Is it 'ard to learn readin' I mean for sumbody like me, for instance?'

Connie was more than taken by surprise. Here was one of the toughest girls in the place asking her, of all people, about reading. The fact that Marie had admitted she could not read was astounding to her.

'It isn't exactly hard, Marie. It's just that you've got to stick to it once you've started. It's no good doing a bit and expecting you can tackle all sorts in the first few weeks.' Connie felt very privileged that Marie had confided in her and hastened to add, 'Don't worry, Marie, I'll not tell any-body, you can count on that.'

Marie looked surprised. 'They all know round the werks, Connie, it's no bloody secret. In any case I'm not the only pebble on the beach, ther's another girl in packin' and stampin' who can't read even 'er own name and ther's a fella on the top floor, but 'e doesn't count really because 'e 'as a teacher who cums round just to 'ear 'im read, that's in 'is own 'owse. It's sum sort of course thing for the government, you know, yew must 'ave seen it on the telly?'

Connie nodded, rather put off her stroke by Marie's nonchalance at the problem.

'Are you thinking of going on the same course, Marie?'

'Good God, no. It's just that now and again I think it would be nice to be able to read one of them love books, you know, the ones with no pictures in, so yer can imagine what goes on, an' all that. Fer everythin' else yew don't 'ave ter read, now do yer? There's telly, and there's records and dancin'.' She smiled. 'Anyhow, who tests yer readin' when yer've gorra fella an 'e puts the light out?'

They both laughed inward little grunts, conscious still that they were on the edge of a world of malevolent beings.

'I think you'll be O.K. now, don't you? At least, the rest will come off with a bit of hot water, but you still look a little pale. Perhaps we ought to wait until the blood comes back to your nose.' Connie had gone down a step or two to retrieve the lantern. 'We better get back now. We must have sat down here for a quarter of an hour, maybe even longer, I've not got a watch.'

Back on the factory floor they were the heroines of the hour. Each time they told the story it was embroidered more finely as the day wore on, until at last it stood unaided like a bishop's cope, textured, and full with mind-catching incident. The girls in the canteen waited avidly for details of the massacre. Some days later the rat man was sent for and laid strips of noxious-looking stuff round the factory, which was to prove harmless when it was discovered that someone with a grudge had given the manager a dose of it.

In the centre of the first floor of the factory stood the huge chute that spewed forth sacks from the floor above, where most of the men worked. Connie stood at the end of her part of the bench, binding the sacks as they were given to her. The girls swapped jokes of a dedicated lavatory humour. Connie remembered some from school and told them with as much conviction as she could, but she soon realised that the quality of the joke didn't matter much at all. It was the telling of them that was important, a ritualistic blending of herself with the whole. She managed to convince the girls on her bench that she enjoyed every mindless moment.

During an afternoon break some time later, one of the women who had just finished carrying bundles of sacks to the hoist fell to her knees in a faint. No one moved. The girls watched the young woman's distress from an uninvolved distance so that whatever pity they had to spare could be dispensed without moving. Most of the girls knew the woman concerned. They were all aware she was not strong and that she badly needed money. Everyone knew but no one wanted to involve themselves with her problems. They could not afford the emotional blood-letting that went with it. As a result they tried to register surprise rather than guilt.

Her dark blood flowed down her skinny legs in a thin stream, rounded her heel and dripped into her broken working shoes. Painfully, she was visible to all until the nurse came out of the sanctuary of the office with a grey army blanket and covered the woman with it, in a quiet display of tenderness. Eventually, the inert body of the young woman was lifted from the moat-filled patch it occupied by a young man in high wellington boots. His oatmeal-coloured socks were rolled over the tops. The woman's hair unfurled over his left shoulder like a silk flag. The blood continued to flow as the man carried her gently to the waiting taxi that the manager had summoned from his office.

'Poor little sod!' The quiet had been broken by Marie who was the first to speak. 'She didn't want anybody ter know she was up the stick. 'Er 'usband's frigged off, yer know. Bastard, but perhaps it's a good job about the kid not stickin' the pace. She's got one poor little buggar already, she duzzen wan another one yet any 'ow.'

Connie was surprised at this tender rasp. Marie had always seemed to Connie the sort of girl who looked upon other people's misfortunes as entirely their own fault. Connie smiled down at her bench. Marie was in the same game as herself. Fancy, all this time she had imagined that Marie was a member of a new super-race of tough 'no tears', 'account to no one', 'befriend no one unless they can do you a turn' women. She had believed that Marie had covered herself in spines because she could not read, but the unveiling of her own illiteracy had been performed with such take-it-or-leave-it matter-of-factness that Connie realised it was a challenge to her.

What faults and worries she had Connie preferred to keep hidden from others who would perhaps be critical but Marie, it now seemed, had a much more feet-on-the-ground approach to the same problem. Marie's brand of gentle seething formic sincerity made a strange but acceptable mixture. Connie admired Marie because she did not feel the need to struggle from her background, where she was held in position like a butterfly in a display cabinet, by ideas and prejudices as tight as whalebone corsets.

When Connie had begun working at the factory she had thought of herself as the only sensitive flower in a world of soulless mutants. Now she realised this was not true. But the realisation did not bring the expected comforts and only made more urgent the desire to escape. Connie looked out hopefully from the spattered windows on an afternoon bright with unaccustomed sun, and found herself concerned with the idea that one day Marie might find herself reading and discovering things about herself she had previously tried to conceal. She thought about her raging quietly in the middle of the night over some half-grasped concept, and was glad she was not likely to be there when the metamorphosis took place, if it ever did.

Monday morning arrived and Connie thought it was warm enough to walk to work. The frost of the night before had clung firmly to the few plants of a sickly, town green that she noticed struggling up between the bars of the old iron areas around the cobbled yard of the factory. It was a minute or two to eight on a sun-gilded morning and Connie left off examining the serrated leaves of a wild berry plant she had found struggling for survival between the sticky black-painted wastepipe and porous pale ochre and orange brickwork. Turning her head she squinted up at the sun through half-closed eyes. She recognised the awkward figure of Sandra running hell for leather towards her. As Sandra got closer she slowed down to her distinctive humping walk and waved a spidery arm over her head. Connie waved back, thinking that Sandra looked for all the world like a spiny anteater she had seen in Chester Zoo.

'Hi San,' she called out to the girl who speeded up, urged

on by Connie's voice and the freshness of the morning.

'Hi ya, isn't it a lovely day terday, Con?' Sandra pressed her arm in a comforting kind of way. 'Look, I've found this in the square gardens on the way to work. It must be the first one in the whole of Liverpool.' Sandra put both hands in the big shopping bag she always carried and pressed open the sides, showing the greeny gold of an immature daffodil. It lay on its side as if sleeping, still in its bud. They looked at it but did not touch it, as if in so doing the magic would slip away from them. Sandra closed the bag.

'Good God, Sandra, so it's you that pulls the heads of the daffs in the park, is it? Never mind, kid, they can't touch you for it.' Both girls laughed and whirled around holding hands like little girls in a school playground until they were both dizzy and clung breathlessly to the railings.

'Con, are you gettin' anythin' for Marie for 'er birthday?'

'Didn't know it was her birthday, Sandra. How old is she?'

'It's 'er eighteenth on Thursday. She's told me you're cummin to the party at 'er Mam's flat. It's all right, 'er Mam and Dad won't be there, they go out to the pub, they're very good like that, they don't sit round puttin' a damper on the show, know what I mean?'

'Yes, I know what you mean.' Connie looked down at her dark brown working shoes and twitched her toes inside them.

Now other girls could be seen gathering in twos and threes around the main gate, although the majority of the work force had gone inside and were in the process of clocking on, lined up, card in hand, ready to record themselves for the day. The factory hooter went dead on eight and the queue of waiting girls concertina'd into the arch of the main entrance.

Connie and Sandra followed the rest, Sandra holding the secret daffodil in her bag — a little bit of the spring, a little sign that she was alive, inside her stiff denim overall. Connie knew she would not take out the flower and put it in water. Sandra was no braver than she was. Connie imagined the flower lying in Sandra's bag, stifling among perfume-soaked Kleenex and crushed by Sandra's customary bacon butties wrapped, British Rail style, in unbreakable polythene film. She knew that by dinner-time the daffodil would have all but expired in the airless heat; but she was glad that

Sandra had bothered anyway. She felt it was a sign of some sort. She could still see the amazing light of the morning through the dirty windows as they passed into the factory and up the staircase to the floor on which they both worked.

Thursday arrived, although both Connie and Sandra had, earlier in the week, suspected that Thursday had been cancelled. Connie had packed her blue duffle bag with a black dress she had bought specially in the dinner hour the day before. She had even bought some new make-up just for the occasion. Both girls were very excitable all day and, whenever they got the chance, could talk of nothing else. During the afternoon break Connie slipped out to the shops at the top of the road opposite the bus terminal. She knew that, even if she only brought Marie a bar of soap, she would love it and keep the bag it came wrapped in for ever. Connie felt a little strange going into the shop in her overall and still wearing her white head-scarf. There had been no time for her to take them off and in the excitement she had completely forgotten her untidy appearance.

She bought Marie the blue silk blouse that all the girls had admired in the shop window. She recalled Marie saying, 'Just look at that there, it's bloody luvly that is, isn't it, I'd give me right arm!' Connie knew that Marie had to support her father's alcoholic wanderings. She admitted to sometimes having to give him as much as twelve pounds out of her own wages. It pleased Connie to be able to give Marie a present that she knew would be appreciated. She glowed with the feeling and enjoyed it thoroughly all the way back to the factory. Running breathlessly into the cloakroom she hid the parcel inside an old plastic carrier from a record shop. There she knew it would be safe from Marie and from the girls who were suspected of having sticky fingers.

The afternoon seemed to be endless. Connie found herself watching the dirty-faced clock that hung over the manager's office like a dead planet. At last they were released by the sounding of the buzzer and ran to queue at the old-fashioned railway-type ticket hatch for the secretary to hand them their wage packets. Connie had never seen the fabulous secretary. She was always obscured from the common view by the frosted glass of the hatch door which was kept as low as possible, everybody supposed for security purposes. The secretary never spoke. Any queries were passed on silently to a male clerk. All anyone ever saw were her hands, slender like a medieval lady's in a rose bower, the skin pale, young and fine-textured, her nails painted deep, frosted pink. She was a candy woman, gift-wrapped in her sanctuary of an office. Sometimes it had occurred to Connie to grasp the delicate hand and see if any of the fingers would snap off like Southport rock. She suspected that inside would be written, right through to the bone, 'I love Adrian'.

She took her money and passed out of the door and down the steps, looking over her shoulder to see if Sandra or Marie could be identified in the swollen crowd of girls eddying around the office hatch.

'Hi ya kid!' It was Marie followed by Sandra, busy fishing around in her shopping bag.

'I thought you'd never get here, I seem to have been waiting here for hours.'

'Hi ya!' said Sandra, crushing the dead daffodil and chucking it behind three cardboard boxes that waited patiently to be shifted inside.

Marie did not notice Sandra's action, but Connie did. Her eyes followed the curve the daffodil made in the air before disappearing behind the shiny pale brown cardboard boxes. She thought of it lying there, the last of its life sap oozing out through the dark green tunnels of the stem.

'Mam, we're 'ere,' Marie shouted through the letterbox of the flat. The door opened and Connie caught sight of Marie's mam on her way back to what looked like the kitchen area. A disembodied voice which carved a path over their heads told the girls to close the door behind them. 'No need to shout, Mam, we 'erd you, anythin' to eat or do we 'ave to go down the chippy? It's all right, we don't mind do we, girls?'

'Oh, get in you lot, there's sum dinner for you all in the oven.' Marie's Mam came out from the kitchen.

'You're Mam looks very young, Marie,' Connie said in a whisper.

'Don't let 'er know that, she's big-'edded enough without all that carry on, keeps goin' on about 'er bein a child bride. She wasn't married when she 'ad me, but she likes me to think it. Me real Dad cum from one of the American bases, you know it was love at first sight.' Connie wondered at how Marie, after so many opportunities to talk about her family, had suddenly decided to tell this to both herself and Sandra in the cramped living-room of her mother's flat.

Marie's Mam came in with her head swathed in a magenta towel. A wisp of peroxide-blonde hair strayed from the taut towel, and dripped on to the black shiny robe she wore. Standing by the gas fire she reached for her cigarettes and lighter which stood on a sort of bookshelf-cum-mantelpiece festooned with small pot dogs, a glass swan and a musical cigarette box in the form of a grand piano that played *Edelweiss* every time Mam reached for a fag. The lower shelves were filled with the more familiar rubbish of every-day living — matchboxes, a cup with a broken handle containing an assortment of elastic bands of different sizes, a hairnet and a handful of kirby grips, some green and white cleaning tickets, and just the hint of a buff letter with O.H.M.S. stamped in the corner.

Connie was intrigued by Marie's Mam. She was reminded of her own mother.

'I'm Alice,' Marie's Mam said, without looking at any of them and drawing on her cigarette with pale, cracked lips. Sandra and Connie sat down on the moquette couch. They were both riveted by the woman. 'Well now!' Alice rubbed her hair with the magenta towel, eventually shaking her head and leaving the towel draped across her shoulders. Holding the damp hair away from her forehead she pressed another cigarette between her lips, continuing to talk as she lit it. 'You both work with our kid? Or is it just you, Sandra?'

Sandra was ill-equipped to answer. Her mouth hung open, moist and shiny like the centre of an exotic bloom.

'Yes, we both work in the same room with Marie.' Connie was used to helping Sandra out on occasions like these when she could not get her mouth to work at the same time as her brain. Sandra closed her mouth and smiled.

'Marie, go and get your dinner out of the oven. Do you want to change after?' Alice said to Connie and Sandra, placing her cigarette in the Worthington ashtray and pulling the robe tighter around her waist, holding it on her left hip with her right hand as if she were deciding whether or not to fling it wide open in a blinding flash of white, fire-patterned thighs. Alice combed her thin hair and rolled up the sections of it in soft, plastic foam rollers. This done, she began to pluck out stray hairs that deviated from the fine-pencilled arch of her brows. Connie noticed that, while she performed this task before her small hand mirror which she had propped up on the table, she made exactly the same vacant face that Sandra had made a moment before.

The two girls continued to watch Alice as she powdered and preened before her hand mirror. Taking up her lipstick she filled in the cracks of her kiss-wounded lips with the colour of rich burgundy. They heard Marie call from the kitchen, 'Cum on you two, it's out on the table gettin' cold.' Connie and Sandra got up from the couch and walked silently into the kitchen to where Marie had put out the meal on the perky melamine table. Alice took no notice of them after that and continued to prepare herself for her usual pay day night out with her temporary husband, Jimmy, part-time kleptomaniac and full-time alcoholic. The girls ate their meal in the quiet kitchen: the only noises their stainless steel steak knives on the stamped tines of discoloured forks. Connie wondered what Marie's stepfather would be like. She thought of Marie's tales of him going to Woolworth's and stealing Mars bars and liquorice bootlaces from the sweet counters. She smiled to herself as she imagined this 'cry for help'. He was never caught; so she supposed his cry went unheard.

Alice went out at last, leaving the girls dressed in their finery and feeling like shaken-up pop bottles. Marie brought out the food from the kitchen cabinet and the other two girls helped to set it out in the front room on the cracked smoky glass dining-table, repaired with Sellotape. Alice had thoughtfully borrowed some chairs for them from the pub on the corner along with two dozen wine glasses. Connie rinsed the wine glasses and set them sparkling on the white paper tablecloth.

'Doesn't everything look great?' said Sandra, clasping her red hands together like a faithful servant pleased at her lady's pleasure even though she was to have none herself. Marie whirled around filling the small floor space with the spread of her new red skirt.

'All we gorra do now is wait for the punters t' turn up,' she said, calming down the flurry of the folds with her hands and plumping down in a big easy chair which was just behind the door.

Sandra turned suddenly, a look of disbelief on her face. 'Christ, Marie, we've forgotten the soddin' booze.'

At 10.30 the alarm Sandra had raised over the booze had been remedied by twenty-five or so guests who had brought liquor of all forms and potent qualities, which they added to the stock bought in haste and on tick from the same pub that had lent them the chairs.

Connie sat in the big chair watching the other guests dance on the twelve square feet of the front room. There was an extraordinary boy of about nineteen who kept pointing to the nicotine-stained ceiling above him like some erstwhile saint, while at the same time he revolved his buttocks independently of one another as if he had been coached by a female tassle dancer who did not know the difference, or perhaps did not care.

She wished that he would dance every time. He was so struttingly amusing, she had to suck in her bottom lip to stop herself from laughing. At 11.30 the young dancer left with two other boys and they drove off in a taxi, talking loudly all the time of going to some other place.

'Did you know them, Marie, or were they gate-crashers?'

Marie looked drunkenly towards Connie's face from where she suspected the sound was coming. She was draped over a very randy-looking boy with tight trousers and white tennis socks and pumps. His head was patterned all over with signs of the zodiac in a kind of light dye. Connie thought that his head was probably more interesting on the outside than it was on the inside. She smiled at him and watched as he blindly groped at her friend's left breast. Marie tried to ignore the thick palm that passed brusquely across her breast. 'That fella, 'e always does a turn, doesn't 'e, Arn?' She pushed Arn's hand down to a more conversational level. 'Con, I'm sorry, this is Arnold Marks, only 'e likes bein' called Arn better.'

'Glad to meet you, Arn.'

Arn took his hand from Marie's hip and stuck it out in front. Connie took it and he squeezed her hand until her mouth opened with the pain. Releasing her, he laughed appreciatively at himself.

'Come on, Arn, you didn't have to hurt Connie.' Marie slapped him, but safely, not on his face, and then kissed him in spite of it.

'It's O.K. Marie. It looks as if it's made him come to life anyway.'

Connie thought it was a good idea to find a corner where she could carry on observing without either being crushed or bitten by cheerfully drunken partygoers. She was glad that she had been offered a camp bed in Marie's bedroom. She sat on one of the hard pub chairs by the table and watched as exponents of the dance shuffled and crashed into one another like blindfolded toddlers. Wine glasses knocked and spilled against each other as they were placed on the table by careless revellers. Hands came from somewhere above her and put out cigarettes in the lees of wine and flat, abandoned beer. She was reminded of Beatrice's habit with her morning tea. A set of pretty fingers carefully placed a cigarette end, sizzling point first, into a plunge of whipped cream cheese. Others followed her example until the little bowl had the appearance of a Sargasso sea of dying butts, steaming and hissing at each other.

Nothing remarkable happened. No one talked, not even to introduce themselves. They were all young, but looked tired and bored, even with themselves. She drifted out of the room and was waylaid by two boys who had not brought anyone and felt she was fair game. Promising to bring them back a bottle of whisky if they would let her pass, Connie escaped down the hallway and into the small bedroom where she locked the door and lay on the camp bed, exhausted by nothing, and no more friendly with Sandra, who had disappeared outside to be sick against a wall, than with Marie, who preferred the company of Arn, the expressionist man with the cruel streak and the Saggitarius ear-rings. Consciousness drifted from her, but she continued to half-hear the music and crude articulations of the guests as their taxis finally arrived. Slowly the night simmered down to a dull throb.

Connie heard Marie's voice calling through the plywood door, 'Con, you awake? Let me in, kid, I'm buggered. Arn's gone off in a huff because you're in 'ere.' Connie got out of the low cot and opened the bedroom door.

'Well, sod 'im, any'ow, 'e's a swine if 'e can't get 'is own way, do 'im good to wait for a bit, do 'im good.' Marie's tears had been waiting for a curtain call all night, and now they rushed, carrying all before them. Eye-shadow and mascara left a blackened trail of havoc down her night-white face.

Connie sat on the big bed and took Marie's hands. 'Come on, whatever's happened to the birthday girl? Cheer up, love, it was a lovely party!' She lied but felt it was a good lie. 'Do you know something, Marie?'

'What?' Marie blubbered abandonedly.

'Well, I've still got your birthday present in my bag. You've not seen it yet. I'll get it now.' Connie got up and took the present out of the bag. 'Happy birthday, Marie love, happy birthday!' She placed the present in Marie's outstretched hands.

Marie opened it and unfolded the blue blouse and stroked it as she held it close to her. 'Oh Connie, you are a love, it's the most luvly thing I've ever 'ad off anybody.'

'I only hope we all live to enjoy it,' Connie said, getting back into the camp bed and pulling the down quilt over her head. Under her snow blanket she could hear Marie's muffled laugh. Marie put out the light and they went to sleep.

The buzzer had gone and most of the girls had dashed off in great eagerness to begin their weekend. Connie was also glad of the temporary release. The wage in her pocket would go into the Post Office savings account she had kept open from her stay in the house in Hesketh Street. She took pains to keep thoughts of her two aunts at bay but she often, as now, wondered about Frank and if he ever remembered her with anything like the affection he had showed himself capable of in their last hours together.

'Hey gurl, wait for me!' Connie turned to look back into the late afternoon sun at the thin figure of Marie in full flight behind her. 'Cum on, hurry up, we'll miss the bus,'

Marie said arriving at Connie's side, panting with the effort of the inclining cobbled road. 'Christ, I've gone and bust my heel on them bloody cobbles again, they were new last Friday an' all, sod!' She stamped hard to drive the heel more firmly on to the body of the shoe. 'You'd have thought they would have put down proper flags by this time. Them things 'ave been down since Donnelley docked.'

Connie laughed and turned around to do a spot of backward walking, to be able to face her friend while they talked. 'Are you going to the new disco on Saturday, Marie? It's supposed to be great, that's if you know all the dances like you do.'

Marie shoved out her bottom lip, looking coyly at Connie. 'Gettaway, gurl, I know the 'ustle, but that's all, even that's not much fun cos my fellah's so bloody left-footed 'e can only pogo, an that's a big pity cos it's gone outa style now, an 'e can't do anythin' else. Well it serves 'im right, the stupid get, I keep tellin 'im but 'e won't listen.'

Connie sucked in her upper lip and held it with her teeth in a frantic effort to avoid laughing at the idea of Arn pogoing regardless of what everyone else was doing. She pushed down her calf-length blue dress that had been blown up about her thighs by a mischievous wind. 'God, I should have put a petticoat on. I'm always getting caught out in the rain with no coat or up to my ears in woolly jumpers in the middle of a heatwave.'

'Yeah, you're a bit like that aren't you, Connie? Me Mam calls it bein' three sheets t' wind, or if yer want it cold, a bit cracked.'

'Thanks very much,' said Connie, a look of mock hurt on her face as she continued to paddle backwards up the street to the bus stop where they would part, to stand in opposite queues making faces at each other until the first bus came.

'About that disco, Connie, it's a nice idea but it's too expensive and I've gorra get a new coat before this one slides off me back in disgust.'

'Well, I promised old Ma Oldshaw I'd do Saturday night in the chippy, Marie, so we couldn't have made it anyway this weekend.'

'I'd love t' see these two old things yew live wid, they must be way out. Carn I cum up one day an' see dem in der natural surroundin's? It must be like livin' in the Stone Age wid dem. Me Mam's bad enough, she gets on me nerves fer ever goin' on about 'ow fantastic 'er youth was an' 'er pictures of Cliff Richard still stuck up in the kitchen. God, it gets right up me nostrils, all that stuff about the marvellous boyfriend she was supposed to 'ave. 'E was supposed to 'ave 'ad this gang of Teddy lads. 'E was the 'ard nut of Toxteth to 'ear 'er talk.'

'The Oldshaws aren't so bad. They're a bit religious but they don't force it down your throat. It's a sort of everyday thing with them, and you get used to it all after a bit. Anyway I like them, and they've been good to me.'

Connie was surprised to find herself defending the old couple so vigorously, and realised that she would defend them staunchly even to the point of risking severing her tenuous links with Marie. Connie liked Marie and she was sure Marie liked her, but she could not see herself following Marie and going to discos every other night, and never doing anything that did not fit in with Marie's idea of a good time. Also she regarded herself as being rather more of a loner from choice. Preferring the company of older people helped her create a certain stability in her life. She knew that, although on occasions she felt an acute need to be nothing more than light-headedly youthful and seek the company and friendship of people of her own age, sooner or later the powerfully private side of her would emerge, and it was the ability to have those feelings that she wished to protect. Poems and older people, however pleasant and interesting, would never appeal to Marie. Connie knew she would have a dedicated teacher in Marie's particular brand of blasphemy, and a happy helper at the British Sherry bottle in the person of Sandra, but there were too many good things, too many quietly promising things to give up.

'Marie, I don't think you had better come. It's not that I want to put you off for ever, but I honestly think you'd be bored after the first five minutes, and there's nothing glam about looking after the chippy. It's just a lot of hard work.'

'God, I'm bored ter death already an' I 'aven't even been yet. O.K., Connie, I get yer drift, I'm not daft you know, not altogether any 'ow.'

Connie was glad that she had successfully put Marie off

without having to hurt her feelings. The two girls stood at their separate bus stops and grinned at each other from behind the other people in the orderly queues. Marie caught sight of the factory's night watchman with his air rifle slung over his shoulder. They both waved until he responded with a pallid, little gesture. 'Wouldn't like 'is job, sittin in our place an' taking' pot shots at our little furry bruthers all night. Mind yew, the munny's not bad so I've 'erd. Suppose that's all 'e does it for, the bleedin munney, don't you?'

The bus came and carried a waving Marie back to her mother's flat in Aigburth Vale.

SEVEN

During the journey back to the Oldshaws', Connie half wished she had the courage to go to the new disco everyone had been so enthusiastic about, but somehow it always happened that, at the last moment, whatever courage she had managed to gather during the week fled from her. She hated to admit to herself that she preferred the company of the Oldshaws to that of Marie and girls of her own age. She lied furiously about a string of non-existent boyfriends, often going as far as creating involved affairs, where, of course, there were none. Admitting the truth would have meant putting up with being the main source of amusement until something more meaty came along, and she was not brave or self-confident enough to do it.

Connie shooed away a dog bent almost double in its efforts to rid itself of a herculean stool at the front of the chip shop. At that point Mrs Oldshaw came out with a bucket of disinfected water and engulfed the dog who, in spite of the attack, remained in the same position looking sadly over its shoulder.

'It must be Adolphe, it must be able to smell him. There's a lot think he's a bitch. I get fed up with dogs weeing on the step, some don't want to go really, you can see them screwing up their eyes to squeeze a drop out, dirty things!' Mrs Oldshaw brought out the stiff yard brush to erase the traces of the offending animal.

'I've had an awful day today, Connie.' Mrs Oldshaw waddled back into the shop shaking her polished head from side to side in a gesture of patient despair.

'What's the matter?' Connie walked into the shop behind her landlady, unwinding her long multi-coloured scarf.

'Oh, just some young yobbos, most of them not more than twelve. They came in just when I was getting ready to close up after the dinner-time trade.' Mrs Oldshaw sat down and rubbed her forearm with her left hand as if she were cold. 'They took to spitting on the floor of the shop, nasty little devils, but then I wasn't going to stand for that and I told them to get out, but do you know, the oldest one just stuck up two fingers in front of my face and said, 'Up yours Mrs.' Lizzie Oldshaw looked hurt and bewildered. 'They said they'd come back and break the window if I told on them.'

'Don't worry, Mrs Oldshaw, it's only bravado. They won't be back. Well not until they're sixteen anyway.' She was struggling to lift the old woman out of her depression, but the mood was firmly entrenched and there was no shifting it. 'Come on, Mrs Oldshaw, you go and have a cup of tea with Mr, and I'll see to tonight's opening.'

'Thank you, dear, everything's ready. You don't have to go through to the yard, everything is at the side of the fryer, in the usual place.' Mrs Oldshaw smiled a tired but welcoming smile. 'Oh Connie, sometimes I feel we put on you too much, I think you're too good-natured for your own good.'

'Rubbish, Mrs Oldshaw, I wouldn't offer if I didn't mean it. Besides, I like to feel that I'm some use now and again, and it does help with the rent, you know.'

'But it doesn't seem fair to ask you after you've done a day's work already.'

Connie took hold of Lizzie Oldshaw's coarse apron and pretended to pull her into the back room by the long tapes dangling at the front.

'Well, I'll go just for a bit, put my feet up for a while and finish off Daddy's latest thriller for him.'

Connie stayed behind the counter for the rest of the evening, reading snatches of her book when things were slack. She was tired but wild horses would not have induced her to admit it. From time to time she looked in on the Oldshaws. They were both sleeping soundly. The book was open on Mrs Oldshaw's knees — she had been so tired that she had fallen asleep with the apron still tied about her stomach. Ernest Oldshaw, his head pushed forward on to his chest, breathed with such effort that it seemed to Connie that he might even forget how to go on. He had deteriorated in both his condition and his spirit in the last week or two. She had noticed that Adolphe now got the upper hand in any argument. The elderly couple lay, propping each other up, in the gloom of the back parlour. Connie let the curtain fall across the scene and went back to the shop.

After packing up for the night in the chippy, Connie made tea for the Oldshaws and sat with them silently drinking by the fire. Connie could feel they were all tired and a little depressed. Lizzie Oldshaw took off her apron at last and passed it over to Connie to hang behind the door.

'Thanks a lot, love. I don't think I could have faced it tonight. Daddy was up most of last night with his chest. The nurse says it's fluid again.'

Connie nodded. 'Is he all right? I mean, is he going to get better?'

'To tell you the truth, Connie love, I don't know. The nurse said he ought to be in hospital but he won't go. We've never been parted, you see, and he thinks that if he goes to hospital away from me he won't come back. You can see the sense in that, really, can't you?'

Connie felt disturbed and touched by Mrs Oldshaw's admission. She liked the old couple very much but did not want to feel emotionally responsible or bound to them. Yet she could feel the bonds tightening and the obligations become more and more demanding. She thought of her life slipping quietly away under an avalanche of commitments.

Finishing her Snoopy-mug of tea, she placed it on the tin tray and collected the other mugs from the Oldshaws, and the bread plate, and took them out into the cold kitchen.

'Leave them things, Connie, I'll do them in the morning. I don't feel I've the energy to move at the moment.'

'It's all right, Mrs Oldshaw, I'll do them. I might as well, I've got them in the bowl now.' Connie ran the hot water, that had been left in the kettle for the purpose, over the bread plate, sweeping the crumbs off the shining porcelain with an arc-like movement of her arm. She could hear Mrs Oldshaw drawing in her breath in sharp, tear-interrupted bursts. Washing the dishes as vigorously as she dared, Connie wished she could blot out the old woman's crying. She had no desire to invade what little privacy Lizzie Oldshaw had left to her, but she was tired and wanted to get up to her room. At last she heard Mrs Oldshaw's weight being spread over the small wooden seat that was kept tucked underneath the harmonium. Connie wiped her hands on the cold wet dish towel and was glad that she had done her usual trick of popping out to the pub across the road to visit the toilet there before closing-time. The thought of stalking past Adolphe in the half-light filled her with trepidation.

Walking quietly back into the living-room she stood calmly at the bottom of the bed looking at Ernest Oldshaw as he lay whitely against his pillows, like a human iceberg. Connie had not been aware of the music until she turned to see Lizzie Oldshaw looking at her with a knowing smile full of sticky sentiment. Connie smiled back at her, a smile she felt was more like the grimace of a wounded animal than the greeting of a human. Lizzie Oldshaw continued to pump *Abide with Me* on the valiant little harmonium, while the tears she so much wished to conceal at last flowed unrestrained down to the lover's leap of her chin where they were hurled off into the void.

'I'm going off up to bed now, Mrs Oldshaw. Say goodnight to Mr for me, won't you?' Mrs Oldshaw did not reply. She had begun already, in her mind's eye, to sail down a sinister corridor while her fingers, looking like old tallow candles, played the signature tune which announced the quiet accompanying angel.

Lying in bed at last, Connie felt worn down and demoralised. It seemed to her that everything that had happened over the months she had spent on her own was pushing her inexorably to the brink of some unknown disaster. Even the darkened room conspired to feed her misery. She heard Adolphe bark outside and the noise of his jumping on to the top of his kennel. The chain made its familiar scraping sound as he tried to pull it round the corner of the wall. She half-expected to hear Mr Oldshaw bang on the window, but tonight she knew that Adolphe could bark and rattle his chain as much as he liked. There was to be no cowing voice, full of Yorkshire blood and threatened thunder — just the old clock on the wall of the landing outside her room. The sound of the harmonium died away into the dark as the hymn came to its glorious end. Connie listened to the clock and felt her pulse beat in time with it. She had deliberately not closed the curtains as she enjoyed watching the tree in the garden next door beating the sky to a froth with its long dark fingers.

The moon had risen directly outside her window and hung framed in the top pane, a pale, silver disc, a flattened milk bottle top, suspended like a sign in the sky. She stared at the moon until the entire room was filled with the navy-blue cotton wool of the night.

Saturday mornings always began in exactly the same way. Because it was a big night in the fish and chip calendar there was a great deal of preparation to be done. As a result, Mrs Oldshaw was rarely seen in the living-room. She spent the first few hours before opening filleting the fish and cutting them into portions ready to be coated in the batter mixture which she had to make freshly each day. Connie could hear her filtering the fat from the enormous fryers. The smell almost always did the trick of waking Connie from whatever level of sleep she had attained.

The day was wide-eyed and beautiful. The back yard seemed alive with bird life. Connie got out of bed and stumbled over to the window. Flicking the catch, she raised the window some two feet to let out the stale, sad air of the previous night. Leaning on the small table that stood in front of the window, she could see sparrows and pigeons exulting in the bright suddenness of a show of spring. It amused her to see them launching themselves into the air to swoop like acrobats just above Adolphe's kennel. Light streamed in and laid itself in a graceful curve over the table and then over her clothes which had been placed on the back of the chair. The tree outside had broken out in a rash of small, green buds barely visible on the tiny finger-ends of branches bouncing joyously in the fresh, picture-book blue of the sky. Connie hung over the sill trying to tempt small birds with a large, unbroken crust. Eventually, it dropped down into the yard below her and was promptly eaten by Adolphe. Looking down into the pit of the yard, she made a face like a medieval gargoyle at the dog, but this did nothing to deter Adolphe from his usual belligerence. Standing almost upright, his thin paws splayed apart on the whitewashed wall, he barked and leaped in his determination to get at Connie, trampolining off the potato sacks on the top of his kennel. After a while, he gave a cursory snarl and gave up. His walnut of a brain was covered by the veil of forgetfulness and he strutted over to the potato chipper and sprayed the iron leg with his own brand of lustral water. Connie laughed out loud, he looked at her but did not bark again.

Connie put on her black, three-tiered, broderie Anglaise skirt, and a fluffy, pale fawn, mohair sweater. She was pleased by the way the sweater clung to her body. She had bought it from Sandra who had owned it for a week before she had become fed up with it and offered it to Connie at a reduced price. Sandra was thinner than Connie, so the sweater was one size smaller than usual, but this did not deter Connie — she liked the feel of it and the way it accentuated her small waist. Sitting on the chair by her bed, she squeezed on her high tan wedges, stood up and stamped on the rag rug. Hurriedly straightening the bed and smoothing down the candlewick bedspread, she took up her black plastic toilet bag from the hook behind the door and jogged downstairs to wash in the kitchen. Stopping outside the green curtains as she usually did, she tapped on the lintel.

'Come in, Connie love.' It was Mr Oldshaw. She had gone to bed the night before thinking she would not see him again.

Connie lifted the dark green curtain and looked in underneath her outstretched arm. 'Hello, Mr Oldshaw. You sound a lot better today. Have you had your medicine yet?'

'No, Connie love, I've been waitin on you coming down,' he said with undisguised pleasure. She noticed that he was still a little breathless when he spoke. He wrinkled his nose like an elephant seal about to do battle, and waited with his mouth slightly open, the bottom lip pulsating pinkly. He pointed to his mouth and chuckled, ''Urry up lass, I'll get lockjaw or summat stuck 'ere like this.'

Connie let the curtain fall, cutting them off from sight of the chippy. 'O.K. It's coming right away so hold on.'

Ernest Oldshaw screwed up his eyes until the lines at the sides bleached white with pressure. His bottom lip trembled with anticipation of the vile taste of the yellow medicine. Connie hurriedly uncorked the bottle and launched herself across the room with the tablespoon held firmly in the fingers of her left hand. As she tipped the contents of the spoon into Ernest Oldshaw's mouth, Connie could feel herself grasped by his bottle-topped hands and palpated like a child's first balloon.

'Mr Oldshaw, you are a naughty boy,' Connie found herself saying in mock annoyance. 'I really will have to do something about you, you know.'

It was to no avail. Ernest Oldshaw was in the throes of a Wagnerian mystic experience. He held her firmly, his eyes closed like a blind man. His still apparently sensitive fingers began slowly to probe and feel around her body. They rounded her thighs, her waist, and reached like a supplicant to her breasts. Connie could not escape him without making things more difficult for them all. His appreciation of her did not disgust her as she had thought it might when the idea of his touching her had slid through her mind in past moments of proximity. She thought it not so serious for her as it would be for him if they were discovered by a suddenly alerted Lizzie Oldshaw. She felt sorry for him, and somehow felt glad to be able to offer him a small amount of pleasure from her store of youth and unmarked perfection. Standing silently at the side of his bed she let him smooth his big hands avidly over her, eagerly seeking out those little pockets of pleasure that for so long, she felt sure, must have been denied him.

She cut herself off from his enjoyment of her, looking down on the top of his head as he coaxed one of her breasts out from her fluffy fawn sweater.

Ernest Oldshaw held her breast for a moment in a vast, trembling hand. Strangely detached, she watched the pink cushions of his open lips moistened by a quick tongue, plunge towards her and close over her pale nipple, sucking it into the vast cavern of his almost toothless mouth. Closing her eyes, she was clothed by blackness from the blushing silence of the moment. Ernest Oldshaw released her breast and, opening her eyes, she looked down on it, shining and moist with his saliva while he continued to knead her buttocks with his hands. She stroked his remaining hair while he made quiet little grunts of realised pleasure and rolled his head from side to side on her soft stomach, until at last he was quiet.

Connie pushed Ernest Oldshaw gently back on to his pillows.

'Oh, you are wunderful, Connie Marlowe, you are a good girl to me!'

He was pink and breathless, and he reached again for the comforting breast he had only just relinquished. Taking his hand she placed it on top of the sheet. 'It's all right, Mr Oldshaw, don't worry about anything. Just you get better! I don't mind and I'm not shocked or anything daft like that.' She straightened out the sheet he had threshed up in his efforts at tumescence.

Connie pushed her jumper back into place and rearranged her skirt which lay spread out like a black cloud on the top of Mr Oldshaw's sheet. She smiled a gentle, reassuring smile and helped him on with his glasses which had fallen off in his excitement.

'Can't believe your luck, I know, but I bet that does you more good than whatever that old nurse gives you.' Ernest Oldshaw was still looking at her as if she had just announced that she had been sent from heaven. His eyes were full to the reddened brims with grateful tears. 'Come on now, Mr Oldshaw, don't upset yourself. It's supposed to make the blood flow in your veins, not make you cry.' She was about to put the yellow medicine back on the shelf when the curtain was brushed aside by Mrs Oldshaw, who came into the living-room, heaving herself around the furniture, the orange chip bucket in her right hand.

'Hello, Connie love, I could hear you were down. Thought you were reading to Daddy. Has he had his medicine yet?'

Connie looked at Mr Oldshaw and winked cheekily as Lizzie Oldshaw's broad back disappeared into the kitchen. 'Oh yes, he's had his medicine, haven't you, Mr Oldshaw?' He participated in the game by sticking out his tongue and waggling the tip of it suggestively at Connie before answering in the affirmative.

The experience had not been a blow to Connie, who viewed the semi-sex act as nothing but a kindness on her part. In a way, she was even glad that it had happened because, as things stood, she had great difficulty in finding anyone she liked enough to have a sex relationship with and, when she did, her doubts and fears held her back so that the day she would get involved seemed to escape and get further than ever from her. It would be useful to be able to fantasise about its having happened with a handsome boy, perhaps at the pictures or at his mother's house while everyone was out. The other girls at the factory would not want to know the name and address, only the salacious details. She admitted to herself that she had even quite enjoyed it in a carefully controlled way. Perhaps, she thought, she would allow him other treats next time. Treats kept hidden from his curious fingers by her closed thighs. She went into the kitchen and washed herself, putting on a bright, plum-coloured mouth with a final flourish.

Mrs Oldshaw came back in from the yard as Connie was tipping out the lukewarm water she had used for washing.

'I'll be out all day, Mrs Oldshaw. I've changed my mind. I'm fed up working night and day and watching the telly in between. I'm going to visit some relatives.'

Mrs Oldshaw looked surprised but pleased, breaking the austerity of her face with a smile. 'Oh, Connie, I am glad for you! I'm sure they'll be very pleased to see you after all this time!' Still smiling, she put down the chip bucket on the table and rested her large blue-veined arms on the rim. Ernest Oldshaw lay still, feigning sleep, his spectacles hanging on the bulbous point of his nose. Connie could see his eyelids fluttering almost imperceptibly as they spoke.

When she had left Hesketh Street, Connie had had no intention of contacting any of her relatives. But recently, the feeling of the snare tightening round her, forced her to hope that somewhere in the city there was ready-made companionship and perhaps a family feeling of caring tenderness which was waiting to be collected like a long-forgotten inheritance.

'Yes, I know where they've moved to, it's by the Park. They were re-housed a few years ago, I think it's Faulkner Square Gardens. I only went there once. I was about twelve, I suppose. They're all new flats but not the twelve-storey ones. They are just like small houses really — all facing inwards in the shape of a square. They looked very nice when I saw them, but, like I said it was a long time ago.'

She had picked up her black plastic sponge-bag and was swinging it slowly backwards and forwards on a clean finger.

Mrs Oldshaw patted Connie on the shoulder as she passed her on the way to the chip shop to get on with the lunchtime preparation. 'Looks as if Daddy's all right now,' she said as she sailed through the green curtain and into the shop. 'You go ahead, love, enjoy yourself. You've done enough in here for a bit, and now that Daddy seems a lot better I can cope.'

Connie smiled slyly at the inert form of Ernest Oldshaw in the knowledge that what the old woman had said was true. Collecting her towel and toothbrush from the draining board she walked silently through the living-room. Looking back over her shoulder, she saw Ernest Oldshaw open an eye like a sleeping whale lying on the bottom of his sea-blue interior-sprung bed. Now he was quietly saying goodbye with a hand raised like a flag in appreciation of her. She dropped the curtain on Ernest Oldshaw, cutting him off with a heavy swathe of green.

Upstairs in her room, she took her coat off the back of the door and put it on, although she felt she did not need it, the day was so fine. She put away her toilet things, and the remains of her garlic sausage and bread and butter in a plastic container, tossing the crumbs out of the window for the birds who waited noisily on the tree outside. The window closed on its old rope sashes with very little effort or sound. The room looked fairly neat, but she cursed under her breath when she realised she had not yet made the fire ready to be lit when she came home at night. Pulling out the ash can from under the fire bowl, she riddled all but the larger clinkers through the fire basket that looked like a set of very angry teeth. Taking up an old copy of the *Sun*, she made tight little sausages of newsprint and rolled them into curls, tucking the tails inside, and put them in place. Finally, she placed the last of the bundle of firewood in a crossword puzzle pattern on top of the paper. After brushing the remaining ash dust back under the firebowl and putting the lid back on the bucket she stood up and dusted herself free from imaginary ash. Connie inspected her hands but they were quite clean in spite of the job she had been doing. She opened the drawer at the top of her small bureau and took out the purse that usually hung from her neck on a leather thong, a handkerchief and a few pounds from her wage packet which she always kept inside her Post Office savings book. Her modest account had by this time swelled to a very satisfying amount and she lovingly touched the outer cover of the blue, plastic book before she closed the drawer.

Connie paraded down the street, nodding occasionally to people she recognised as customers at the chip shop. Catching the bus at the main road stop, she sat on one of the high seats at the back and watched everyone from behind a copy of *Cosmopolitan*. The bus took her into the centre of Saturday Liverpool where she stepped off as near as she could to the covered market. She found a café and went in and sat by the window where she could watch the passing mêlée of frenetic shoppers all carrying impossible bundles of shopping like leaf cutter ants intent on their acquisitive destiny.

In seeking out her relatives, Connie knew she was tempting fate to deal badly with her, but she was prepared to take the risk. She wanted allegiances to be reformed and, inside, she waited for the flood of natural warmth and affection to seep into her receptive nerve-endings that were becoming more and more aware of their appetite for real love.

She stayed in the café for as long as she possibly could, even reading her magazine twice. At last she got up to go, leaving the magazine on the table with the remains of the cellophane-covered salad she had eaten for her dinner. After three, the frenzy of the shopping madness had died down. There were only a few people standing at the stop where she waited for a bus that would take her toward Sefton Park and the new brick flats which she half-remembered from an occasion when she had gone with her mother to see Aunt Justina and her cousins Uleka and Joan.

Released from the stale, malodorous atmosphere of the pea-green bus, its windows all but obliterated by a thick film of dust, Connie walked through a stretch of knee-high corporation bushes, then past a brick island, planted with struggling rose trees in arid, pale soil watered with cigarette ends, sweet wrappers, used condoms and bus tickets.

Around the entrance to the flats, the sun glistened on an array of deliberately smashed milk bottles. They lay in shiny speckles around the bases of the mottled concrete bollards, that stood in the entrances to the paved courts which belonged to the flats. Connie noticed a little black girl with her hair plaited in decorative, thin loops around her head. Smiling at the child, she bent down and asked, 'Do you know where the Murreys live, love?'

'They live at number sixty-four, two doors up.'

Connie turned. The voice had come from a pretty, brown girl who held a small baby in her arms. She hoisted the struggling infant up on to a more comfortable position on her hip.

'Thanks,' said Connie.

She knocked at number sixty-four with some reticence. The varnished door was opened by a leggy black youth wearing sawn-off jeans and a tee-shirt that proclaimed, 'I'm Dennis, fly me'. Looking her up and down, he turned his head and shouted over his shoulder into the dark of the entrance hall, 'Auntie Justa, there's some woman at the front door, you better come!'

Connie folded her arms and rested her bum against the doorpost, scanning the patch of blue sky above the square, but there were no birds and no trees.

After some time the boy finished staring, closed his mouth and sat on the step to tie up his left baseball boot. 'She won't be long, it's 'er leg, she's gorra bad leg.' The boy stood up, said 'Tarra', and bounced rangily off to join some other boys who had been sitting on a low wall opposite the flat. She watched them leave the square, practising karate kicks to the head as they went along.

Swallowing hard, Connie turned around to see a tall, black woman of about forty-three at the doorway. Connie recognised her because of her striking height — she was about six feet two. The tallest in the entire family, Justina had dwarfed her brothers, especially Connie's father who had only reached the height of five feet three inches — two inches shorter than his wife. Connie remembered the stories her Dad had told her about Justina protecting her brothers from attack on the way home from their school.

'Hello, Auntie Justina, I don't suppose you recognise me now. It's Connie, Connie Marlowe. I think you saw me last when I got chicken pox.'

For what seemed an age, the woman's face remained impassive, her eyes full of suspicion but, to Connie's relief, her aunt's mouth began to stretch in a wide, pleasant smile.

'Well, if it isn't Teddy's girl. Come in, Connie love, whatever are you doin' round here? That grandma of yours let you escape?' She laughed from a great height, her gold and black kaftan juddering with her amusement. 'Come in girl, don't mind the mess, these kids are always leavin' their stuff in the hall for me to break my neck on. Did you see Dennis? He thinks he's a real tough guy, but one day he'll meet his match.'

'He didn't look so tough to me, Auntie Justina. He looked like an average sort of thirteen-year-old. That's how old he is now, isn't it?'

'Yes, but he's a big stiff around here, always hustlin' me for money, and if I don't give it to him sometin' goes missin' around the place.' Aunt Justina sighed deeply and then broke out in blisters of small chuckles, as Connie followed her into the front room.

Connie's basic shyness returned for a while and she sat silently in a big wickerwork chair beside the gas fire.

'I'll go and get us sometin' to drink — tea I mean. Your Uncle Sam still don't approve of drink in any form.' Justina giggled again. 'Mind you, those aren't my sentiments. I like a little drink once in a while, and, after all, Connie, even the Bible says, 'Take a little wine for thy stomach's sake'!' She grinned, showing teeth that looked as though they had been carved out of calcium tablets.

Connie self-consciously passed a tongue over her own teeth behind closed lips. 'Yes, I think I remember something about that,' she answered nervously. 'Is Uncle Sam working at the same place?'

'Yes, Connie, he's been there almost eighteen years now. He's never cared for it much, but work's work and everybody's got to do it.' She paused in the doorway. 'Well, I must say, I'm surprised to be seein' you, Connie Marlowe. Nobody thought we would ever see you again after your dad died.' Aunt Justina's voice sounded strained. 'It was a big shock to us all. He was only a young man, but to go and take his own life like that. Your other grandma has never got over it yet; it's hard to know how she feels because she hasn't spoken to anyone since it happened.'

'I haven't quite got over it myself, Auntie. But why isn't Grandma Marlowe speaking? Did she have a stroke?'

'No, Connie, she just decided she wasn't going to speak any more. The doctor says there's nothing he can do at her age but give her Valium and hope for the best, but he says there's nothing wrong with her, it's something to do with her deep grief. She never cried like we all did at the time. Everyone thought she was blaming him for goin' against God and that was why she didn't care about him dying, but her hurt was too deep. That's what none of us realised.'

'I'd like to go and see her,' said Connie, holding the arm of the wicker chair so hard that she could feel the impression of the pattern on the heel of her hand. She was trying not to cry, and the only way she knew to prevent herself from letting her eyes fill with confusing tears was deliberately to hurt herself. In rehearsing her visit, she had not prepared herself to talk about her father. He had remained swaddled with love, hidden away in a segment of her mind, his memory sealed from all further harm. It was both distressing and comforting to her to be sitting listening to her father's sister, to someone who really knew him and had loved him.

'What's Rita doing now?' her aunt asked, a note of irony in her voice. 'I heard on the grapevine she was gettin' married again, some young bloke, isn't it?' Justina put down her cup and saucer with fingers cool and long like polished lengths of dark Colombian onyx.

'Yes, but I don't know if they did get married or not. I've been living on my own for quite a long time now.' Connie took away her hand from the corner of the chair and rubbed it against the other to encourage the circulation in her finger-ends.

'You mean you finally got away from that grandmother of yours?' Justina smiled. 'I can hardly believe it. Whatever did you do, Connie, to break your chain?'

'Oh, Auntie, she wasn't all that bad. She was strict and had some funny ideas, but she was O.K. really.'

'Connie Marlowe, I hope for your sake you never come across another bad-mouthin', soul-sellin' woman like that in your life. Well, I don't want to go into all that woman done to our Teddy or said about his family but, believe me, she is a wicked woman, make no mistake.'

Connie listened to her aunt's gentle tirade with a feeling of humility, as if the whole affair had somehow been her fault, but she did not feel that admitting her grandmother to be the most bigoted woman in the city would help her get closer to Justina. So she did not pursue the conversation about her grandmother.

'I have my own place and a job that pays reasonable wages. I manage to save nearly half my wages most weeks because I don't go out very much, and one day it may come in handy, who knows?'

Justina had gone into the small back kitchen to make a fresh pot of tea. She was out of sight but still talking. 'Connie, you take sugar?'

'No Auntie, thanks anyway.'

'Right, I'll bring the scones the girls made yesterday. They're still fresh enough and they'll be disappointed if I don't eat them.' Her voice seemed suddenly nearer and Connie felt as if she were being observed from a position behind the door jamb. 'Don't suppose you saw Uleka and Joan on your way here? They went into town to do some shoppin' for me. Dr Smyth says it will be bad for me to go out until the ulcer on my leg heals up.'

Justina emerged like a decorated bat from the obscurity of the flat's gloomy hall. Coming into the room that, by contrast, was full of sunlight, she set down a fibreglass tray that appeared translucent against the light streaming in through the flock-printed nylon net curtain. Auntie Justina sat down with a grace unexpected in a woman of her height and weight.

'Look at this poor, old leg, Connie!' Justina hoisted her leg up and put it on the black vinyl couch opposite her easy chair. In its depression the couch breathed out a great sigh. Connie looked down at the leg which swelled ominously beneath the crepe bandage that had been carefully bound round it. Whatever was lurking underneath, she was grateful she was not going to be forced to admire it. Justina poured out the dark tea into the bone china cups that were covered from rim to base with ornate gold and vermilion decoration. Connie's eyes kept coming compulsively back to the carpet, until she believed herself about to be sick. The carpet swam around in large circles of gold cinema-acanthus on a crimson and chrome-orange background. 'Have a scone, Connie, go on help yourself!'

'No thanks, I'm not really hungry, but don't let me stop you, Auntie.'

She watched her aunt as she ate two scones in rapid succession. She thought that perhaps Justina had been at least partially right in her criticism of her grandmother, as she vividly recalled how Grandma had unkindly described Justina as looking like 'an educated mountain gorilla.' To her maternal grandmother, black people were only one step up from monkeys. It was one of her regular complaints that, when Britain was entertaining a black head of state, Her Majesty had actually to steel herself to shake hands with them. Connie remembered her Grandma sagely shaking her head and explaining to her, 'Of course, they always burn those long gloves she wears afterwards, you know, you'd never know what germs they might be carrying from those hot countries. Leprosy, I shouldn't wonder.' For years, her Grandma had implanted in her a deep suspicion of the members of her black family. She remembered how, as a small child, she had feared being left alone with her cousins on the few occasions they had met lest they should revert to their arboreal habits and carry her off swinging through the trees of Sefton Park like jubilant orangs. She smiled at the childish but damaging ideas she had entertained.

The doorbell rang and her aunt heaved her leg off the shiny, black couch to limp slowly to the front door. Through the open door, Connie could hear someone giggling at the other end of the hall. 'Forgotten the three pound bag of flour and the bath-size toilet soap Mam, sorry.' The other voice giggled as if keen to begin the joke again. 'We'll go later just before the shop on the corner shuts. It's O.K., they're open till eight.' The voices were in the hall now and Connie could see Uleka and her sister Joan put down the shopping bags and follow their mother into the front room where they sat down on the couch.

Connie was sitting in the high-backed wicker chair opposite the couch which had its back to the window. She held her red and gold cup of tea in nervous fingers. Uleka ignored Connie, closing her eyes and putting her hands behind her head on the back of the couch. Joan leaned forward towards her mother and asked in a confidential manner, 'Isn't this Uncle Teddy's girl, Mam?'

'Yes, it is, and after all this time too!' Justina opened her mouth to take a bite out of a third scone. Her green-painted lids were closed against the light from the window as she spoke.

Connie thought the girls, Uleka and Joan, were being deliberately off-hand and she had at least expected them to appear friendly. Joan poured herself a cup of tea while Connie scrutinised them both as discreetly as possible. Joan wore denims that were patched with contrasting shades of blue in the same material, a long, hip length, dark-brown sweater, a bit like her own, and a white collarless shirt beneath. Her face was very pretty, dark and passively round like a Burmese girl. Her hair was arranged in a series of tiny plaits around her head, each of them terminating in a set of glossy blue and white beads, that made gentle rattling sounds as she moved. Connie thought she looked exotic and aristocratically aloof. Uleka was still resting with her hands behind her head, which she moved from time to time as if she were in pain, creasing her mouth up and furrowing her otherwise bland forehead.

'These boots are killin' me, Connie,' she said at last with an expression of utter agony on her face. She held a leg up towards Connie. 'Help me off wid them, will yeh, I carn' stand them any longer. Me feet feel like two squashed corn beef butties. There was me thinkin' I wuz clever an' breakin' them in for goin' out tonight, but they've nearly killed me.'

Taking hold of the outstretched leg, trapped in its corset of a boot, Connie gave a sharp tug. Uleka held her bottom lip with her teeth and, shutting her eyes hard with effort, pulled against Connie to escape the grip of the boot. Suddenly released from constricting leather, Uleka gasped and smiled over to Connie, enthroned in her wicker seat.

'Shall we do the other one, Uleka, or is that all you can take for now?'

'No, might as well get it over with. Here!' Uleka planted the stacked heel of her boot in Connie's palm like a gift. The boot came off a little less reluctantly than its brother. Uleka leaned over and massaged her aching toes. 'Thanks, Connie, let's have another cup of tea. Any left in the pot, Mam? I'm parched after all that dashin' around Lewis's lookin' for lippy for our Joan.' She turned to her sister and nudged her with a very pointed elbow, and smiled with her as if there were something secret between them. Joan looked out across the landscape of the carpet to a point just above the wood surround of the gas fire where there hung a picture which had caught Connie's attention.

Aunt Justina noticed Connie looking at it. 'Are you interested in that picture, Connie? Unusual, isn't it? Grandad Marlowe painted it just before he died. It's some workers in the cane field. He took me there once but I was too little to remember it much.' Leaning back, she rubbed her leg. 'What I wouldn't do now for some of that Jamaican sun to heal this leg of mine.' Connie thought the picture not bad for an amateur, for it appeared to have all the qualities of intense light and darks that were inclined to be purple in their density. Here was a small piece of family archeology, something with substance where before there had only been a dream.

'What's the matter, Connie?' her aunt said, laughing and making the long string of amber beads on her bosom bounce about in disorder. 'You look as if you've swallowed the Blue Bird of Happiness!' Her aunt's hand was on her arm. She had leaned over and was looking into Connie's face.

'It's just the picture. I don't think I've ever seen anything that made me feel like that before. I'd love to be there, now.' She stopped suddenly because she felt she sounded foolish.

'Whitey isn't very welcome at the moment, anyway, Connie.'

'Uleka!' Aunt Justina had reared up in her chair, 'I'll have none of that kind of talk, not to Connie. You can say what you like in private in the bathroom but none of that talk in the house, O.K.?'

Uleka made a face when her mother looked aside. 'O.K. Mam, but it's true. I know some of the boys that have just come back, and, let's face things like they are, Connie is a white girl. Every bit that wasn't has been carefully rubbed away by that old bag of a grandmother of hers.'

Connie looked down at her lap and studied the fine cotton embroidery of her skirt. She began to cut herself off from the unpleasantness as she always did when things got out of control. She had not expected her father's kin to welcome her with open arms but she had not expected them to accuse her of being white. It was, after all, something she could not exactly help. All Connie had wanted was to be one of those lucky people drowned in family affection. Even second-hand love would do. She had put away the proud resistance she had felt in the past about seeking out the pockets of people who were supposed by ties of blood to have affection for her. She had come here wanting to give herself the chance to be black. After all, she was her father's child, whatever her cousin Uleka was saying. That part was not going to be altered. She had not meant to upset them. She felt fragmented.

'I'm sorry, I didn't mean you should argue over me. I only came to visit.' She spoke softly like a child disturbed from sleep. 'Thanks for the tea, Auntie, I'll see you again sometime.' Getting up from her wicker chair, she straightened out her skirt and put on her jacket which had been laid out over a small chair in the corner of the room.

Noticing her mother's bubbling anger, and rather than face her after Connie had left, Uleka decided to throw out an apology. She performed this in exactly the same way as she might dispose of a paper handkerchief. 'Oh, look, Connie, it's nothin' against you personally but, like the man said, where've you been all my life? You can hardly claim to have been a constant visitor or anythin', can you?'

'No, it's funny isn't it, Uleka? For ages I've worried about coming round to see you and Joan because I thought you might not want me to. Now I know for certain, don't I? So all that rubbish I went through worrying was a waste of time, anyway.'

'Look,' said Joan who had all the time been watching Connie and her sister, 'let's all calm down, eh? Come on now, Uleka, let's get rid of all these plasticine principles of yours for five minutes. Ever since you've been goin' with those lads that say they're goin' back to Ethiopia, the mother country, you've been gettin' as hard as nails. Anyway, those lads have never been further than Birkenhead, and they were born here, not bleedin' Jamaica.' Joan put out her hand to Connie to prevent her from leaving. 'Sit down, Connie, take no notice. She doesn't really mean it.'

Uleka stood looking out through the large front window of the flat. 'I'm goin' to get ready to go out to the club after, are you comin' or not?' Uleka was calmer. Her face had returned to its previous, placid beauty.

'Yes, of course, I'm coming. Connie's coming too, aren't you, Con?'

Connie was bewildered. Auntie Justina, who had seemed to provide her with some defence against Uleka's aggressiveness, had left them to it, preferring the companionable opiate of an afternoon's television programme in the room across the hall. Connie clung to the emotional lifeline thrown her by Joan. 'Yes, I'd like to. I can always get a taxi back home.' She and Joan smiled at each other as if they had just signed a non-aggression pact. Connie sat down, her hands underneath her on the red cushion of the chair. Her enthusiasm for the now ailing relationship she was attempting to form was fast waning. All the same, she thought, it would be a good idea to try to part on a more friendly basis than the one on which they had begun. Uleka gathered the tea cups together and took them into the kitchen.

'Come on Connie, she'll get over it all, sooner or later. It's Grandma. Uleka's very fond of her and she blames your Mam for it all.'

'How's that?' Connie could feel herself becoming openly defensive even to Joan who appeared to want to be friendly.

'Well, you know that Grandma Marlowe hasn't spoken to anyone since your dad died?' Connie nodded and watched as Joan took some cigarettes out of the big leather handbag at her feet. 'It's just that Uleka thinks that your Mam drove him to do it because she'd got herself this young fellah, and, let's face it, your grandma didn't exactly pour oil on troubled waters, did she? She was a cow, to put it mildly, right?' Joan closed the flap of her handbag and slung it on the back of the vinyl couch she was sitting on. 'Smoke, Connie?' She offered the packet to Connie, shaking one out from the silver foil inside. Connie reached for the smooth, white tube offered her as if it were going to anaesthetise all her wounds at one go.

Uleka came back and, seeing Connie sitting in the big wicker chair with the cigarette held limply in her hand, took a lighter from her pocket and held it like a statement in front of Connie's face. Then, grinning, she said, 'You're supposed to put those things in your mouth, Connie Marlowe.'

'Oh shut up, for God's sake, Uleka, you're gettin' on me nerves now! A joke's a joke, but you have to go on and on. It's boring.'

Connie drew in the smoke from the cigarette and closed her eyes. Through her closed lids she was still aware of the sunlight that bathed the room. She coughed and opened her eyes again. The smoke swirled around her head like the supposed spirit materialization that Mr Oldshaw had seen emerging from her open mouth on one of their voyages of discovery to the world beyond the veil. She wished she were back there, in the comfortable knowledge that nothing she did not understand would happen to her, where the old couple liked her, and had become dependent on her to a great extent. The Oldshaws, although they were odd, were a greater comfort to her now than she had ever believed they would be.

'Where's Mam, Uleka?'

'Watchin' that quiz game on the telly. She's all right. Has our Dennis gone out for the duration or is he cummin' back for his tea, do you know?'

Joan got up and opened the vent in the top of the picture window. 'Dad hates the smell of fags.' She moved back to the couch and pulled the ashtray toward her on the small glass-topped coffee table. 'Dennis has gone off to arrange the disco at the youth club. He won't be back until they throw him out.' Joan stretched out the palm of her right hand, bringing it down sharply on the arm of the couch.

Three cigarettes later, Connie helped Joan to make tea for Uncle Sam who was expected back at any time. They left it in the oven in the kitchen, and went back into the front room. Uleka was singing upstairs in the bedroom she shared with her sister.

'Joan, will you pass me that lippy out of the bag in the hall, please?' Uleka's voice was less tense and Connie registered this with some relief.

'Comin', I'm lookin' for them now, but I can't see where they are, there's too much stuff in this bag. You can't see the wood for the trees.'

Connie picked up a tiny white packet that had fallen on the carpet at the side of the couch. 'Joan, I think this is what you might be lookin' for.'

Joan stopped rummaging in the bag in the hallway and looked toward Connie inquisitively, her finely plucked brows superarched above wide eyes. 'Connie's found it, Uleka,' she shouted up the stairs to her sister without taking her eyes off Connie who had changed her seat in favour of the vinyl couch.

'Do you mind if I take another?' Connie said, indicating the open packet on the coffee table with a ramrod of a finger.

'Yes, Con, help yourself. Don't ask again. As long as I've got them, you're welcome.'

Connie took the cigarette and lit it with the lighter that Uleka had left on the table. There were no books in the flat — nothing, not even a magazine or a cookbook she could latch on to to get to know her cousins on a level that would be a bit deeper than the scratched surface they were presenting to one another at the moment.

At last the girls were ready to face the evening. Joan had made up her eyes with blue and purple and her lips shone darkest red, like maraschino cherries. She wore black cord jeans with a plum-coloured, ribbed sweater tucked inside them. Around her narrow hips there hung a thick silver belt. Joan could see Connie looking at her belt admiringly.

'Like it, Con? Uleka keeps sayin' I'm goin' to be the only woman in Liverpool to be mugged for a trouser belt.' She giggled and looked at her teeth in the mirror as if she was not sure they would still be there.

Connie wished she had thin legs like Joan and flat, narrow hips that went all the way up to her armpits. She deplored her own pear-shaped bum and well-rounded thighs when she compared herself with her cousin, and thought herself ox-like and frighteningly unsophisticated. Uleka came downstairs at last, wearing a hand-embroidered African shirt in delicate shades of indigo.

At this point Connie wished she had had the foresight to bring a change of clothes. She did have quite a few pretty things, but they were all lying tidily in her chest of drawers back at the Oldshaws'. 'You both look fantastic, I wish I'd something a bit more, well, you know. Will I be O.K. like this?' Connie smoothed out the top layer of her black skirt over her rounded stomach and pulled down the fawn jumper to a point just below her waist.

Joan watched Connie, her eyes half closed to avoid the smoke she had just sent pouring from her narrow high-rise nose. 'You'll be fine, Connie,' Joan said, unrealistically, shaking her head to make the little beaded braids around it disentangle and lie flat. 'It's the Saturday night ritual, we always get tarted up.'

Joan was smiling and bending slightly, so as to be able to see herself properly in the mirror, as she pressed a pair of large, gold hooped ear-rings through holes in her ear lobes. Connie winced as she watched. Pierced ears upset her and she thought of them as being in the same category as body tattooing, a bit like advertising and American sweaters announcing U.C.L.A. and worn by boys who could not count beyond five, and did not care anyway.

She was glad to be going out at last, and with people she was related to, no Marie or Sandra, but people who knew something about her past and would possibly provide some anchor for the future. Sitting in the front room she smoked a further cigarette while waiting for her cousins to be satisfied with their appearances.

'Open the door, Uleka,' Aunt Justina shouted through from the dining-room opposite. 'It's your dad. Quick now, he'll be tired. I always tell him not to work that extra shift but I might as well talk to the wall.'

Connie could hear the difference in her voice as she turned back to view the early evening news on the television, while Uleka strode across the carpet and into the hallway to answer the door. Soon Uleka came back, beating the evening newspaper against her slender calf. 'Dad's gone in to watch telly for a bit, Joan. Will you go and get his dinner out of the oven for him?' She made a sour-looking mouth at her sister as if to indicate the mood she suspected her father of being in.

'Come on, Connie, let's go and see Dad.' Joan took the dinner out of the oven and carried it into the dining-room, followed by Connie. Uncle Sam sat at the table gloomily watching television over Justina's head. Joan placed the plate in front of him between his knife and fork. He mumbled, 'Thanks, Joan girl,' without looking up at his daughter or registering Connie's presence behind her. Joan nudged Connie and made a thumbs-down sign. Connie backed out of the small, furniture-stacked room. Justina sat very still on a low wooden couch with purple cushions and did not speak to the girls, as if she did not want to involve herself in their affairs. Joan closed the door on her parents, and the two girls joined Uleka who already had her coat on and was waiting for them.

Out on the street, Connie's two cousins walked as if they were always aware of their wonderful long limbs. However much of an effort Connie made to keep up, they were ever just that little bit ahead of her. They walked disdainfully, heads held high on delicately turned necks, eyelids drooping as if they did not always believe what they saw. Several times Connie took a long stride, but she never seemed able to shorten the gap.

'Joan, where did you say we were going?'

'To the Africa Club, just off Upper Parley.' Joan used the familiar slang abbreviation.

'What's it like?' Connie bounced along by Joan's elbow.

'Oh, it's O.K., good music, but late on, you know, nothing decent before eleven at night. It's all records until the band turns up. Never mind, there'll be plenty of fellahs to get the drinks in.' Joan turned to Uleka and the two girls laughed warmly.

They walked on in silence until they turned the corner of the old Rialto with its once attractive marble façade. The columns were plastered with notices, with long gone dates and forgotten venues. Shredded papers bowled over the wide, shallow white marble steps and on to the gritty street. Connie knew the names of several of the clubs in the area. She had often said the names over and over to herself while journeying home from the factory. She enjoyed such names, and the exotic external decoration that often accompanied them. Doors would sometimes be bright green or pink, with pale, dusty, orange window sills. Here and there, old crusty brickwork had been painted blue or yellow.

Uleka lit a cigarette. 'It's still very early, Joan. Do you think anyone will be there yet?' She stuffed the packet and lighter back into her bag and re-slung it over her shoulder, leaving the cigarette to fend for itself in the corner of her mouth.

Joan did not bother to answer but seemed to be thinking of something much more absorbing than who would be there.

They jaunted on down the great sweep of the road toward the river, turning eventually up a side street already dark with the beginnings of the night. They stopped outside one of the large, three-storey brick terraced houses, and Uleka led the way up the wide, white-painted steps to the open front door. At the top of the steps there was a plump, middle-aged black man. He leaned against the yellow lintel of the door as if he were vaguely trying to drop off to sleep. Connie noticed he had on a dark navy knitted hat, which made him look, in the half light, as though he had ribbed hair. The hat was pulled down to a point just above his ear. She could see that in his left ear he wore an ear-ring, which, because it had obviously been pulled at some time in the past, had torn a hole in the lobe with the weight. The ear-ring consisted of a short piece of copper tubing about an inch in diameter with a fifty pence piece either glued or braised to it. He wore a dark-blue, padded jacket that made him look like a Michelin man.

The girls stopped at the top of the stairs. 'Hi ya, Lucky!' Uleka put her arm around the man's broad back, nuzzling him affectionately.

He remained quite calm as though he were used to Uleka's displays. 'Hi, you delicious woman.' He took Uleka's hands and kissed them on the palms. She giggled. 'Hi, Joan!' He rubbed his own hands together, blowing on the knuckles as if he were about to throw dice. He waved enthusiastically to a couple of younger men who passed by on the other side of the wide street. Thrusting his hands deep into the pockets of the ski jacket Lucky snorted, 'God, I'm cold. I think I will away inside with the ladies.'

Connie thought he looked very friendly, and his strangely formal yet deliberately joking manner amused her. He went on, 'But tell me, fair Uleka, who is this pale damsel?' As he spoke, he lowered his voice, curling his upper lip slightly, and rolled his eyes toward Connie, blowing secretively on his knuckles to hide his mouth.

Uleka laughed and threw back her head theatrically. 'Lucky, this is our cousin, Connie Marlowe, my Mam's brother's girl.' Joan brought Connie round from behind Lucky, holding her by the arm as if she were about to bolt.

'Hello!' Connie smiled brightly at Lucky and at the same

time twisted the strap of her shoulder bag around her hand.

Lucky examined Connie with his quick, brown eyes. 'You're very pale, my lady, are you sick or summat?'

Joan put out a restraining hand on his arm. 'Don't be a silly bugger, Lucky. Her Mam's a white girl. You know that anyway, you wicked sod!'

Connie watched her cousin Joan show her displeasure at Lucky's choice of words. She appeared to care more about people's feelings than her sister Uleka who thought everything that happened to everyone else was hysterically funny. Even from Connie's fringe observations of them both, this much was clear to her. Yet, however close Connie felt Joan might want to be, it had not been hard to detect the note of apology in her voice.

'Come in ladies, anyway.'

'You're not going to charge us, are you, Lucky?' Joan put down her big patchwork bag on the table just inside the door.

'Oh, come on now, girls, you wouldn't get me in trouble with the boss now, would you?'

'Come off it, Lucky, you are the boss.' All three laughed, except Connie who still stood uncomfortably by the doorway.

Connie followed Uleka and Joan down the narrow staircase to the basement club. The atmosphere was laden with the scent of Indian perfume. Connie liked the musky odour that rushed up to greet them from below. At the bottom of the stairs, the heavy door opened and closed regularly as, from time to time, people squeezed out to seek lungfuls of air on the cool stairway. As they waited their turn to progress, Connie heard little bursts of music come from behind its studded surface like small exhalations of magic breath.

'Haven't seen you for a few weeks, Lucky. You've done the place up nice, I bet it cost at least ten quid.' Uleka cast a glance over her shoulder at the figure of Lucky behind her.

'Why don't you re-name the place Dulcimena's Palace?'

'Good idea, have to give it a bit of thought.' Grinning at Joan, Lucky pulled down his hat over his remarkable ear ornament and, opening the door politely, swept the three girls inside. The room, flickering with red and orange lights, throbbed relentlessly with reggae. Lights from the band area slicked around the room over tables and across backs and arms as if on search and destroy missions. Connie stayed discreetly behind her cousins who were greeting some of their friends. She thought perhaps she would recognise in some of the assembled faces the Marlowe nose and high cheekbones that made most of the family she had seen so far look like black Arabs.

'Take your coat off, Con. Here give it to me. I'll put it with mine on the corner of this seat. You can put your bag with mine, too, if you like, only don't forget where you've put it, O.K.?'

Connie nodded and took off her coat, passing it over the table to her cousin. Uleka waved a slender arm to where she thought Connie should sit. 'I like this place in the corner, it's not too far from the band when they turn up.'

Connie passed her bag across the empty table. 'Are they good, Uleka?'

'Good? You must be joking. They're better than the Wailers, and they take some knocking about.'

Connie did not press Uleka to reveal the identity of the Wailers but pretended a slight knowledge of the group by nodding and then letting a short sigh escape her lips, as if she had just that moment reminded herself. As she spent most of her life walking the tight-rope between absolute ignorance and absolute lies, the execution of this gesture was a simple matter.

Uleka got up and left their table for the small bar behind the place where they were sitting. 'Con, you sure you don't want anythin' more interestin' than gin and pineapple?' She made a face as though it was beyond her to understand such bad taste.

'Yes, please, I'm used to it.'

'God, rather you than me, girl. Like rum and black myself, why don't you try it? Go on, be a devil!' Without waiting for an answer she turned abruptly back to the bar.

Joan took out a packet of cigarettes. Taking one, she left the packet on the top of the table and slid it along to Connie. 'Go on Connie, have one, girl, you look as though you've been to a funeral. For God's sake, cheer up! It may never happen, or then again, perhaps it already has.'

Connie smiled at Joan and took up her offer of a cigarette. 'It's not that I'm born miserable, Joan, it's well, I don't know any of the people here, and Uleka can live without my company.' She lit the cigarette.

Connie felt sure that there was some small link between herself and Joan, and, although it was fine like a strand of spun sugar in a candy floss machine, she was happy at this moment to believe it had the tensile strength of spider silk. Even though Connie knew that Joan was being only a little more than kindly polite, she felt that during the afternoon there had been indications of some underlying feeling that was below the stratum of her cousin's good manners and natural friendliness. Connie, although provided with sparse material, was more than willing to work on the little she had to improve her relationship with Joan.

'Don't let Uleka get on your wick. She's always like that with everyone. She likes to turn the spit and hear you yell.'

Connie looked around her, almost imperceptibly, her cigarette held in front of her like a disguise. Her eyes, heavy with smoke, expressed nothing of her feelings of loneliness, made more acute because she could see no one who looked remotely as white-skinned as herself. All the dancers, all the drinkers at the bar, all the people sitting at conversational tables were either black or, like her cousins, dark brown.

It was as if Joan had read her thoughts. 'No white people come here as a rule, Con. A few years back it was different. But black lads don't like white girls since they discovered their own. If they come it's O.K. but Lucky don't encourage them, if you get what I mean.'

Connie felt herself flush under the amber lights. 'Yes, I know what you mean.' She was grateful for the drink that arrived in front of her on the table.

'Cheers!' said Uleka, bending over the back of her chair and raising her glass.

Connie felt that her cousins were exhibiting her to their friends and that to them she was little more than a Barnum and Bailey production. There was not the love she had hoped for as her father's child. She could not postpone the realisation that her father's death had robbed her of any future relationship with his family. Connie grieved in silence, and drank her drink, avoiding any further dollops of the small talk that kept them together like children's glue, weakly made with flour and water. She continued to sit with her cousins because, although she felt she would rather leave, she did not know how to go about the operation without further embarrassment to herself and without making her cousins more scornful of her than they already were.

'Hello, Uleka! Joan! I'm afraid I don't know . . .'

The young man who had joined them at their table and who was so overwhelmingly polite was carefully interrupted by Joan. 'It's our cousin, Connie. Connie, this is Ramone.' Ramone shoved his posterior along the shiny seat until he was sitting next to Connie. She could feel the warmth of his lean body against her thigh. He put his elbows on the table and took of his National Health steel-rimmed spectacles and rubbed the bridge of his nose wearily.

'You looked tired, would you like a cigarette?' Connie opened the packet on the table and offered it to Ramone.

Ramone chuckled silently and took one of the offered cigarettes. 'I was hopin' it didn't show. I've been up all night working on a disco lights show for a wedding party next week.' He smiled at Connie. 'Got to get everythin' taped, can't leave anything to chance, at least I don't. I got to work at it until I know it's all wrapped up, then I'll allow myself a drink or somethin'.'

Uleka leaned over the chair. 'An' we all know what that somethin' is, don't we, Ramone?'

Connie began actively to dislike Uleka who could not, it seemed, let anyone begin a conversation without it having to include herself.

Ramone lowered his head on to his forearms and giggled, shaking his head from side to side. 'You know you must make allowances for Uleka, sometimes she opens her mouth and falls right in.' Connie liked Ramone if only for his observations on Uleka. He had on a black cotton shirt that was all but transparent, and it was torn at the shoulder so that she could see his collar bone and the slight hollow underneath it which pulsed with his life. She tried not to look at his hair but felt herself fascinated by its odd convolutions. It was long and held out stiffly from his head in a series of thick braids. Each one of the plaits was individually wrapped with black wool. On top of the black wool there were other strands in alternating shades of orange and brown. The percolating heat of the smoke-filled room made Ramone's high cheeks glisten with a fine dew of perspiration. Connie looked past him at the dancers and then at the wall beyond the band area which had been painted with scenes of black life in bright, pure colour. Connie felt Ramone nudge her gently.

'C'mon Connie, you're dreamin', aren't you? I can tell the way your fag's burnt down to the quick, you got somtin' on your mind, right?'

Connie smiled and made a show of collecting herself — sitting up straight and folding her arms as if she had just been told to pay attention by a teacher.

'No, Ramone, I'm fine, honest. It's just my way of relaxing. I just go out there somewhere.' She indicated vaguely with an outstretched hand a portion of smoky blue atmosphere between them. She was glad she had met Ramone — he was the only person she had met during the entire evening who had not brought up the subject of her paleness of skin. By the time he had come along she was determined to tell the next person who alluded to her colour that she looked the way she did because she had just finished a gaol sentence. She was thoroughly sick of it all, and wanted nothing more than to plunge back into the darkness of her solitary room above the chip shop.

Ramone reminded her a bit of Frank. She wished Frank were there. He would give her confidence and protect her from baleful stares and misunderstandings. Half-closing her eyes, she tried to imagine Frank, and wondered if, after all this time, his face had healed of the silver ribbon scars that laced his black skin. She sat there, slowly realising that what she felt for Frank was almost love, but love from a safe distance. She had no idea at all if Frank had ever given her a second thought once the chase had ended. Remembering how the scalding tears of mute rage had run into his cuts was too painful, so she sealed him up once more to lie dormant in her head.

After a while, Ramone got up and backed away from the girls, smiling and saying he was 'bushed' and would have to go to bed.

'He's a nice feller,' Connie said, amiably folding her hands under her chin.

'Oh, you mean Ramone. Yes, he's all right, but he's quiet tonight. You should see him when he's on about the brothers and sisters being black Ethiopians and going back to bloody

Africa!' Joan pushed her chin back and laughed sarcastically. 'You'd think the bloody Africans would want looneys like Ramone and his mates! They've got their own problems, and, let's face it, if any of us did ever manage to get back to Africa, we'd be a minority over there so it would all start over again. We'd take poverty with us. Black people over here are a different kettle of fish to the boys in the West Indies.'

'Yes, I can see your point,' Connie said, feeling her isolation and loneliness more and more clearly defined by her remoteness from any such problems.

'I don't mind them romancin' about Africa, but apart from makin' them feel good, it's all bloody pie in the sky. They'd be about as welcome as a plague of locusts.' Joan, still smiling, lit a cigarette and offered one to Connie.

'No thanks, Joan.' Connie looked over to where she last remembered seeing Uleka. She was no longer at the bar but was dancing with Ramone and one of his friends, right in the middle of the small dance area, their legs lit from underneath by the orange lights beneath the opaque glass floor. Uleka was enjoying herself hugely as she was the centre of almost all attention. The two girls waved to her.

'Uleka believes in all that Africa shit,' Joan said, looking at her sister and nodding and smiling as though she were just idly inquiring the time of day from Connie. Connie listened. She had hoped for some immediate identity with her cousins but she recognised that the ideas Joan was unfolding to her meant that they did not even consider her seriously as belonging to them.

'I don't. I think I'd go as far as going back to the West Indies perhaps, to teach or nurse, if I manage to qualify, but Africa — well that's different. We're too much of a racial cauldron, know what I mean?'

'Yes, I know,' Connie answered, trying not to give any indication of the misery she was feeling.

'Anyway, like I say, at the moment it's all pie in the sky.'

Two more drinks appeared on their table as they were watching Uleka and Ramone.

'Who are these drinks from?' Connie looked at the gin which had been put down in front of her with a total lack of desire. She associated the drinks with the fruitless prolongation of time, and she knew that to stay longer would only be to compound her loneliness with boredom.

'I've no idea. Just drink it and see if another one comes to replace it. It's a game with some of these guys, they like mysteries.'

'Joan, will you tell Uleka — it looks as if she's occupied — I think I'll have to get back now.'

Joan passed over Connie's bag and coat from the corner. She did not seem surprised. 'I'll get Lucky to get you a taxi. Shouldn't cost you much, have you got any money with you?'

'Yes, I brought a tenner out with me just in case. I always prepare myself for 'overkill'!' Connie put on her coat and was watched by the three people at the next table.

'Lucky says there's a taxi outside right now, Connie, so I guess it's tarra kid, we'll see you some other time, O.K.'

Lucky steered Connie out of the room and up the stairs.

EIGHT

Connie became suddenly conscious of Sunday morning. The bells of the nearby Catholic church were pealing out over the rooftops of all the Saturday night people half asleep in their beds and dying from the riotous noise of religion. Flicking the quilt over her head, she sank down in the scented warmth created by her body. Somewhere in the muffled distance she could hear Mrs Oldshaw's voice. She threw the covers from her face and listened.

'Connie, Connie love, do you want a cup of tea? I've just put the kettle on.' The landlady's voice came up the stairs and into her room, a welcome sound.

'Yes, Mrs Oldshaw, I'll be down as soon as I'm dressed. Isn't it a lovely day?' she shouted over the short bannister at the top of the landing, and meant what she said. The events of the previous night had been painfully analysed as they had happened, and the marks left on her had all been carefully eased away and lay in the wastepaper basket by the side of her bed, a mound of crumpled paper tears.

The birds had done with singing their territorial round and she was dressed in the black dress she had worn at Marie's birthday party. Looking at herself in the mirror, she laughed at the way her hair had been forced up into a crest by her sleep so that she looked like a surprised squirrel. After brushing her hair she saw that her eyes, puffed and sore, had the appearance of cowrie shells. She sat down on the corner of her bed and held cream-soaked cotton wool over each eye in turn until some of the split-skin feeling had gone away.

'Well now, Connie, you do look pretty in that dress,' said Mrs Oldshaw, pretending that she had not seen or recognised Connie's tear-swelled eyes. 'Look, Daddy, isn't it a lovely dress? You could wear that on any sort of occasion and it would look good.'

Connie looked toward Ernest Oldshaw. He was sitting up as usual and holding his big, black, old Bible. He smiled weakly at her as if he were too tired even to speak. He closed his eyes and his spectacles fell down to a point just on the very tip of his nose which looked as though it had been coloured with a bright felt tip pen. Mrs Oldshaw seemed nervous and, kept on chattering about Connie's dress as she made the promised tea.

'Isn't Mr Oldshaw very well?' She looked over to where he lay, white and swaddled, a giant infant asleep, his bed a monumental crib. The light from the whitewashed yard outside touched the tops of the hillocks of undulating, white, snowcovered candlewick. He was like a gentle landscape. The seeds of his ravaging illness populated him, and went about the business of cell destruction silently and without outward offence. She saw him growing and dividing before her, a colony of new life, misunderstood and given small sacrifices of drugs to dull all knowledge of them in the hollow places in his bones. There were no secret places hidden from them in him now. Valves and capillaries had carried them willingly on voyages of discovery to the ends of his toes. He had been occupied by a new creation. Ultimately he would be devoured by God, the substance of his being sucked out and dry-cleaned ready for a joyous joining under a celestial canopy.

'Connie' — Mrs Oldshaw was standing over her with the tea in the familiar Snoopy mug — 'Connie love, you know how you like poetry?'

'Yes, Mrs Oldshaw.'

'Well now, in the paper last night there was an advert about some club or other, to do with poetry. It says they're meeting tonight in a pub in the town. I thought of you immediately.'

Mrs Oldshaw fished around inside the big black rexine carrier bag she kept hanging on the back of the door to hold such odds and ends. 'Look, here it is. Oh do go, it would do you no end of good Connie, you might meet someone nice there, who knows?'

Connie took the cutting from the paper handed to her by the old woman's rather shaky hand. 'You are what they call an incurable romantic, Mrs Oldshaw,' she said, laughing as she read the advertisement. 'It sounds interesting though. There's a meeting tonight at seven at O'Casey's pub on the corner of Husskison Street, although I don't think I'll take any of my jottings along until I've seen what the others do. Anyway, I'm not as confident about them now as I used to be.' She folded the two-inch piece of paper and put it in her pocket.

Her landlady poured out a second cup for them both. 'You know, he worries me, Connie. He's had no breakfast apart from a bit of Bemax I got down him, but only after a struggle. I could tell he didn't want it really, he kept pushing my hand away with the spoon.' They both looked at Ernest Oldshaw who gave no indication whatever that he was even aware of their presence. 'It's a good job the nurse comes tomorrow, perhaps he needs more of those pain killers they've started giving him. The doctor said he'd need them all his life. He does look poorly though, doesn't he?'

Connie wished she could say otherwise but she knew the old woman would not believe her, and she did not want to begin telling deliberate lies to this woman who had cared about her.

'Are you having a session today, or are you not bothering, with Mr Oldshaw being a bit off colour?'

'No, it's been cancelled until he can join us again. There's only Martha George up the road, you know, her whose husband passed away a year ago this coming April. She wanted to see if he could come through, but she's not a religious woman so it will be all the more difficult for her. When Daddy gets better, perhaps you would help me with her, Connie, it's bound to be a hard job even for two.'

'Of course, I'll help. You know I don't mind any time, you only have to ask.' The two women sat drinking, their black dresses hard-edged against the soft, patterned wallpaper, like professional mourners waiting for the procession to begin. The tree outside had its brave show of light, green buds which had grown noticeably since the week before when she had first seen them out of the window of her back room.

'You wouldn't think it was nearly the end of March would you? It was so mild last week, that's why the tree decided to bud, but now it feels really cold.' Connie shivered, but she only used the cold as an excuse for what she really felt.

'I tell you what, would Mr Oldshaw like me to read something from his Bible? I'd like to read him something, to make him feel better.' She crossed the small room and took Mr Oldshaw's right hand from the Bible where he had kept it pressed to his stomach as if it were his entire life savings. He opened his eyes and looked at her steadily. 'Oh, it's only you, is it Connie love? I'm sorry, I'm a bit sleepy today that's all. Tell you the truth, I didn't sleep much at all last night. Sometimes my old pins hurt something cruel, you know, it's all I can do to put up with it all. Last night I asked God if I could go, I was right fed up, love.' A tear formed in his right eye which he brushed away as soon as he was aware of it with an embarrassed movement of his hand.

'Now then,' Connie said softy, as if she were speaking to a sick child.

'Now then, Daddy, don't go and upset yourself. Connie'll give you some of the new tablets, though you're not supposed to have more than two, you know.' Mrs Oldshaw went into the kitchen to deposit the dishes on the draining board. The tin tray made a high-pitched squeak as it was scraped over the shallow metal ridges.

Connie reached for the tablets on the medicine shelf and opened the white plastic drum. Shaking out a couple, she picked one up and placed it on the tip of Mr Oldshaw's tongue, carefully avoiding touching it. 'Hang on Mr O.,' she said, flurrying into the kitchen. 'I'll get you some water to chase it down with.'

'Here you are, Connie, I've filled one already for you.'

'Thanks, Mrs Oldshaw, I'll sit and read a bit to him when he's settled down. Perhaps he'll get off to sleep easier if I read his library book instead of the Bible, that's if you think he'd like it.'

'Yes, Con, you go ahead and read him his library book. He gets so depressed about the burden of his sin when he reads the Bible.' She bit her trembling bottom lip. 'Stuck there like that for fifteen years. Do you know, I can tell you now, we've not had any connections with one another for twenty years.' The old woman sucked in her cheek, a sign, Connie knew, of her embarrassment. 'Imagine, Connie, poor thing, worrying about the stains on his soul. I'd be surprised if he's got so much as a smudge.' She went on chuntering to herself as Connie went to help Mr Oldshaw with the glass of water.

'I'm sorry, Mr O., I was talking to Mrs.' Connie placed the cold went rim of the glass against his hot, bottom lip, tipping the liquid into his mouth. She was upset at how lethargic the old man had become in so short a time. His head lolled back on the pillow and his hand fell away from the glass and dropped hotly by his side on the white bedspread.

'Mrs Oldshaw,' Connie shouted through to the old woman who had just that moment begun to sing *Amazing Grace*.

'What is it, Connie?' Coming back into the living-room, she stood with Connie at the top of the bed nearest her husband's head. Taking his hand, she felt for the pulse in his wrist, and listened attentatively for the familiar muffled drumming of his heart's echo. 'His pulse is steady Connie, but he is very hot. You're right, if the temperature doesn't go down, I'll have to telephone the doctor.' Smoothing the bed covers, she took one of the pillows away and Ernest Oldshaw slid down. His head slightly inclined, he rested with his eyes closed and his mouth open. His lips were dry and the usually delicate pink had turned to a shade of pale violet.

Connie brought some water in a pyrex bowl and, with a small amount of cotton wool which she had soaked in it, wiped first his lips and then his perspiring forehead. 'Please rest now, Mr O. Do you want me to read or not?' She stroked his wisps of hair over the age-mottled pink of his scalp.

He opened his eyes. 'Connie. Yes, read to me, will you, lass, and let me hold your hand, please.'

'Of course, I will, I'll do better than that, I'll sit on the bed and put my arm around you, that'll be nice with a pennorth of *Murder Go Lightly*, won't it?'

Ernest Oldshaw moved his huge shoulder just enough to allow her to sit by him on the edge of his bed. Putting her right arm under his neck until her hand rested on his shoulder next to the wall, she picked up the thriller with her left hand from the shelf at the side of the bed and let it fall open at the place where Mr Oldshaw had turned down the top of the page to form a grubby triangle. He seemed less hot now. He held her hand inside his cage of swollen fingers. She was happy that his contact seemed to give him the confidence to rest.

Mrs Oldshaw came in and hung up her pinafore on the back of the door. 'He looks a much better colour now, doesn't he Connie? You know where you're best off, Ernest Oldshaw, lying there letting Connie cuddle you to sleep.'

Ernest Oldshaw smiled as his wife affectionately chided him.

'Now I know he's all right, Connie, I think I'll go to this morning's service, that's if you don't mind.' She looked at Connie as she took down her coat from the kitchen door holding it in mid air as she waited for the go ahead from Connie.

'Go on, of course I don't mind. We'll just sit here and read quietly, won't we?' Connie turned to Mr Oldshaw who was looking out of the window at the budding back yard tree.

Mrs Oldshaw resumed the business of putting on her coat. 'I'll just go upstairs for my hat, Connie.'

Connie joined Mr Oldshaw in his pleasure of the tree. She remained motionless, her thumb over the page keeping the place. Upstairs she traced the clumsy stumbling of Mrs Oldshaw as she heard her pull open the big wardrobe door with its antique squeak. The footsteps crossed the ceiling and came down the gritty, lino-covered stairs. The old woman raised the green curtain with a P.V.C. gloved hand; the other was holding a black shiny straw hat that perched on her head like a mutated spider.

'Going now then. You be all right, Daddy? Are you sure?'

'Ay, I'm all right, Lizzie lass, you trot along. You'll be late, it must be gettin' on now. Me and Connie, we'll be fine, won't we Connie?'

Connie waved. 'Ta-ta, Mrs Oldshaw, I'll look after him, don't worry.' The old man closed his eyes as the curtain dropped and Connie could hear the shop door close after Mrs Oldshaw. Still holding his hand she raised the book and began reading. Very soon the old man's fingers relaxed and he began to breathe heavily. Connie put down the book and sat looking out of the window at the tree which moved almost imperceptibly in the small fresh gusts of wind. It seemed a long way to the yard or indeed to the outside world. She thought about the evening at the pub, and promised herself nothing.

At half-past six Connie had caught the bus and was sitting alone on the bench seat nearest to the faded conductor. He had a look on his face as if he were dreaming of his holiday in Spain. She could see it all in the space between his eyes. During the short journey she read and re-read the six poems she had brought with her until they sounded dull and uninspired. Realising that she was killing them stone dead with her anxiety, she put them back into the buff folder, smoothing out the flap and trying to look out of the dusty window.

'Did you say you wanted Husskison, love?' The conductor's hand rested on her arm.

She looked at him as if he had awakened her from a deep sleep. 'Oh sorry, I was miles away. Yes, it's Husskison Street I want. There's a pub by the bus stop, isn't there?'

'Yes, love,' he said, holding on to the metal bar as the bus rolled to the stop, and stooping to point out of the lower window at a place where some wag had written 'Clean Me for God's sake'.

Connie lowered her head and squinted at whatever the conductor had been indicating.

'Near as dammit, quarter to seven.' He winked at her as she got off the platform and stood on the pavement. 'Don't worry, love, he'll wait, won't he?' Then, stretching up to ring the bell, he bared a set of wobbling false teeth in a gurgling laugh.

She watched as he was whisked round the corner, standing on the ticket-littered platform, his legs apart inside tubular trousers.

Connie had been glad of the uneventful ride on the bus. She hated being jostled or followed by jeering youths as sometimes happened to her. Tonight she was lucky. There were only a couple of kids sitting on top of the pillar box eating crisps. As she passed the children she was hit on the shoulder by a black pump.

'Ay girl, 'ave yer got the time?'

Looking round, she found herself face to face with a child of indeterminate sex who peered at her through sore-looking blue eyes. 'Yes, it's just coming up to ten to seven, lovvey.' The other child giggled and almost lost its grip on the top of the pillar box. He clutched the first child around the waist and shuffled his bottom into a more secure position. 'What are you doing on top of there?' Fishing in her bag she found two five-pence pieces and pressed them into the children's already open hands.

'Me Mam and 'er fella, thee've gone in fer a drink.'

'De won't be long, thee always tell us t'stop 'ere.' The other child added his voice to the explanation. 'Thanks, girl,' he said, pocketing his five pence, holding the bag of crisps in his mouth in order to have his hands free.

Connie patted his bony little knees as he continued to drum his heels energetically against the open mouth of the post box. 'Tarra, then.' She raised her hand and spread out the fingers in farewell.

Inside the pub, she was raked by eyes that waited for other people or were just curious about newcomers. The place was almost full, mostly with housewives out with their girl-friends, sitting in twos and threes, some of them wearing old-fashioned mini-skirts and tight jumpers to make the most of their low-slung breasts. After buying a drink, she sat down and smoked a cigarette, pressing her head against the padded back of the long seat on which she was sitting. Above the bar, there was a crudely written notice. 'Poetry reading, see Mr Amersham at bar 7pm'. Connie put out her cigarette in the green glass ash tray in front of her, and stood up. Her head pierced the cloud of blue-tinted cigarette smoke that hung above her in the still atmosphere. She went across to the bar and waited, resting her elbows on the padded arm-rest in front of the strip of beaten copper where the barman stood the glasses. Above her, a ceiling of glass tankards hung, glittering in the light from two pink electric light bulbs. The mirror at the back of the bar gave the white, plastic chrysanthemums a rosy glow of near-life on their wire stalks. She saw herself reflected in the mirrored tiles, and gazed at her face which seemed paler than usual. She held her eyes wide open and then closed them slowly, watching her lashes close over her grey eyes. Moistening her bottom lip with her tongue she pressed her lips together. Her lipstick had all worn away, but she thought, looking at herself, that it made her appear all the more interesting.

'Yes, love?' The barman was in front of her, blocking her. view. He wiped the counter between them automatically. 'Yes, love, can I get you anythink?' he asked, a note of irritation in his rather feminine voice.

Connie pointed up to the sign. 'Sorry, I wasn't thinking. You Mr Amersham?' The barman nodded, his arms folded, his chin pressed back against his Adam's apple. 'I've come for the poetry meeting. Is it upstairs? Do you have to pay anything?' He looked down his large, Greek nose.

'Yes, I'm Mr Amersham, and yes, the poetry meeting is upstairs, in the back room, the second door off the landing.' He polished the spot directly in front of him and stared at her from under his animated eyebrows as if he did not approve of the 'goings on' in the upstairs backroom.

'Thanks,' Connie said, already on her way up the stairs at the side of the bar. At the top of the stairs the opening was doorless and covered by the same kind of cloth the Oldshaws used to screen their living-room from the chippy. She pulled it to one side and stood on the landing. The small passageway had been given the flavour of a nineteenth-century brothel. Red flock-printed acanthus leaves swarmed up to the cornice on a golden background. The two wall lights were copies of old gas lamps. They were so good that Connie looked underneath at the forty-watt bulbs as she passed them. The red carpet licked up the sound from under her feet as she walked up the passage until she reached the door.

The door opened suddenly without her touching it. 'Magic,' she thought, but then a woman pushed apologetically past her, a sheaf of papers held in the crook of her arm. Waving back at Connie, she pointed with her biro in the direction of the open door.

'Do go on in, Mr Harrison is still taking names,' she said, and then, smiling widely, showing even, unnaturally pink gums, she disappeared behind the burgundy curtain.

Walking into the big room, Connie made her way over to where there was a small group of people clustered around a thin, rather spiky looking, little man who appeared friendly and fiftyish. She stood and waited patiently until finally it was her turn.

'Hello, dear,' the little man said. 'Can I take your name and address and, of course, there is the fifty pence for the rent?' He chuckled to himself. 'I wish it could be free but we have to pay the landlord something for the room you know.'

Connie filled in the card which Mr Harrison had passed over the table to her, and he signed it and gave it her back.

'Got something to read there, have you? We will be reading later, after all the business is done and we've had our coffee.'

This startled Connie for, although she was quite proud of the things she had inside the folder, she did not think they were strong enough to be read in a public meeting. In fact, she really did not know why she had bothered to bring them at all. She pulled out her purse and offered Mr Harrison the fifty pence, eyeing him carefully as if at any moment he might snatch her buff envelope from her and parade round the room spouting the contents and laughing between stanzas. She smiled nervously and, holding her precious envelope close to her body, found a wooden, slatted seat at the back of the room and sat on it as if she expected it to collapse under her. Taking out a cigarette, Connie looked around hoping to see someone else smoking. She put the cigarette in the side of her mouth and opened her bag wider to look for her matches. The buff envelope which she had so jealously guarded only moments before fell to the floor, and she watched in disbelief as the contents appeared and fanned out on the polished surface. From somewhere behind her, an arm groped for the papers that lay scattered under the chair that was next to hers.

'Here you are. I think they're all there, aren't they?'

Connie turned and looked into the face of a youngish man who had bent right over the chair in front of him to retrieve her papers. 'Thanks very much. Yes, they're all there. It doesn't much matter if they're not really. It was a bit big-headed of me to bring them anyway.'

The youngish man came from behind her and sat down on the empty chair beside her. 'Oh, come on now.' He grinned at her from under his Che moustache and interlocked his fingers, pushing the palms outwards toward the seat in front. 'Anyway, you need a light, don't you?' Disengaging his fingers, he fumbled in the tight top pocket of his pants and produced a cheap, yellow, plastic lighter. Holding the flame in front of her, he waited for her to put the tip of the cigarette into the flame. As she took in the first shallow breaths, Connie examined him thoroughly. His hair was fine and light brown, reaching his shoulders which, although fairly broad, were more than slightly hunched. He wore a fine, hand-embroidered shirt tucked smoothly into the denim jeans which, in turn, terminated in the tops of his calf-length, black, cowboy boots. She thought he was overdoing the 'Look at me, I'm beautiful' bit but she liked his face, his greenish eyes and the burnt-toast moustache that rested regally on his upper lip.

The evening passed in a haze of nicotine and a sprinkling of good poetry. But most of the poetry, although honest, had little else to commend it. Connie thought it wiser not to broadcast her own brand of sentimental verbiage. However, she regarded the meeting as a useful exercise, especially her encounter with the young man who had introduced himself at coffee time as Jeremy Allan. She was leaning back in her chair and thinking about Jeremy, who had gone to get another two cups of coffee from the lady with the tin Samovar who stood in the corner dispensing drinks and ginger biscuits, when Mr Harrison stood up waving his green tweed arms in the pall of stagnant smoke. 'Will everyone please return to their seats. We are about to resume reading. I think, yes, it's Joan, isn't it?' He indicated a youngish woman who stood and turned shyly to face the rest of the group. At this point the coffee lady decided it was time to trundle her way across the back of the room, which seemed to glean the last vestiges of confidence from the attempting reader. Colouring, and putting her hand up to her half-open mouth she mumbled an apology and sat down heavily. Mr Harrison then asked if anyone else wished to read, and several arms were raised. Some were chosen and read anonymously.

'Here's your coffee, Connie.' Jeremy had passed her the cup but was whispering as it had become the turn of the Dunnock-brown woman to read.

While Connie smoked nervously, Jeremy insisted quietly on pulling the buff envelope from under her arm. She was about to protest loudly when she was silenced by his gentle finger against her lips and the slight shaking of his head. She turned her attention to Mrs 'Dunnock' who was standing up at the front of the group reading about a love lost in the Metro. Connie looked at Jeremy. He had slid out the five pieces of paper from the buff envelope and was reading the top one. Although she liked him, she hardly felt that a cup of coffee and a half-hour chat entitled him to pry into her treasured buff envelope. Acutely embarrassed, she hid herself in pretended interest, clapping vigorously when Mrs 'Dunnock' sat down, not realising that no one else had thought of doing so. Almost everyone turned toward the sound of Connie's applause. She bit her bottom lip and closed her eyes until she felt the rumble of amusement die down.

At half-past nine the group dispersed with smiles and hand-shaking promises of telephone calls and exchanges of addresses. Some left without a word, silenced into speechlessness and resolved never to return for another spiritual bruising. Connie and Jeremy made their way down to the pub and sat at the bar.

'What'll you have, Connie?' Jeremy asked, as Mr Amersham approached, polishing as he moved.

'Only a fruit juice, please, Jeremy. I've got to get the bus soon and I don't want to get chucked off for being drunk and disorderly.' They both smiled, first at each other and then at Mr Amersham.

'All that doin's finished up there?' he asked, jerking his head in the direction of the staircase.

'Yes, they're all finished up there now,' said Jeremy, smirking at Connie momentarily from behind his pint mug.

'Get some funny ones now and again. But it's a schoolmaster's in charge of this group so the wife tells me.'

Jeremy could hardly contain himself. 'Silly bastard,' he muttered, giving Mr Amersham a furtive sidelong glance. 'Don't people like that get on your nerves, Connie?' He wiped the beer foam from his moustache with the back of his hand.

'No, it doesn't really bother me. In any case I've had to get used to much worse than Mr Amersham.' Connie drank the last of the tomato juice that she had been thoughtfully warming in her hands.

'Who says you're going home on the bus, Connie? Not while I've got my old Esmeralda in good fettle. I'll have you know we'd be most upset if you were reduced to placing that beautiful body in the hands of Corporation transport.'

He stood back, eyes blazing with mock heroics, and she enjoyed it immensely. She could sense he was excited by her, in the way he displayed like a beautiful honeysipper, cresting air around her. She believed herself beyond resistance and, already, her imagination had got the better of her in plunges of wild romanticism.

Jeremy put her coat about her shoulders and laid his arm across her back, his hand over the round of her hip. They walked out of the pub and he steered her to the passenger door of his battered Renault 4L. The drive back to the chippy was uneventful, except that once he touched her face gently as if she were a small child. They sat outside the chippy. There was no light on in the upstairs bedroom which meant that Mrs Oldshaw was not yet in bed.

'I'm sorry, Jeremy, I can't invite you in, I only lodge here. The Oldshaws aren't relatives or anything, and I don't really like putting on them. They're very good to me.'

'It's all right, Connie, don't worry. I've got to take some kids out on a school trip tomorrow. A conducted tour of the Liver buildings finishing up at the Town Hall, would you believe?' He laughed and nuzzled her.

'What do you teach?' She felt somehow shy. To Connie, teachers were synonymous with cheque books, colour tellys in the kitchen and big houses with net curtains in Woolton.

'Well, Connie, my story is a sad one. I'm supposed to teach English, but, unfortunately, the R.E. wallah died last September and I was lumbered with the task of lightening the darkness of the lower orders of the school.' He shook his head and sighed like one who knows his doom is just around the corner. 'I suppose they gave it to me because I was one of the youngest and the least likely to make waves. It's all to do with the promotional merry-go-round, and I don't think you'd understand that. I hardly do myself. The funny part about it is that the kids I've got, well, one's a Jew; there are three Catholics; and about four are our coloured brothers, little Pakies, and that means half the bloody class is excluded and have to have different work. God it's a mess!' He looked exhausted just thinking about it.

Connie tried to put from her mind the vehemence with which he had mentioned the Pakistani lads. Tiredness, she thought, and he is fed up with being put on. Connie watched him as he sat with his eyes closed, his head back on the seat. She could not imagine the teachers at her old school swearing like she did herself or wearing the clothes that he wore, but she wondered if he ever turned up for work in the gear he was wearing that night.

'Well, Connie, don't forget I'll pick you up next Sunday and we'll go to my folks for tea. Now don't go back on your word, promise? I can only stand them if I've got somebody with me. It should be quite funny!'

Suddenly she was aware of him kissing her, opening her soft lips with his tongue and invading her mouth until she thought he was about to choke her. She withdrew from him, leaving a thin spider's trail of silk spittle linking their mouths.

'What's the matter, Connie, too rough?' He looked slightly hurt.

'No, it's just that, well I might as well be honest, I've never really kissed anyone like that. You know what I mean!' She was embarrassed but she knew he would suspect her naïvete sooner or later and she wanted to get over the shame of admitting to being a technical virgin. Putting her hand on the drawstring door she prepared herself for the sound of hearty laughter which she knew must inevitably come.

Jeremy put his hand up to her face and held her by the jaw saying tightly, 'Christ, Connie, you need a keeper! Fancy doing that to me! You know I could have taken more than a kiss for granted. You are a silly, but very charming little cow.' Moving across to her he dropped his hand and, pulling her softly toward him, kissed her again in the same way.

Connie got out and blew a childish kiss as the little camel of a car drew away from the kerb. Jeremy waved solemnly out of the window until he was at last out of sight. Turning to the door she let herself into the chippy.

NINE

As she lay on her bed, Connie could hear that the Oldshaws were still up, although it was late for them. She waited for her thoughts to settle down. Sandra had been right. It was not at all hard to get a man really interested. She felt smug and happy, but still forced herself to admit that she was flattered by his attraction to her. Lying very still, she thought about the meeting that was promised for the following Sunday. She wished things would go at a steady pace and not at full gallop as she had thought they would when he kissed her in the car. She did not want to become obsessed with him, as she feared she might if she went to bed with him. She had hoped she could keep sex peripheral, as easy to withdraw from before total committal as the kind she had so far experienced, something she could feel genererous about, something that would evolve slowly enough for her to understand and appreciate. She needed a relationship in which she could avoid annihilation of the kind she had seen her father subjected to.

Connie remembered her father crawling around outside the small bedroom door when her mother locked herself in from time to time to punish him, because she objected to his emotionalism and entire need of her. Connie had sat on the edge of her bed in the dark and watched her father weep and plead and make rich promises which indicated his complete subservience in the face of her cruelty. Sometimes Connie had tried to imagine her mother behind the locked door, impassively massaging her neck or varnishing her day-chipped nails a brighter shade of red. Inside, on the spare bed, her mother had lain smiling, a Mantis, implacable and in the process of sucking him dry, until he was to hang, a paper-thin, emotional ghost of a man, acquiescent both to her demands and her lovers, neglected in spite of his own beauty in an emotional desert she had created especially for him. Connie felt her tears, brought on by the sadness of her recollections, chew their way from under her eyelids. She recognised that, at the end of all her resolutions, if Jeremy wanted her, she would dissolve before him, willingly entrapping herself in the pretty nooses he would leave in his tracks.

It all seemed utterly hopeless to resolve. She felt badly equipped to deal with a simple explanation of basic facts such as having a black father. She wondered if his remarks about the Pakistani boys had been anything more than thoughtlessly made remarks that had meant nothing, or whether it could have been that they were the tip of his own emotional iceberg. She did not know, and could only find out if she let herself get close to him.

Putting on the light, she looked down on her slender, white arms. She stood, looking at the pale mask of her face in the mirror. With a sure finger she traced the straightness of her nose. With her other hand she lifted her hair which, after eight months, had grown long enough to brush the collar of the black dress. Her hair fell back into place as her fingers swam through its dark richness. Connie's eyes had taken on an eerie brilliance glazed with her tears. The mascara tracks which had begun to descend her cheeks she swept away with a hot index finger. Picking the hem of her dress up, she held it over her forefinger to absorb the last of her tears. She drew the shape of her full mouth, now pouted with her waning distress, on the mirror in the dew of her breath.

Connie slept badly. Her emotions lashed her. She felt like the lion which the ancients believed had a spine in the tuft at the end of its tail for the sole purpose of beating itself into a self-inflicted fury. She smiled at the idea that there, in the dark of a Liverpool bedsitter, there was a classical hybrid shaking itself to pieces.

Woken by an alien sound, Connie reared up in her bed like a mechanical doll, pale and listening. From somewhere beneath her she heard a regular, low wailing. She listened to the noise of developing crisis until she could ignore it no longer. Getting out of bed, she put the top quilt around her and walked to the door of her room. Somewhere in the back-yard, Adolphe was scratching insistently at the kitchen door and snivelling, his black, scarred nose stuck as far as it would go under the crack of the door. Connie stood at the top of the landing, her whole body activated to absorb the slightest sound from below. Leaning over the bannister, she could see that the light was still on in the Oldshaws' living-room. The clock ticked on and was somehow a pleasant reminder of all the ordinary things that continued as usual in life. There were no terrors for her at night. The things in her room were always in the same position so, if necessary, she could always find her way about in the dark without displacing anything. The night was kind and always, when she had found the events of the day insupportable, had prepared a mind-clouding salve for her. She wondered what was happening down the twelve stairs and behind the green chenille curtain.

The noise went on, and at last she walked down the stairs and stood at the bottom. She knocked as she usually did on the lintel of the doorway. The green chenille curtain was swept away by a white arm. It was the nurse.

'You live with them, don't you, dear?' she said, pertly rolling down her navy blue sleeves in a matter-of-fact sort of way, and fastening the white cuffs with dry fingers. 'Come in, anyway. It'll be up to you to help Mrs Oldshaw now,' she said, still blocking Connie's view of the interior of the room.

'What's the matter? Is it Mr Oldshaw? What's happened?' Connie squeezed past the nurse, her blanket quilt still held around her like a ceremonial cloak.

'Couldn't do much for Mr, I'm afraid. He should have been in hospital, but you can see the obvious difficulty and he wasn't keen on being separated from Mrs Oldshaw really. I can tell you, anyway, dear, it was only a matter of time before it happened. I shall miss the old chap myself. Put up with a lot, he did. Well, the doctor's been and the death certificate's seen to and everything, so I'd be glad if you'd stay with the old lady. There's no family, I understand.' The nurse continued to pack her bag and put away her phials of pain-killers that had proved insufficient.

'I thought he'd be all right. I wouldn't have gone out if I'd known.' Connie was amazed that she had been sleeping while so much had been going on in the house.

The nurse had put on her dark blue coat. She laid her hand on Connie's shoulder, firm yet comforting. 'Look, love, it's no one's fault. It just happens. He was a religious man and that helped. It was all over very quickly. He just lay there trying to smile at me for the few moments that he was conscious. There was no pain. He was too full of stuff for that.'

Connie wanted to cry but knew she must not. She stood in the middle of the room looking at the bed where lay the body of Ernest Oldshaw, his jaw tied up with a bandage, but otherwise looking as if he were pretending and at any moment might haul himself up in his bank of pillows as he always did. Mrs Oldshaw was seated on the harmonium stool, her head rested on her arm. She did not move except to continue sobbing rhythmically. Her black, shiny head bobbed up and down in time with each jerk of distress.

'I should leave her for a bit, love. Let her get rid of as much of it as you can. It makes it all last longer if they get too much sympathy too soon.'

Connie wanted the nurse to stay, and to keep pouring out her common sense before them, but she knew the nurse would leave now that she had done her duty. 'Yes, I'll just sit with her. I'm not going to work now in any case. Thanks for looking after him. He was a good old man.' Connie pulled the quilt around her, shielding herself from the life-stalker who might yet be about.

The nurse left two tablets under a water glass in the middle of the table. 'Doctor said she was to take one of these tablets tonight and, if she was still unable to sleep, the other one too, but at least four hours after the first one. O.K.?'

'I'll see to it. Powerful are they?' Connie asked the nurse hopefully.

'Oh yes, they're proper knockout drops, so be careful!' The nurse smiled at Connie and winked a gentian violet eye at her and, lifting the green curtain, disappeared like a music-hall turn.

Connie's attention was fixed on the still undulating shoulders of Mrs Oldshaw, who remained slumped over the keyboard of the harmonium. Connie made up the fire until it was in danger of searing the quilt which she still had draped around her. Putting away the fire irons, she sat up again on the chair by the round table. The fire glow gave her a new awareness of the dead body in the bed. Ernest Oldshaw was illumined by the flames. Connie had put out the harsh overhead light in the hope that Lizzie Oldshaw would find it easier to go to sleep. Connie put her fears of a rapidly decaying body warmed to putrescence by the fire to the back of her mind. To her mind his soul was still in his body waiting to be released. The nurse had kept closed its escape route by the tight bandage that was tied around his head. She planned to untie it later and to open his mouth so that his soul could fly free.

'Mrs Oldshaw, come on please, I'll stay with him. You go on upstairs and try to get some sleep. There's a lot you have to do tomorrow, please.' Connie left the quilt on the chair and went into the kitchen to get a glass of water for Lizzie Oldshaw to take the first of the tablets. Coming back from the kitchen Connie took one of the tablets from under the glass and raised Mrs Oldshaw from her entrenchment on the harmonium. Peeling her head back from her arm, Connie placed the tablet in Mrs Oldshaw's mouth.

'Come on, Mrs O, I'll take you up now.' She bent over the old lady and pulled her to her feet. Connie had some difficulty as Mrs Oldshaw threw her arms around in her grief and continued to press her head down on to her forearm. Forcing her to stand, Connie stumbled over the rag rug with her arm around Mrs Oldshaw's back. She guided her to the door where the nurse had lifted the curtain. Connie pushed Mrs Oldshaw up the stairs from behind, her hands planted firmly in the small of the old woman's back, fingers fixed firmly in the ridge at the top of her corset which Connie could feel under the Sunday best, polka-dot dress that Lizzie wore.

It was the first time that Connie had ever been in Lizzie Oldshaw's bedroom. The key was in the bicycle chain lock so it was an easy matter to open the door and shove the still weeping woman inside.

'Come on, Mrs O, we won't bother to undress you. Just put your feet up on the bed, that's it, I'll take your slippers off. I'm going to cover you with the bedspread, all right? You go to sleep now, promise?' Mopping Mrs Oldshaw's face which was sprayed with a mixture of tears and saliva and felt like a cold guppy, Connie shaded the old lady's eyes from the light with her hand and watched until at last the tide of emotion abated and she fell into the sleep exhaustion demanded. She drew the curtains on the first light that was already shining through the window and on to the wardrobe mirror. Connie left the light on, as if Lizzie Oldshaw were a sickening child and, before leaving the room, draped it with the cream silk scarf that the old lady had left out from the night before. Connie smiled at the habit the woman had of shading the central light with the scarf to create an atmosphere for her spirits which she believed could emerge at any time, and sometimes did. Connie had often heard her landlady late at night, after a good bout of hymn singing, cry out as if startled by some sudden presence in her room. Then, quite often, she would sing for a while and rapidly chant the Twenty-Third Psalm as if she were running out of breath and feared to stop in case some unholy conjuration would drag her screaming through the darkened wardrobe door. Often Connie, her veins pumping with adrenalin, would venture as far as the padlock on the door and try to listen to the spiritual commerce which she knew was taking place inside.

Shutting the door gently, Connie padded barefoot along the landing to her own room. She looked over the bannister rail at the clock. It was almost six in the morning. She did not feel at all tired but seemed to have the energy of a thwarted spider keen to get on with the job of repairing its shattered web. She dressed in her room, and thought it a suitable occasion to wear her dark skirt and blouse. After tidying her room, she opened the window and fed the birds with the remains of the brown loaf in her bread bin. The crust she threw down to land on the top of Adolphe's head. She watched as the dog shook off the crust and turned round to devour it. It had rained overnight and the young leaves on the tree looked shrivelled and frost retarded. The spiny limbs, hung with the recent rain, juddered in the slight, morning wind. She closed the window. It did not seem proper to let in the outside air.

Going downstairs, Connie closed the curtain on the long glass panel in the front door and then lowered the blind in the shop window, turning the sign around to show 'Closed'. There were a few men and women on their way to work. She watched them scurrying, heads down against the slight, wind-blown drizzle, her fingers holding open the yellow, plastic blind.

She went into the living-room behind the shop and looked at Ernest Oldshaw lying in the light of the fire. Connie picked up the quilt and folded it neatly, placing it on the chair. She emptied the bowl that the nurse had used and put on the kettle. Opening the curtains that hung over the sink in the back kitchen, she sliced the dogmeat up with the butcher's knife with which Mrs Oldshaw sometimes filleted the fish. She liked the clean way it stroked through the offal. She liked things that did their job properly. She stopped short because she remembered the strips of mutilated flesh that had hung from Frank's face. She put the meat into the dog bowl with the saved crusts from the loaf, hurriedly shoving the uncut portion into the fridge with bloodied hands. Washing away the red under the cold water tap, Connie took off the kettle and re-filled the bowl, placing the sponge and soap on a small plate decorated with pink roses and leaves. She took it all into the living-room and, putting it down on the round table, dashed back into the kitchen for the bottle of Dettol. She thought Ernest Oldshaw would last longer if he were bathed in a solution of it. She poured it into the bowl until the water clouded milky white, and the satisfying smell rose as usual from the hot water. She was not at all afraid. She stripped Mr Oldshaw of his lion-patterned pyjamas, and began washing him as she would manage a helpless child. The lather she had created on his chest crept down until it reached to the towel she had placed over his loins. Connie dried the cold flesh and then reached under the towel with the sponge, doing her best to do the necessary job with dignity. Then she went upstairs and looked in the chest of drawers in Mrs Oldshaw's bedroom and found a nightshirt which she put under her arm. Then, looking at Lizzie to make sure she was sleeping all right, she closed the door and went downstairs. She put the open neck of the nightshirt over Mr Oldshaw's head. After pushing the bloated arms through the large armholes of the shirt, she pulled it down as far as she could until only his feet stuck out from under it, the skin flaking and the colour turned grey-veined blue. Getting some fresh water, she took off the bandage from around his head and washed his face. The nurse had thoughtfully closed his eyes and plugged his nostrils with cotton wool. Connie dried his face and combed the few wisps of his hair neatly into place with her own tortoiseshell comb. She opened his mouth to let his spirit fly from its fleshy prison.

Later, when she judged that the spirit had flown, she forced the thickening muscles to close the mouth and once more tied the bandage firmly around the chin. She put his spectacles on the bridge of his nose and slid the arms underneath the bandage that passed over his temples. Having taken everything away into the kitchen to wash, she came back and pulled the white candlewick bedspread up over the body until it reached his chest. She tucked it in to the top of the mattress all around the bed. Then, sitting down, she reached out and turned on the small tablelamp which was on the medicine shelf which the nurse had cleared before leaving. She thought he looked much as he had always done. The blood settled in his nose as it always did when he lay down. Bending over him, she kissed him softly on the mouth which was puckered somewhat by the firm bandaging. His lips were blanched with death, although she wished with all her heart she did not have to admit it.

Connie opened the big Bible and read. 'I will extol Thee, O Lord for Thou hast raised me up, and hast not made my foes to rejoice over me. O Lord my God, I cried unto Thee, and Thou hast healed me. O Lord, Thou hast brought up my soul from Sheol: Thou hast kept me alive, that I should not go down to the pit.'

After reading, she rose from the chair and went into the kitchen to get the butcher's knife and a saucer. Lighting a candle, she held a match over the bottom until the wax had melted enough to be able to stick it to the white saucer. The smoke from the match-flame marred the white of the candle, making it look like dirty marble. The flame shuddered as she stood by it with religious resolution made more significent by the sacred and just spoken words that she could feel hanging in the air about them as if waiting for her to give them something of herself.

Taking the scalpel-sharp butcher's knife she slowly pushed the very tip into the flesh of her forearm and then withdrew it to lay it quietly down against the edge of the saucer. Holding her hand to her face, she let the blood drip down her arm and on to the rim of the candle where it fizzled and spat and smelled like the place next door to the meat factory where she had worked. It was the old slaughter house where the unusable parts were burnt along with the big thigh bones she had seen sticking out of the aluminium drums in the bleak yard. Here she was, burning her blood to appease Ernest Oldshaw's God, his terrible Lord so swift to punish but so sweetly loved. She felt she owed it to the old man, and she had tried to love his God and this gift of her warm life would fly up directly to soothe and placate the passage of Ernest Oldshaw's soul. After a few minutes she took her arm away and tied a piece of bandage around it tightly so that the flow stopped and she was able to pull down her sleeve and fasten the cuff as though she had been engaged in nothing more serious than washing a few dishes.

Connie put out the candle in the kitchen and, standing on the kitchen stool, placed it with the saucer on the highest shelf possible.

Much later in the day there came a procession of people, including the undertakers who went about the business of preserving, to some extent, the mortal remains. Mrs Oldshaw slept well on into the day and it seemed to Connie's mind she had somewhat recovered from the bloated crying of the night before. Connie wished she could cry more easily than she did. She felt she was acquiring too much pride and would one day explode with preserved tears. Connie watched the quiet people come and go. The woman from the corner shop came and fussed mightily like some overpoweringly maternal animal. Her head was bowed and she wore misery on her face like a painted mask.

Connie let her take over. She was tired and she had said her goodbyes privately. She felt that Ernest Oldshaw's body had, now that his soul had flown, fallen into the hands of the despoilers. She could hear them whispering behind the green curtain as she passed on her way out of the house. She smiled and wished she had the courage to throw back the green and shout, 'Ernest Oldshaw, arise, the Amalekites are come down from the hills and are upon ye!' He would have understood the joke, she thought to herself, as she took down her coat from the back of the door and pushed her arms into the cool sleeves.

She walked in the park for several hours in the afternoon. It seemed to her too nice a day for someone to die. Birds stood in the bony trees, opening their wings and bathing in the sunlight like miniature Phoenixes. She liked the starlings best. The spectacular, jewel colours in their coal-black feathers glittered in the sun as she watched them. She was envious of the little they seemed to need to be beautiful and to survive. The sky was a dusty orange over the trees, the light turning the sparse grass brown and bronzing the leaves of the dusky rhododendrons that she passed on her way back to the chip shop.

TEN

The shop was to remain closed. Connie looked out of her window at the back of the house at the man who had been specially brought in to break down part of the backyard wall. The funeral was to take place early in the week, as Ernest Oldshaw had had to be left lying in his huge coffin in the back room.

The undertakers had been distraught at the idea of a renegade body lying in its own home instead of in their sickly Chapel of Rest. Connie smiled to herself as she watched the black-jacketed man pacing nervously up and down the narrow, crowded yard, brandishing an old-fashioned yardstick with a brass tip, with which he measured the gap in the wall from time to time, before continuing to pace up and down, the yardstick under his arm like a conductor's baton. A second man with a sledgehammer had taken out the old wall bin, and was busy enlarging the hole to make it wide enough to take Ernest Oldshaw's coffin.

Connie looked at her travel alarm that stood on the table beside her. It was already half-past eight — barely an hour to get everything organised before leaving for the cemetery. She waited anxiously for a knock on the door that would mean Mr Oldshaw's relatives had arrived. She lit a cigarette and twitched to put on her transistor to break the spell of calm indifference she saw expressed in the faces of the two labourers below her in the yard.

There was a loud knocking. Connie doused her cigarette in the bowl of water she had used to wash herself and raced downstairs to the front door. Opening the door, she stood face to face with Mr Oldshaw's relations.

'Good morning, I'm Mike Oldshaw and this is my wife, Shirley. We've come up for the funeral.'

Connie smiled at the man and his wife and let them inside. Their two little boys appeared suddenly from behind their mother, who bent down and smacked one of them soundly across the back of his legs. Her action made the child turn very pink, but he did not cry. Instead he pushed back his hair with his hand and then, rubbing his leg, glared at his mother balefully, like a malevolent changeling. The other child smiled sweetly up at his mother and took her hand, glancing at his brother with disdain. They all followed Connie into the living-room where Mr Oldshaw lay in his custom-built coffin on the floor directly under the window where the bed had previously been.

'It's disgusting! Fancy leaving him there. Look, Mike, he's on the floor! You'd have thought they could have managed to put him in between a couple of chairs or something wouldn't you?'

Connie tried hard not to laugh at the idea of a twenty-eight stone man plus oak coffin resting respectably between two chairs, only to plummet lino-wards as the legs of the fragile kitchen chairs finally gave out under the load.

'I don't think the undertakers could manage anything better, Mrs Oldshaw. They've been quite upset at not being able to take the body out through the front door to the funeral car; but you can see the point of their taking him out the back, can't you? First of all, it's more private and, second, they'd have to take off two doors and two lintels. They measured the coffin and it was just three inches too big to get through the door. They even tried tilting it but, as you can both appreciate, there's a limit to doing that sort of thing.' Connie bent down and made up the small fire in the grate.

'Would you all like a cup of tea? I'm sorry I should have asked you straight away, actually I've had a kettle on a low light all morning just ready for you, so it's no bother at all.'

'Yes thanks, er, it is Connie, isn't it?'

Connie nodded.

'Could you find a bit of orange juice for the boys? They don't drink tea. Oh, and they like it in a glass, please.'

Connie went into the kitchen, followed by one of the little boys who was curious to get out in the backyard to see what the two labourers were up to. He was called back to sit dolefully by his mother on the chair which had been provided for him.

'Justin, I won't tell you again, come back here and sit down like a good boy or I'll smack your legs again.' The woman's voice rose coldly toward the end of the sentence. The boy, who was about eight years old, kicked the back door and, leaning against it, said, 'Bugger off!' into a crack in the planking before running inside to climb back on his chair and sit there with his arms folded tightly, swinging his little legs rhythmically backward and forward.

'Don't go on at the lad, Shirley! It's only high spirits. After all 'e's never been in a house like this, with an outside toilet and a coal fire.' Mr Oldshaw's nephew leaned over to one side so that he could project his voice to the kitchen where Connie was making the tea. 'Is Lizzie all right? You know, is she well enough to go to the internment? We'd heard all sorts off that neighbour of hers, Mrs George isn't it?'

Connie brought in the cups and saucers piled up on the tray and the big brown pot that Mrs Oldshaw kept for Sunday afternoon sessions.

'Of course she's all right, Mr Oldshaw. She needs a lot of care, though.'

'She'll get that off us all right, won't she Shirley?'

The young Mrs Oldshaw had taken off her navy coat and was sitting on her chair in an unfortunately gay floral dress in shades of pale blue and cream, waiting for her tea.

'I'm going to take Mrs Oldshaw up a cup of tea and tell her that you've arrived. She's dressed and ready except for her hat and coat, but she didn't want to sit with him in the room. It only upsets her more. I've kept her more or less upstairs since it happened.'

Connie looked fixedly at the oak casket lying shinily under the window like an accusation. She passed the tea around to the family sitting in the middle of the room. Mike Oldshaw took the tea from her and snorted his thanks as his thick lips closed over the rim of the cup. Connie had taken an almost instant dislike both to him and to his wife with her cold, scrawny voice and red, puffy elbows.

'I'll take Lizzie her tea up,' Mike spluttered in his tea, then wiped his swollen-looking mouth on the back of a wide, flat hand. His eyes bulged like pale-blue eggs in his sallow face. He sat with his legs apart; his belly flowed out over the top of the too tight but fashionable trousers. He wore a camel coloured overcoat, which he had kept on in spite of being inside the house. The coat more or less covered his brown striped suit. Connie thought him horrendous with his thick fingers and dirty fingernails. In the short time he had been there she had noticed that he had a habit of sitting with his legs apart and his hands placed uncompromisingly on his meaty thighs. He stood up and looked around the living-room as if appraising its future value.

'Didn't go in for decorating much, didn't our Lizzie, did she?' He made a laugh that sounded like an implosion of broken biscuits.

Connie ignored the remark and offered to fill up his wife's tea cup. Mike Oldshaw stood in the middle of the room, slowly turning around, so that he reminded Connie of the music box she had seen at Marie's mother's flat. The elder boy was kneeling on top of Mr Oldshaw's coffin in order to have a better view out of the window.

Shirley Oldshaw noticed Connie's agitation and pulled the child off the polished coffin. 'Get off, Darren, you ought to have more sense! Here, take our Justin and go down to the shop on the corner and get some sweets!' She fished in her handbag for her purse, opened it and, bringing out some money, gave it to Darren who, grinning, pushed his younger brother off his seat and prodded him out into the chip shop. Connie listened to make sure the door was closed.

'I could have done without bringing the boys, Mike. We should have let your mum look after them. They're all over the place.'

'Don't you worry, Shirl, the lads are only having a bit of fun, it's only natural, they'll be all right.' Mike looked at the watch that nestled on a bed of wiry black hairs on the back of his hand.

'Time's getting on, Connie. I better take her tea up.'

She poured out a cup and passed it over to Mike Oldshaw, avoiding any contact with the thick, stubby fingers that curled fatly about the saucer. Connie watched him disappear behind the green curtain, and sat down by Shirley Oldshaw who sat looking out of the window, her mouth held slightly open like a small child. They had sat there for some time before Mike came back into the living-room. There was a knock at the front door.

'I'll go, shall I?' Connie got up and moved slowly past Mike Oldshaw who stood in the doorway looking bored and holding the empty tea cup. 'It's probably the undertaker with the cars, for us to go to the cemetery, it's about time now.'

She glanced out of the back window at the progress that had been made in the yard in time to see the last few bricks come bursting out from the wall as though the only thing that had kept them together was the thick coat of blued white-wash and the hairs torn out from the brush it was painted with. She went through into the chip shop and opened the door to the undertaker, his two feckless looking assistants and Mr Audley from the paper shop a little further down the street.

'Please come in. Mrs Oldshaw's upstairs but the relatives are in the back room. I'll stay here a while, because you'll want to talk privately, won't you?'

'Thank you, Miss.'

'Connie, Connie Marlowe.' Connie held up the green curtain as the three men dressed in their ceremonial black stooped to enter.

'Am I glad you've turned up, Mr Audley. Everything's all right except for Adolphe. He can't get at anyone where he is but the minute they begin to take Mr Oldshaw's coffin out they'll be in trouble.'

Mr Audley smiled smoothly at Connie, pleased to be of some help. Darren and Justin came running through the open front door, their small fists bunched greedily over bags of sweets.

'Shh, lads, be quieter will you!' Connie gently admonished them for their youthful noise. Mr Audley put his finger up to his lips as they scrambled past. Darren stood in the door-way to the living-room, his arm around Justin's neck. His left hand, about to lift the curtain, made a V-sign instead. Then both boys lunged through the green velvet and back to safety.

'That's very nice, I must say, 'ave they been like that since they came?'

'No, Mr Audley, but I suppose there's still time.'

'I'd let their dad know. 'E doesn't look like a man that'll stand for much carryin' on from kids.'

'No, I can't be bothered with the hassle, Mr Audley. They'll be gone soon. It can't get much worse.'

'I'll go and get our Paul to look after the business of the dog, and I'll come back and bring some chairs. You'll need chairs, especially afterwards when they all come back for their tea.'

Mr Audley passed her a wreath of bright yellow marigolds and freesias. Connie took it, holding it by the wire loop at the back, and laid it on the counter of the chip shop. The marigolds glowed marvellously and made Connie feel quite sad for the first time in the whole morning. She could hear that Darren and his brother Justin had got into the storeroom upstairs and were playing riotous games, jumping on the stacked plastic cartons. After a short while, their father called them downstairs and down they came with some of the wooden forks that were usually used to eat the chips, stuck in the lapels of their smart little men's suits like an array of badges.

Connie went upstairs and sat down by her window, looking out on to the yard. Soon she saw Paul, Mr Audley's red-necked son, come into the backyard by leaping through the hole in the wall, and heard him tell the labourers, 'It's all right, mate, I've come to put the dog away for you.'

She could see that the men were laughing as they drank their tea out of the chipped enamel mugs they had brought with them. Their hair was full of whitewash dust from the wall. She did not feel sad any more. This was Ernest Oldshaw's triumph, his Jericho, and she was glad he was giving them all a bit of trouble in his death. He never had in life.

Connie watched Mr Audley's son grasp Adolphe firmly with his big swallow-tattooed hands, and, flinging him into the outside lavatory, lock the door. Then he stood outside the door, his arms folded over his dark green jacket, from which his chest seemed to sprout pigeon-like and full of self-appointed pomp. Connie imagined the floor show inside: Adolphe standing on the scrubbed, white, old seat, his thin, muscular front paws hard against the green painted door, chewing at the soft wood of the centre panel and whining with impatience to get out and be about the dog-like business of biting somebody.

There were no pearls of potatoes lying drowned in the bath of cold water outside. All had been neatly disposed of by Mr Audley and his son the night before, but Mr Oldshaw's divan, its legs unscrewed and lying in a plastic bag beside it, was propped up against the chip fryer as if he had forgotten to take it with him on his journey.

Connie put on her coat and, leaving her room, shut the door behind her. She went into the bedroom where Mrs Oldshaw was still sitting quietly, her Bible open on her knee and her head bowed over it. Connie put one hand on her shoulder and, with the other, she gently drew the Bible from Mrs Oldshaw's grasp.

'Time to go now, Mrs O!'

Connie went over to Mrs Oldshaw's bed and picked up her coat from over the corner of the headboard. She held open the coat while Mrs Oldshaw pushed in first one arm and then the other like a weakly child. The old woman stood quite still while Connie tied the belt around her middle and adjusted the dark, imitation fur collar.

'I won't put my hat on, Connie, not until I'm downstairs.'

'That's all right, Mrs O, you do what you want.' Connie passed Mrs Oldshaw her navy-blue straw hat. 'Come on, then, we'll have to go now. They're almost ready downstairs.'

Connie led Mrs Oldshaw downstairs, just barely supporting her by her elbow. Once they were at the bottom of the stairs, Connie sat her down on one of the chairs thoughtfully provided by Mr Audley. Mrs Oldshaw put on her Sunday straw hat and picked away nervously at imaginary dust on the skirt of her coat. The front door was open and occasionally the small face of a child would appear and stare in at them. Connie could see the funeral car outside, waiting without noise to toil down the hill with its load, like a giant Scarabeus, its humped, shiny back glistening in the mid-morning sun.

Connie left Lizzie Oldshaw waiting by the door while she went back to her room to get her scarf. Looking down on the scene in the backyard, she was just in time to see the monstrous coffin emerge like a gigantic stool from the wide open window immediately below her. Disembodied hands fed it out to the small band of black-coated men in the yard. Then they valiantly bore the twenty-eight stones of Ernest Oldshaw over to the prepared gap in the wall. Connie watched as the men, after thrusting the coffin through the hole in the wall, opened the backyard door and, stepping aristocratically outside, between them lifted the scratched oak box on to the trolley that had been waiting to bear away Mr Oldshaw's body since 8.30 that morning when the undertaker had realised that the casket was three inches bigger than the front door.

Ernest Oldshaw was taken out into the back entry and pushed around to the front of the shop. Connie rushed across the landing and into Mrs Oldshaw's bedroom and squinted through the closed curtains. From this vantage point she saw the coffin arrive slowly and, with great stateliness, turn the corner, supported on either side by four of the undertaker's assistants. They lifted the box impassively and slid it into the gaping mouth of the limousine. The small, chattering crowd fell silent as they turned to watch one of the men placing the wreaths on top of the coffin.

Connie came down and stood by Mrs Oldshaw's chair in the chip shop. Putting her hand out, she stilled Lizzie Oldshaw's hand that flicked to and fro before her eyes like a returning shuttle.

'It'll be all right, Mrs O. Shall I stay with you or will you be O.K. with Mr and Mrs Oldshaw? Just say, I won't mind if you want to be on your own or with them, nice of them to come all that way to see Mr Oldshaw off, wasn't it?' She held Lizzie's hand tightly to reassure her. 'Did they say they'd come all the way up from Cornwall? Is that where they're living now?'

Lizzie Oldshaw did not answer but, instead, clutched at Connie's hand and pressed it hard as if she wished to say, 'Oh yes, stay with me, please.'

Connie noticed that the car bearing the coffin had pulled away from the kerb only to be replaced by another. The driver got out and opened the door. Connie led Mrs Oldshaw from the shop and helped her to the car. Lizzie Oldshaw got inside and was swallowed up by the healing dark. Connie prepared to follow her but turned as she felt a hand on her arm.

'Look, Connie, isn't it? I'll get in this car with the wife, if you don't mind, love.'

Mike Oldshaw was smiling at her, but it was not at all a pleasant smile. She stepped down and away from the car.

'Yes, of course, I never thought, sorry.' She lathered him with her apologies while he ignored her, ushering his two boys and their floral mother into the car.

'Come with us, Connie!' A voice called out from among the confused tangle of people standing on the steps of the shop. Swinging around, she could see that it was Mrs George who lived only a few doors up the street from the chip shop.

'Come with us, Connie! My son's taking his car. Mike only ordered one car to follow.'

'Thanks, Mrs George,' Connie muttered, bewildered by the flow of faces that swam before her. She shut the front door of the shop and followed Mrs George and her bovine son into his vermilion Ford Escort that smelled of warm vinyl and stale cigarettes.

As they followed the cortége to the cemetery, Mrs George's son wound down his window and tipped out the ashtray into the slipstream. No one spoke.

The cars wound through the cemetery gates and past the tombstones that stuck up out of grass-trimmed gums like old stumps of teeth. The close-cut grass reminded her of the green curtain that had separated Mr Oldshaw from the public gaze of the shop. Here he would get familiar with another separating green. She felt that it should rain as it always did in films at dank gravesides, but was glad it did not as no one had brought an umbrella anyway. Instead, the sun was gloriously shining on the assembly who were shuffling around waiting for the minister and feeling uncomfortable in the warmth.

Connie stood under an elm tree and wondered if it were the last elm in robust health in the entire British Isles. She did not want to see the coffin lowered and all the rigmarole that went with it. She preferred to look into the boughs of the trees and watch the small spring clouds shunting across the skies like playful children. She tried to be elsewhere in her thoughts. Ernest Oldshaw had gone, had slipped away from the graveside crowd and was swanning around in his own spiritual paradise. It was the first time she had been quiet enough to think of Jeremy who was somewhere in a school in Old Swan doing projects with the kids on the Town Hall they had seen on their trip only a few days before.

There was a sudden shadow across the baby blue of the sky like a frown. It was all over. The wreaths were left to rot by the graveside or until someone who cared came and took them away. The Oldshaw's relatives and Mrs Oldshaw got back into the hired car and were whisked out of the grounds before Connie was able to make her way over to Lizzie to speak to her.

Mrs George took Connie's arm. 'Are you all right, Connie? You can come back with us if you like. Our Annie's makin' the tea at Lizzie's for the visitors so there's nothing to do. You look tired, luvvy. You look as though you could do with a sleep yourself.' Mrs George screwed up her miserable-looking face and leaned over Connie sympathetically. 'I don't suppose it's been easy for you with Lizzie like she is.' They walked over the path of green chippings that stuck in their shoes and stood waiting to be let into the vermilion Escort. Connie took a deep breath of the fresh air and plunged inside to exhale as slowly as she possibly could before taking her first breath of essence of fag ash and stale cosmetics.

Inside the Oldshaws' living-room there were about half a dozen people all mumbling quietly as they sat around the oval table eating their portions of chicken and salad and bridge rolls. Later, the sherry was passed around in an assortment of glasses, and even in one or two cups which were passed out of the window to the men who were re-building the ravaged wall.

Connie helped Mrs George to tidy the things away while Mr Oldshaw's nephew sat with his arm around Lizzie affecting sudden concern. She could hear him through the half-open door.

'Now, Auntie Lizzie, you just leave everything to me and Shirley. We'll look after the estate and all that sort of thing, so you don't have to concern yourself with it at all. I always did look up to Uncle Ernie. I think he'd trust me to do things right, don't you?'

'I'll have to leave you to see to everything, Mike, I just don't know enough about it to cope. Anyway, I'm past caring now.'

Connie and Mrs George looked pointedly at one another as they heard Lizzie begin to cry again.

'You wouldn't think she 'ad any tears still left in 'er, would you?' Mrs George said, passing over a soapy dish to Connie and wiping her foam-flecked hands on the coarse apron that hung from the back of the kitchen door. Tossing her head back and sniffing as if she knew something secret of which Connie was unaware, she began stacking the plates on the shelves in the pantry. 'If you ask me,' said Mrs George in a grating whisper, 'I think this place'll be closed down for good now. She's not got the 'art to go on, not without the old man, and in any case they've not got two ha'pennies to rub together. To be honest, that nephew's in for a shock if 'e thinks there's any money there to be picked up.' She laughed a throaty, satisfied laugh and stroked her fluffy, pink cardie sleeves with her stubby, age-spotted fingers.

Connie steered a course past the harmonium and the oval table and made her way upstairs, followed by the curious little boys who stopped from time to time on their way to gasp with laughter at the sight her swirling skirt afforded of her legs. She hated Mr Oldshaw's relatives and wanted them to go and to stop polluting the house with false feeling. Sitting up in her room, she wondered how Lizzie would fare in her bewilderment. She felt she had abandoned Lizzie, but there was nothing she could do to prevent it happening. There were few times in the immediate past when she had felt quite so out of things as she did this day. She had loved the old man with a genuine and kind affection, and it had sometimes pleased her to think of the old couple as her adoptive parents. They had certainly treated her like the daughter they had lost all those years ago, and she had loved letting them pretend. She was glad that she had given Ernest Oldshaw the comfort and warmth of her body before he had died. She did not regret it. It was her gift to him, and had seemed far from profane at the time of the gentle giving.

Later in the evening, when Connie heard Mr Oldshaw's relations leave in their shiny blue Cortina with the plastic skeleton dangling over the fun fur dashboard, Connie went downstairs into the gloomy living-room where she could just see the dim figure of Lizzie Oldshaw, sitting stock still on the easy chair that had been brought from the upstairs bedroom when a neighbour had taken the bed up to the spare room to be out of the way. She stood watching from the doorway for a moment, debating whether or not to put on the light.

'Come in, Connie, love, I'm all right now. Mike and Shirley are going to come up and see to everything next week.'

'That's fine, Mrs O. Would you like me to get you a drink, perhaps there's a bit left in the sherry bottle?' Going into the kitchen, Connie got out the bottle from the door of the fridge and closed the door with her hip while she examined the level inside.

'Mind if I put the light on, Mrs O?' She came into the living-room carrying the bottle and a couple of the glasses from the draining board. Connie switched on the light with a free finger, and put down the glasses and the bottle on the round table, where she began to pour out the pale sherry. Some tiny pearls lay on the surface of the pile of the blue velvet. Connie brushed them off before the surface tension broke and they sank into the cloth. 'Bloody hell, I would do that, clumsy sod!' she mumbled, her head turned away from Lizzie Oldshaw who, Connie felt, would have been shocked to hear her words. Turning, she held out a glass in the direction of the armchair. 'Mrs O . . . Mrs O?' She put down the glass on the mantelshelf by the left-hand Staffordshire dog that stared out at her from fire-glittering gilded lids. Lizzie Oldshaw's head was lolling on the back of the chintz cover of the easy chair. She was sleeping like a dark stone at the bottom of a slow stream. Mouth open, her tongue rattling in her throat. Lizzie Oldshaw slept away the pain of the present, making it, after a few moments, a bearable past.

Connie drank the contents of the two glasses and placed a blanket over Lizzie's knees, tucking it in to the sides of the chair. The day of the funeral was over for all of them.

The curtains remained closed. Connie cared for Lizzie Oldshaw for a couple of days and, when at last she remembered to go back to her job, Mrs George took over. Connie did not like leaving Lizzie as the old woman seemed to get more and more disorientated. Her grief had got her stuck firmly in the past and, when Connie came home towards the end of the week, she found Lizzie had put on a dress that was meant for a much younger woman and was busying herself taking an array of pies and cakes out of the oven. Connie looked down at Lizzie's back where the zipper had refused to be pulled over a roll of her pallid flesh, and had split open.

'Come on, Mrs O. What's all this baking for? If we ate all this we'd burst!' Connie tried to laugh unsuccessfully.

'They're not for us, Connie, Oh no, but the lads are coming round tonight. Don't you remember,the dance.' And then, all big-eyed and strangely coy, she smiled and pressed her several chins on to her chest, her head to one side. Mrs Oldshaw's hair had been let out of its usual tight bun at the back of her neck and was hanging in thin, greasy coils about her neck. Connie knew that, although she could not see her eyes, they were underneath the Medusa-like coils, shining and strange with another reality.

'Oh yes,' Connie said, as though she had been reminded of something so important that she should have remembered it. 'O.K. Mrs O, you get on with that and I'll put the new cloth on the table and set the places. How many?' She wanted the old woman to be happy in her fantasy. It was easy to join in and pretend it was something they both shared; but Connie knew the symptoms of too much unhappiness and realised she must get help.

'I'm just going over to the paper shop to see if they've got some silver doilies for the cake stand. It would be nice to have that out on the table again, wouldn't it?' Connie knew that the china cake stand had been Mrs Oldshaw's pride, carefully preserved for over forty years for this occasion.

'Won't be long, promise,' she called, putting on her coat. She waited, hand over the lock, for an answer that did not come. Lizie Oldshaw was preparing her feast and had no time to do anything but forge ahead with her plans for guests who would never arrive.

ELEVEN

The day she had most looked forward to had arrived. She had done little else but manufacture scenes of perfected and unhurried love in her mind's eye all week. Connie had worked automatically, her eyes from time to time searching the clock face over the manager's cage of an office for some slight signs of movement. She had even refused an invitation to Sandra's flat to hear her new tape of some old Buddy Holly tracks. Marie had been sullen for quite a while and was keeping herself apart from everyone when they went to the canteen. The events and disturbances of the past days were now smarting less in her memory. Mrs Oldshaw was sedated most of the nights and, during the day, would sit in front of the small television in the cave-like living-room and watch vacantly, her brain slushing around inside a Librium-coated skull, until Connie came back home from work in the evening when she would haltingly offer her the first few words of her day.

Connie looked through the net curtains of Mrs Oldshaw's bedroom window, holding the heavy russet curtain aside with one hand. There was no one in the street. The paper shop had closed its bright red door. Even the bells of the Catholic church had fallen silent. 'It must be gone eleven,' Connie said to herself. 'Perhaps he's forgotten. Perhaps he's in prison. Perhaps he's been killed on a fairground machine.' There were a lot of perhapses in Connie's mind and they were all good reasons for Jeremy's not being able to come to pick her up as he had said he would. She never imagined for five minutes that he would not come because he had not been serious in the first place. Letting the curtain fall back into position she went downstairs and took the tray from in front of Mrs Oldshaw.

'Aren't you having anything to eat, Connie?'

'No, Mrs O. Remember, I'm going out with someone. We're going to have our dinner at his parents' house. You feel O.K. now, don't you?'

Connie felt a bit mean leaving the old woman alone in the house, but she was not going to give up the chance of going out with Jeremy if he did turn up. Connie looked at Lizzie Oldshaw, who sat slumped in her veridian nylon-quilted housecoat in front of the fire as solidly as if she might never move again. One of the tartan slippers had come off her foot and Connie bent over and slid it back on again almost without her noticing. Connie did not like Lizzie's twisted toes with the long misshapen nails, but she quickly forgot such things, preferring to believe that older people were just young people, gone wrong.

'What time will you be back, Connie love?' The old woman looked agitated and afraid.

'I can't tell you just like that, Mrs O, but I will be back in time to get you a nice hot drink. Would you like me to get you another bottle of sherry?'

'No love, I'll manage, I've got half a bottle in the cupboard still and the doctor said I mustn't have above one or two when I take those pills he gave me. Anyway I'm going to try not to drink so much as I've been doing. People will think I'm a right old alcoholic.'

'If they do, they'll have me to deal with. I'd just like to see them. They'd bite off more than they could chew, make no mistake!' Knowing that Lizzie Oldshaw would be comforted by her defence of her right to drink, Connie went into the kitchen with the tray of lukewarm tea and leftover dinner.

'Shall I give these bits to Adolphe, Mrs O?' Connie called from the cold kitchen, already taking the answer for granted and scraping the unwanted food into the dish reserved for Adolphe.

'Yes, Connie, and give him that sausage you made for my breakfast. I'll not eat it now, I've not got any appetitie for food yet, just don't seem to want anything, know what I mean?'

Connie slid the bowl primed with food out of the kitchen door with a long handled wooden ladle from above the sink. Adolphe was not a dog to be trifled with. It was as if the old brute had actually realised that the man with whom he had shared life as an affliction had gone to the big kennel in the sky, and was jealous. Even Mrs George's minator-like son could not get near him to unhook the big chain from his collar. So, for the last few days, he had been left to himself until it could be decided what should be done with him.

Connie could hear someone tapping on the glass panelling of the front door and leapt to her feet, almost closing the backyard door on her fingers in her haste to shut it. She was sure it was Jeremy.

'Going now, Mrs O. Shall I put the telly on for you, or do you just want to have a sleep?' There was more knocking. She lifted the green curtain and went through to the shop. The old woman did not answer her but watched her go through the curtain, her heavy head resting on the back of the chair.

Connie could see through the wavy glass of the front door that it was Jeremy. He put his nose on the glass and made a face, spreading his mouth like a limpet's foot on the door. Laughing, she pulled the door open toward her.

'Hello, Connie, pleased to see me, I hope?' He smiled confidently at her and, folding his arms, leaned on the right-hand lintel of the door as if he were waiting for her to faint with delight at his sheer presence.

'I'll just get my coat, won't be a min.'

He went back to the car and leaned against it while he waited.

'Have a nice rest, Mrs O. See you soon. I'm going now Jeremy's come. I'll have to go now, don't want to keep him waiting. Bye.'

'Bye, bye, love, have a nice time!' Lizzie Oldshaw raised her hand weakly and the fingers fluttered like pale, transparent feathers held against the light. The green curtain came down and wiped her out. Skipping out of the front door, her coat held over her arm, Connie closed the door temporarily on her troubles. Jeremy held out his hand and she ran toward him over the small strip of pavement that was between them. He held her hand momentarily and pressed her fingers gently with his own, a kind of loving signal. She felt they were like two birds touching and calling to each other, dancing over old, imprinted display patterns until finally accepting each other as mates.

She sat beside him quietly and felt him smile at her as the little car started up noisily and pushed forward on the beginning of their journey.

Connie knew she looked her best wearing her black, embroidered skirt and her new pin-tucked, beige, forties-style blouse she had bought on her way home from work the night before. There was a little mirror embedded in the cream plastic sunvisor that was just above her head in front of the windscreen. From time to time she took furtive glances at herself in the mirror. She was pleased with herself. Her hair, dark and thickly curling, looked like stylised Baroque woodcarving around her pale, oval face. Her eyes, fringed with dark lashes, the lids painted blue and white, gave her the look of a Mexican madonna. She held her black, calf-skin handbag close to her thigh beside her on the seat. She thought of nothing other than the effect her instinct told her she must be having on Jeremy.

'Jesus, now they've jiggered about with the wavelengths you can't get any decent reception of Radio 3 anymore!'

'I think it's O.K. Anyway you can never get radios to work in traffic. I know that from when I took my tranny to work. I could only get it working indoors.'

He gave her a puzzled glance before his eyes once more turned to the uncluttered Sunday-afternoon road.

'Where do your parents live, Jeremy? I've never been this far out of the city before.' She glanced out of the window at her side at the surprising flashes of green and bands of regularly cut hedges.

'We're moving out of Woolton right at this very moment, then on, thrusting deep into the topiary towers of Hunts Cross.' He spoke with comic pompousness, his voice deepening towards the end of the sentence.

Connie felt unsure of him for the first time since they had met. Taking her little, black handbag on her knee she clutched it like a lap dog for the rest of the journey trying to get involved with the fluctuating strength of Mahler whose work was offered, gift-wrapped, through the dented mesh of the radio under the dashboard, and flowed into their laps.

Connie felt the car turn slowly round its last corner. She had been listening to the music with her eyes shut and posing so that everytime she felt him looking at her she would be as beautiful and composed as possible. Opening her eyes, she was just in time to see a big yew tree that stood on the right hand side of the wide drive that curved like an ochre crescent moon in front of the house. They passed a sign in cedarwood that hung from a white post. The sign had painted on it in Gothic script 'Montpellier'. The car came to rest just outside the door by the front step.

Jeremy stretched himself and combed his hair roughly with his fingers and looked at himself in the wing mirror. 'Well, we're here. Welcome to the homestead, Connie!' He got out of the car and went round to her side to let her out. 'Don't get a taste for all this stuff, Connie,' he said, winking. 'It's for the old lady's benefit. She likes all this old world, standing for ladies bit.'

'No I won't, but I wondered what you were doing.' Connie got out of the car, glad to be able to move around and concerned at the abundance of creases in the flowing black skirt.

Jeremy thrust his hands deep into the pockets of his suede coat. 'Come on, Connie, they know we're here. Let's go round to the back and head them off at the pass, the old lady loves it when I'm unpredictable.'

Taking hold of her hand, he pulled her behind him along the short gravel path to the conservatory door at the side of the house. Connie could see a big bush of hydrangea inside to the right, and on the shelves there were rows of cacti in mellow, orange pots. The moss that had been encouraged to grow among the small stones in the pots had sometimes spilled over the tops and flowed down the sides to merge into the sandy, old earthenware.

'There's not much going on in here right now,' Jeremy said, reaching into a plant pot for a key to the door that would let them into the house. 'Later on in the year most of these cacti flower and the whole place is a riot of colour. It's Dad's hobby, really.' He turned the key in the lock. 'Funny things cacti. When everything else dies there'll only be cacti and insects left in the entire world.'

Jeremy pushed open the door and pulled Connie into the room after him. 'They've gone round to the front. Sit down, Connie. Like a cigarette?'

Connie took a cigarette from the packet he offered her. 'Thanks, Jeremy.' Drawing in the smoke, Connie, who had seated herself on the edge of one of the big, wine leather chairs, held her bag under her arm in a nervous stranglehold. She could not remember being in anyone else's house before in her whole life. Of course, she had visited schoolfriends and relations who had council flats or rooms which made her aunts' house, bought over thirty years before her birth, seem a freehold paradise. She looked through the conservatory windows at the immense garden with its panoramic display of green. She could not recall ever being in a house with a real garden, and, while she and Jeremy waited for his parents to turn up, she took imaginative trips to the four corners of the shrubberies, and lay naked on the still dewy lawn, her arms and legs spread wide, her flesh stroked by thousands of tiny, damp, green tongues.

Inside, the house was tall ceilinged and coolly aloof as if it were passing judgement on her. All the rooms that she had experienced before in her life had been marked with obvious signs of the people that lived in them. There had been traces everywhere, a book left on the arm of a chair, a pair of tights under a cushion, or unwashed ash trays with discarded fags left in the channels to burn off and get stuck by their tar-congealed paper to the painted tin. Here there were no signs that anyone lived or breathed about the rooms. Everything was neatly squared off and either very new and smart or, like the Grandfather clock standing discreetly in a shaded corner, antique and expensive. She looked at Jeremy and wondered what he might think of her if she admitted that she had never been in such a large room unless it had been a bedsitter for two with a cot stuck in the corner and a sort of tent over it to shade an infant from a blazing central light. He looked perfect to her, and there were times when she felt that he would not care about such things, and would only think it amusing and endearing. But she was not prepared to take the risk.

Jeremy stood up and walked over to the door, holding out his arms in an attitude like a dancer. Turning in her seat, she watched as he strode out across the sand-coloured carpet towards his parents who had appeared in the doorway leading to the hall.

'Jem, how are you love? It's lovely to see you again! You stay away from us too long, you know.'

Jeremy laughed and kissed his mother, holding her in his arms until she had satisfied herself that all was well by touching his face. His father offered a large hand which Jeremy shook vigorously several times, smiling and nodding to each other but not speaking.

'Look Mum, I've brought Connie along for lunch. Sorry I didn't get time to ring you or anything, but, I knew you wouldn't mind.' His words surprised Connie as it was the first inkling she had had that this ceremony he was putting her through was only his idea and not his parents'. Feeling slightly uncomfortable, she looked up at Jeremy's parents from her low seat. Jeremy's description of his mother as the 'old lady' hardly seemed to fit this fairly young and very smart woman who came towards Connie, a slender hand extended in greeting. Jeremy held his mother about the shoulders and guided her towards Connie, who rose from her chair. 'Connie, this is Mum.' Then, turning, 'Dad.'

Connie smiled and shook hands with them both.

'How nice of you to come, Connie. Jem, I'm sure you could have taken Connie to somewhere far more interesting. It's such a beautiful day, isn't it?' Jeremy's mother sat down on the Chesterfield opposite Connie who became suddenly aware that she was being inspected. She did not mind, indeed she had expected to come under the gruelling scrutiny of a woman who was obliged to defend the second man in her life from would-be interlopers.

'Let's have a glass of sherry, shall we?' Jeremy's father had already moved over to a corner cupboard that served as a drinks cabinet and was busily arranging four narrow glasses on a tray. Connie watched him as he poured in the pale, golden sherry. It was the first time she had seen him properly because, as he had never spoken before, all her attention had been riveted on Jeremy's mother. With the last glass filling and the squared decanter held firmly in hands so skilful they did not spill a drop, Connie imagined his sandy hair disappearing and melting into the background of cacti and pale, old terracotta pottery that stood in serried ranks on the green shelves of the conservatory.

Jeremy sat with the fingers of his right hand interlocked with those of his mother's, a childlike accolade of love. Connie, who knew that he privately despised them, wondered at his seemingly deliberately affected *bonhomie* with his parents. As she herself came from a family whose likes and dislikes of one another were displayed openly, she felt a distinct unease, sitting in this polite but parched atmosphere with people who were evidently used to playing elaborate games of cat and mouse. Jeremy's father, a little more predictably conservative in style than his wife, showed a flash of the unconventional in the form of a cream polo necked sweater he wore proudly under a green, tweed jacket with leather patches on the sleeves. Connie thought that he might be the more interesting of the pair to talk to, but was too shy to try. Jeremy and his parents talked together about cacti and the local by-election and about the school where Jeremy taught English. Connie felt like a child with ringworm excluded from school, and, to help herself over the hurdle of boredom that loomed before her, concentrated on the painted dial of the Grandfather clock and waited for it to strike the quarter hour.

'Do you work at the same school as Jem, Connie?'

Jeremy almost leaped out of his seat in his alarm, but checked himself before anyone else noticed. 'No, Mum, Connie works on the other side of the city, er, book-keeping in a shipping office.' He smiled tightly at Connie who was utterly shocked.

Why had he done this to her? She had never worked in an office in her life. She felt waves of cold panic ripple over her and leave marks. However, she was sensible enough to realise she must give them some sort of answer.

'Yes, as a matter of fact I've been there almost two years now.' She saw no alternative to keeping up the pretence begun by Jeremy. As he had instigated the beginning of a battery of lies, she thought there might as well be a few more for good measure, and, if this was the sort of game he enjoyed, well, she would join him in it.

'Oh, that must be interesting, Connie. Do you like it?' His mother tried hard to disguise her distaste.

'Not really, but I must admit the pay is good. That's the main reason I stay, because I get more than most of the men in our office and the boss takes me with him on trips to head office and conferences. I type as well, you see. He says, he couldn't do without me now for these special jobs. It's because I know the business so well now. My boss says I should have been a boy, I've got such a good head for figures.' Connie laughed coyly, and held her head high, looking confidently down the gentle slope of her nose at a point just above the beechwood framed glass coffee table in front of her, with the air of someone who knows her value, just to add a little flush of colour to the soft ground etching of her lies.

She could see that Jeremy was furious with her elaborations. When their eyes had at last met again she tried to make him laugh while his parents were temporarily engaged in the re-filling of their glasses. He gazed back at her with cold eyes.

She enjoyed lying to Jeremy's mother who sat very still, her head cocked on one side with polite interest. From time to time her fingers stroked the narrow glass in between sips as she listened to Connie. Jeremy had taken his hand from his mother's clasp and had sat forward on his seat, elbows on his knees, his hands thrust deep into his thick hair as if he were trying to plug a leak in his head through which the secret of the universe was escaping. Connie knew that he was shielding himself from the exposure of the lies they had both been ladling out to his parents like a thick and nourishing soup.

'Shall we have lunch now?' Jeremy's mother put her glass, held between two dry-cleaned fingers, on to the tray held out by Jeremy's father who had appeared, like 'Abenazzar', from the shadows at the side of the Grandfather clock to collect the empty glasses. He stood by the doorway leading into the hall.

'Come on, you two kids, we don't stand on ceremony here. First come, first served,' he laughed as he disappeared into the hall with his tray.

'George, have a look and see if the beef's done, please. Jeremy, do show Connie where she can freshen up and, for goodness sake, hang up her coat! The poor girl's been sitting with it draped over her knees from the time she came in, really.' She took Connie's coat herself in despair of her son ever having the sense to do anything about it, and left the room. Connie and Jeremy were drenched in embarrassment and found it almost impossible to speak to one another. Connie was fast realising that Jeremy was happy to submerge himself under the family influence. At last the truth was surfacing that, although he was quite pleased to be with her, as she was more than ordinarily attractive, he was certainly always going to be ashamed to acknowledge her real life-style. It had all been a hideous mistake.

Jeremy rose from his seat and came over to where she was sitting. Taking her by the arm he steered her like a blind child to the doorway which led to the hall and stairs. He took her right to the foot of the white wood staircase. His fingers bit into her arm before he saw fit to release her.

'Thanks very much Connie, thanks very, bloody much! You didn't have to take the piss out of the old lady like that, did you?'

'I'm sorry Jeremy, but when people expect things of me I can't help giving them what they want to hear. It's just an intense desire to please, I think. I've always done it. Anyway, you helped. I thought you wanted me to tell her something like that. You can imagine telling that lady where I really work, can't you? She couldn't take it!' Connie moved away from him and felt already separated from him by the wreath of misunderstandings that she had woven with him and laid on the tomb of their stillborn relationship.

'The little girls' room is on the half-landing at the top of this flight. Please don't leave any doors open, Mum's very particular.' He spoke, tight-lipped and unbelievable, and it pained Connie to realise that Jeremy felt about her in the same exasperated way as she had herself felt about Marie and Sandra. She wanted to cry for the first time since the funeral of Mr Oldshaw, although she smarted enough with hurt pride to prevent herself.

'I'll go up now, then, won't be long!'

She went up the stairs holding her black bag tight under her arm, pressing it hard against her ribs to make herself aware of the importance of not crying in front of him.

After locking the bathroom door, she stood stiffly against

the wall and cried silently for two or three minutes. Then, washing her face, she renewed her make-up in the wall of mirrors behind the basin and sat down on the basket chair in the corner by a mock Victorian bidet. Connie usually got over self-pity very quickly; there were no safe periods in which she could indulge in self-recrimination and abandon herself to grief. Now her dissected feelings were closing ranks and re-grouping to give her comfort and strength. She sat for a while rocking herself from side to side as she was accustomed to do when she felt unhappy. She looked angrily at the walls and the curly carpet on the floor saying over and over to herself, 'This isn't somewhere to freshen up, it's a shithouse! It's not a little girls' room, it's a shithouse, a posh shithouse!' Connie took out her lipstick and wrote on the white wall behind the lavatory, 'This lavatory is a shithouse' and all the bawdy remarks she could remember, such as 'Beware of Limbo dancers' and 'If you follow this line you are now shitting at an angle of 45 degrees.' Finally the lipstick broke in two, putting an abrupt halt to her activities. She washed her fingers and put away the mangled lipstick in her black bag. Having closed the door firmly behind her as if nothing had happened, she walked sedately down the stairs. She could see Jeremy's face pale behind the light brown moustache looking up at her through a gap in the bannister, only to disappear again in the shady hall. Jeremy had waited to take her into the dining-room and appeared agitated and unfriendly.

'God, you're really pissing everybody about, aren't you, Connie? Did you have to be so long?' He ran a slim, freckled hand through his hair. Connie had noticed before that he did this when troubled by something or other. His voice had taken on a slightly bitter and unpleasant tone that she had not heard him use before. He took her into the dining-room where his parents were waiting patiently before cooling soup dishes.

'There you are, Connie dear, thought you'd got lost.'

'Sorry to have kept everyone waiting!'

'That's all right, my dear, now sit down and have your soup before it's past redemption.'

Connie was no longer worred about anything — things had got well past that stage. Now she was beginning to relax and behave more naturally, so that when the soup was eventually served she dipped her portion of garlic bread into it and ate with relish. She knew that Jeremy's mother and father were a bit puzzled as to why Jeremy had brought her. Jeremy sat with his hands clasped just in front of his moustache, his elbows resting on the table in front of him. He seemed to be deliberately avoiding looking at Connie.

'Yes, Adrian's doing very well now, Jem.' Adrian, Connie gathered, was Jeremy's elder brother who had emigrated to South Africa. 'He's been promoted to overall manager of the concrete factory, and Candice is expecting her first baby anytime now.' Jeremy's mother smiled on one side of her face as if she were not sure whether she should be pleased to be a grandmother or not.

'That's nice,' said Connie, stuffing the last of the garlic bread into her mouth. 'Wonder what they'll call the baby?' Then, pausing as if suddenly struck by something of great moment, she said, 'Adolphe, now that's a nice name. I've got a very good friend named Adolphe. He keeps everyone on the trot. I've heard he's a real mean boss but he's a lovely fellah underneath it all.' She went on eating her meal without looking up or worrying about the cataclysmic effect she had had on them all. She was glad now that her brush with Jeremy was going to remain stunted and would never amount to anything but a bag of Chinese takeaway, and an off-putting struggle for supremacy in the back of his Renault. She enjoyed the lunch and wondered when anyone would visit the bathroom and see the wall that waited like a Rosetta stone to be deciphered by its speechless discoverer. No one did.

After coffee, Connie volunteered to take herself off back into the city, claiming that she had important office work which she had forgotten about but which must be finished before Monday morning. This left Jeremy a great deal of margin to redeem himself; but he did not. He did, of course, insist on driving her back to the city centre to where she lived, and helped her on with her coat, brought from a cupboard at the foot of the stairs. Standing on the gravel path outside the cream-painted front door, Connie waited for Jeremy to get into the driving seat and open the passenger door. It was chilly and she wished she had put a woolly on top of the new beige blouse and not worried too much about spoiling the effect of it. She shuddered and tied the belt of her coat tightly around her, although it did little to protect her from the vivacious spring wind.

Jeremy's mother stood at the door rubbing her arms against the spirited wind, her aquiline noise pinched and mottled pink and white.

'Thanks for the nice lunch!'

'That's all right, Connie, we were glad to have met you, dear.'

Connie smiled, knowing very well that Jeremy's mother was a past master of the facetious remark and prided herself on its expert delivery.

'Goodbye!' Connie almost felt sorry for the woman who stood so confidently on her front step unaware of the vicious attack that had been made on her middle-class bathroom.

Connie did not begin any healing conversation on the way back into the town centre but sat looking out of the small divided window at the side of her. The characteristic high hedges of the more salubrious parts of the city passed greenly by as she reflected on the depressing events of the afternoon. She blamed herself for not trying hard enough, and could not believe that she had let Jeremy slip away from her by something so tragic and unnecessary as a division by class. Somehow, by the isolation of a single, niggling incident in the day and by enlarging on it until it raced uncontrolled through her consciousness, she had done her share with Jeremy in shredding into a fine mash the many reasons why they should like each other. Now they were both content to let things between them ossify like the bones of some magnificent but long dead beast. Jeremy stopped the car outside the chippy. They both sat still, looking straight ahead out of the front window of the car, both unwilling to be the first to speak. Jeremy sat with his forearms around the suede wheel-glove, his head well back on the head rest of the seat.

'Goodbye, Connie, goodbye, sweet Connie.' Sighing deeply he put two fingers to his lips and, kissing them, transferred the kiss softly to her forehead. Smiling, she accepted the kiss as her severance pay.

Getting out of the car, she ran for the safety of the chippy and did not turn back even when she heard the car start up again and move away from the pavement. Closing the door behind her, she sat and cried, screened by the glass panel. The mottled light rippled over her cheeks, distorting the tears which she shed in a mixture of anger and terror at her renewed isolation and failure. Connie sat huddled by the door, her arms hugging her knees, her head resting against the glass. Her calm face of the afternoon was lacerated by searing tears that ploughed through her so carefully made-up face, and she wiped them away from mascara-muddied eyes with the back of her hand.

'Is that you, Connie love?' She could hear Mrs Oldshaw's voice coming from behind the curtain over the living-room door.

'Yes, Mrs O.' Connie gulped and, getting up on her feet, looked at the sad mess of her face in the fat-spattered mirrors over the chip fryer. 'Just getting the newspaper, Mrs O. The paper lad's shoved it through and ripped it again.' Picking up the Sunday paper from where it had fallen neatly folded on the red lino, Connie tore the front page deliberately to give credibility to her story. She pushed aside the curtain to the living-room and went in.

'For God's sake, Mrs O, why are you sitting here in the dark?'

Connie, realising she had spoken sharply to the old woman, was immediately repentent and, smiling, said, 'I'm sorry, Mrs O, but it's been a bit of a gungy day and I'm too tired to even understand myself. Look, I'll put the telly on and make us a cup of tea, shall I?'

Mrs Oldshaw patted Connie's hand and nodded, without looking up at her. 'Yes, that'll be lovely. I was beginning to get thirsty. I thought I could last until you came back, Connie.'

Connie, smiling at the old woman, pressed the T.V. control and the set bloomed in the corner. Mrs Oldshaw sat watching the flickering movements of cheetahs stalking across exotic African grassland. Connie watched her gazing vacantly at the set with no more intelligence than a pet animal recognising shape. Bringing in the tea, Connie set it down on the blue velvet tablecloth and passed Mrs Oldshaw her familiar mug. 'I think you ought to go to bed after this programme, Mrs O, don't you?'

Lizzie Oldshaw nodded quietly, her head over her cup,

poised to sip. 'Wasn't all he was cracked up to be, eh, Connie love?' Lizzie Oldshaw put out her hand and took Connie's gently, as if she knew everything without being told. She squeezed Connie's hand and then let go, allowing her arm to drop into her lap drained of all energy.

Connie sat with her, patiently willing the strength to return to the old lady. But Lizzie had had her courage cleanly and surgically removed by her loneliness for the old man, who had been her life. Connie felt ashamed that her shattered dreams of love had been allowed to claim emotional priority over Lizzie Oldshaw's bowed grief.

Looking over the top of Lizzie's head at the Staffordshire dogs on the mantelshelf, she saw that the letter was still where she had put it the Friday before when it had arrived. She had realised from the postmark that the letter had come from Mr Oldshaw's nephew Mike, and was probably full of the bad news that she had been trying to avoid thinking about ever since the funeral. Connie felt panic rise in her throat; once more she was about to find herself dispossessed, and she was bitter about it. She had worked so hard at the relationship with the old couple, and now the letter was all that was needed to deal the final blow. All the same she knew that, however she wanted to ignore the letter, she had to make sure Lizzie Oldshaw knew what it contained for her own protection, especially as she did not want the old woman to be put to any needless upset later on. She drew her attention to it now.

'Look, you've never opened that letter you got on Friday. Here, you better read it right away. You are a naughty girl!' Getting the letter from the mantelshelf, Connie passed it to Lizzie and pressed it into her unwilling fingers.

'Oh, Connie love, I can't seem to concentrate these days. Will you read it for me, please?' Lizzie handed back the letter between two shrunken fingers.

'Come on now, Mrs O, I can't do that. It may be private or something. I'd feel embarrassed. No, you must read it.'

Lizzie Oldshaw burst into tears like a child who is told a final no. Connie took the letter and put her face against the old woman's cheek. 'All right, then, now stop crying this moment, otherwise I'll have to put you in a home with your ears tied back.'

Lizzie Oldshaw stopped crying and, looking out from reddened eyes, snuffled a small, wet laugh to show that she was recovering. Connie took the tear-stained, blue envelope and, pushing her thumb under the edge of the flap, prised it open without tearing the paper. Pulling out the piece of buff, lined writing paper that was inside and looked like army issue bog-paper she began to read.

'First of all, it's from Mr Oldshaw's nephew, and he says: "Dear Lizzie, I hope this letter finds you in better spirits than when we had to leave. I thought I better tell you that Shirley and myself will be coming up to stay with you from next Wednesday. To about Saturday or perhaps a bit later. After the sale of the chip shop Lizzie you will of course stay with us, Uncle Ernie would have liked that. In the meantime Auntie Lizzie don't you worry about a thing because its my job as executor to see the solicitor and everything. Anyway I will be there soon to discuss things with you properly so there is no need for you to concern yourself with anything except to tell that girl that lodges with you that she'll have to look for a room somewhere else, because I'd rather you did that than have to do it myself. Your loving nephew, Mike, Shirley and the kids."

Connie let the buff letter rest on her lap. The old woman seemed dazed and did not appear at all to understand the letter that had been read to her, or, if she had understood, she was preferring to push it all to the locked compartment at the back of her mind where all such hurtful things were kept.

'I shan't be able to see you much after this week then, Mrs O, but I can't imagine that happening at all, I'll probably come down to Cornwall to see you and take you out for picnics on the beach. That'll be nice, won't it?' Connie squeezed Mrs Oldshaw's shoulders with a circling arm and dropped her head again to press her cheek against the old woman's face.

'Picnics on the beach, Connie, that's nice love, that's nice.' Lizzie Oldshaw closed her red-rimmed eyes, teetering on the brink of sleep.

Connie removed her arm from her shoulders and pulled up the quilt Lizzie had over her knees, until it came up to her chest. Leaving Lizzie to sleep, she went up the stairs and into her room where she sat down heavily on her bed. Taking the pillow on to her lap, she sat with her radio on, rocking and joining in snatches of songs that she knew to stop herself thinking that her life was once more getting out of her control and speeding on ahead of her. The room was filled with confident D.J.s and reggae throbbed from her lonely walls and receded like a tide of sound back into the cheap tranny. She looked at the small red and chrome radio, its aerial snapped off halfway up the stem. She saw it as just another thing in her life that was doomed to inevitable failure and extinction.

Later that afternoon, Connie began packing the large holdall she had brought from Lewis's only a week before to accommodate her new clothes and bits and pieces. The blue duffle bag held her winter boots and her sandals and the exercise books that she used for her writing. Into the holdall she put her underclothes and the black party dress and pretty fawn sweater and her favourite forties-style blouse. She packed everything as neatly as she could and, leaving the top zipper open, she placed her black toilet bag on the top and pushed her savings book and other personal documents into the side pouch. She had no idea what she was going to do, but the act of filling the two bags with her belongings made the hurt of having to part from Lizzie Oldshaw not quite so acute. She looked around the room at the other things she had bought while she had lived there and thought it would be better to make a clean sweep of it all and consign them either to the kitchen downstairs or to the dustbin in the yard. Putting the bread knife and her knife and fork and her two dishes and the Snoopy mug inside the breadbin, she placed the lot in the blue plastic bowl and took them all down to the kitchen and placed them on a shelf behind the refrigerator.

She behaved as though she was clearing out the room of a person who was already dead, as if she were erasing all trace of herself. Lizzie Oldshaw was still asleep and the white walls of the yard shone moon-struck through the window of the living-room and across the portion of space that had been solely occupied by Ernest Oldshaw. Connie put on the light, wondering why the old woman had switched it off again while she had been upstairs and out of the room. She drew the curtains together and threw out a cupful of scraps into the yard for Adolphe who, she thought, was being extraordinarily quiet. Opening the door, prepared to throw the bits of bacon rind on to the back door step, she saw the dog sitting motionless and silent on top of the potato bags on the roof of his kennel. Placing the empty cup on the window sill, she went over to the dog, expecting that at any moment he would rear up and show his broken teeth. Surprisingly, he did not move toward her outstretched hand. She touched his ruff-like mane of hair that stood out from the studded collar that he wore. There was no response. His fur was cold and damp and, as her fingers tentatively probed his coat she felt flesh below it that was already stiffened.

She laid one of the potato sacks over his body and went back into the kitchen where she washed out his bowl and the cup that had contained the scraps, leaving them on the draining board. Lizzie Oldshaw slept on as Connie crept around her and out through the green curtain and through the chip shop to the front door. Slipping out into the street, Connie left the latch up so that she could get into the house again without waking Mrs Oldshaw. There was a fine mist of drizzle that settled on her dark jumper in tiny gem-like beads as she walked the half dozen houses to Mrs George's. Connie knocked at the door which was opened by Mrs George's mythological son.

'Hello, Connie, haven't seen you all week. You 'aven't been down to the Grapes, 'ave you?' He opened the door wide and, with an arm which seemed to drag along the floor on its knuckles, indicated that she should go inside.

She moved past him, trying not to touch him or any part of his clothing as she went. 'Is your Mam in? I've got to see her about Mrs Oldshaw. It's important.'

'Come in, then, Connie.' She could hear Mrs George's voice from the living-room. She followed the sound and Mrs George's son closed the door behind her and shuffled after her down the cheap rucked carpet of the hallway. 'What's the matter with Lizzie then, Connie? I think we should 'ave got that sod of a nephew to take 'er with 'im. She should never be left like that on 'er own, it's a cryin', bloody shame!' Mrs George came in from her kitchen and sat down heavily for one of her slight build, and rubbed her hands dry on her yellow apron.

'I can't see to her anymore, Mrs George. The nephew

sent Mrs O a letter that says I've got to find another place. He's coming to wind things up on Wednesday and he reckons I've got to be out by then.' Connie found it difficult to prevent herself from weeping but she did. She felt desperately in need of help from someone and had come to the Georges in an attempt to get some assistance for the old woman. Her own position was clear to her and needed no explaining, but someone else had to be recruited to assist in looking after the woman who had cared about her and was now so helpless. 'She's real doolally now, Mrs George. When you talk to her she looks right through you and she cries almost all the time. Those tablets aren't working like they're supposed to. She needs somebody to see to her. Could you please, just for a couple of days until Mr O's nephew comes to sort things out? I'll have to go after work tomorrow probably. It all seems to have happened so quickly, I don't know.' Her voice trailed off toward the end of her sentence in a sort of pleading bleat.

'Sit down, Connie love, it's not fair. You shouldn't have to mess around with all this. But that's what happens with people that are decent, they get put on. Anyway, I suppose I could go and see to Lizzie at night until 'er nephew and that clotheshorse of a wife of his turn up to take over. I know what'll 'appen as well, once that mingy bugger finds out there's no muny except from the shop. E'll put Lizzie away, say she's cracked or somethin', I can see it all. They won't want her on their 'ands like she is. Ooh, I could bloody swing for the pair of them.'

Connie listened with some satisfaction to Mrs George's tirade against Ernest Oldshaw's nephew. It was probably the only form of retribution the old woman would get, and Connie enjoyed the way that Mrs George railed against them both.

'Have a cup of tea with us while you're here, Connie. I've just this minute put the kettle on, it won't be a jiffy.'

Mrs George's son got up and loped toward the kitchen. 'I'll do it, Mum, you take the weight off your feet, you've been at it all day.'

Mrs George sniffed in agreement and made a muff out of her pinny, her hands rolled up inside it. 'Yer a good lad, son. I don't know what I'd do without 'im Connie. Doesn't mind 'ousewerk at all, do you luvvy?' She smiled at him as he grinned on his way into the kitchen. Connie felt quieter inside herself than she had felt all that traumatic day.

'Don't you worry anymore, Connie, I'll take care of Lizzie. You've got enough on your plate, love. 'Ow the 'ell are you going to find another place to live at this kind of notice, Connie? They aren't allowed to put you out just like that you know, love. You could stand up to 'im if you wanted to.' Mrs George looked quizzically up at Connie, her eyes shiny like a couple of glass beads.

'No thanks, Mrs George, I'm going to go back to my aunties' place. I don't fancy it much but I suppose it's been on the cards for quite a while now. Once the hoo-haa has died down they'll be very nice to me. They always have been before.'

Mrs George's son came in carrying a large gilt tray which he rested momentarily on the television before putting it down on the solid oak table in the corner by the window. He passed the fine bone china cups and saucers, first to his mother and then to Connie. 'I'm sorry I can't put you up, Connie, but I could only offer you the couch in the front room. You know 'ow it is.'

'I'll be all right. It's just that I've been so worried about Mrs O. Now that I know she's going to be looked after properly I feel much better.' Connie sipped the tea gratefully. Later, she went back to the chippy and, after putting the old woman to sleep, went to bed herself.

Connie helped Mrs Oldshaw downstairs at about seven the next morning and brought in a bowl of water from the kitchen and washed the old lady's hands and face, as she seemed to have little will to do it for herself. After this she made a breakfast of toast for them both, cutting the crusts off Lizzie's toast before encouraging her to eat by gently pushing a piece of it against her mouth.

'Wakey wakey, Mrs O, come on, be a good girl and eat. I'll have to go in a few minutes.' Connie helped Lizzie to hold her mug of tea and persuaded her to drink. Soon Lizzie put up her hand to prevent the passage of any more food to her mouth. She had eaten very little. Connie took away the breakfast things and tidied up the room. She put the quilt around the old lady after bringing her in from a visit to the cold, outside lavatory. 'You'll be warm again in no time,

Mrs O. I've asked Mrs George to come in at dinner-time and give you your soup.' She kneeled by the old woman's side and put her head down on her lap. 'Oh, I'm so sorry to leave you. You have been so kind, but it's all I can do. You'll both be inside my head for ever, and that's all that counts, isn't it?' Just before Connie could raise her head she felt Lizzie's hand fleetingly touch her hair. It was a goodbye touch. She knew the old woman understood and did not dislike her for what she was doing. Connie did not make any further goodbyes but went straight to where she had left her two bags and opened the door of the shop on to the street.

TWELVE

Connie had felt childishly responsible for the death of Ernest Oldshaw, and the subsequent crack-up of Lizzie. There was an almost constant nagging in the back of her mind that, if she had not gone out with Jeremy on that particular day, she might have been able at least to offer both of them some comfort. She felt mean and selfish, which reinforced the opinion she had been forming of herself that somehow failure was endemic with her.

Jeremy had receded in her memory — a trick she had perfected to cope with the pain of reality.

Now that she had returned to her aunts' house, she had begun to think seriously of developing her relationship with Frank, pinning on him her affections like paper money on a Greek bridegroom. She had painfully been made to realise, through the events of the eight months she had been living on her own, that she needed a durable relationship, one which would create in her a sense of achievement, a joy the possibility of which she feared might soon be lost to her for ever.

The oracular light from the mystic landing shone through the Tiffany lampshade that hung above Connie in the hallway, as she followed her Aunt Beatrice into the living-room where the bowl of electric light blazed down as usual, regardless of either the time of day or the season.

Connie was surprised to see her Aunt Rachel, lying on the couch in front of the fireplace. She could not remember

Rachel appearing before seven in the evening, as she kept such late hours that she almost never woke before three in the afternoon. The rest of the afternoon was spent bathing and making-up in preparation for the night's engagements. Connie had often heard her grandmother refer to Rachel as a 'night stalker' which inferred that her aunt had some sinister purpose to her life. Connie sat down on the very edge of the couch in order not to disturb her aunt or make her less comfortable.

'Well now, Connie Marlowe, what have you been up to since we last saw you?' Rachel caught hold of Connie's arms with her long fingers and Connie froze inside. 'It's all right, my love,' Rachel said. She spoke in a surprisingly warm and affectionate tone which Connie had never heard her use before.

Connie relaxed in the bubble of warm friendliness that Rachel had emitted and thought it easier not to question or probe her reasons. 'Honestly, Auntie, if you only knew. Absolutely nothing happened to me although it wasn't for want of trying. I spent most of the time working, and the bit of time I had left I spent looking after the old couple that I lodged with.' Sighing, she wondered if Mrs George had been in to give Lizzie Oldshaw her dinner, and to turn on the television.

'Beatrice, make some tea will you, love, I'm spitting feathers.'

Aunt Beatrice, although she was slightly annoyed at having her concentration on Connie's affairs broken, shuffled out to the kitchen and complied with her sister's demands.

Rachel pressed Connie's hands gently between her own encouragingly and insisted on hearing the details of her life since they had last seen her. Rachel's brow furrowed slightly as if an unpleasant thought had struck her. 'You're not going steady with anyone, are you, darling? It's the beginning of the end when you're as young as you are. The best thing to do is to keep all your options open.' Rachel leaned forward and lowered her voice. 'Don't you just give it all away for nothing, love, you take notice of what I say. There are just as many nice, rich boys as there are nice, poor boys.' Lighting a cigarette, she frowned again, coughed and held her throat as if she had just that moment made a miraculous escape from the Boston strangler.

Connie smiled, but made sure her aunt did not think it was at her previous comment. 'Can I have a ciggy please, Auntie?' Connie was already reaching for the pack that lay torn open on the top of the blue satin eiderdown that covered her aunt's legs.

'Did you hear that, Beatrice? The girl smokes now!' Rachel wrinkled her nose in an expression of pleasure and pushed Connie softly on the shoulder, until she swayed backwards. Connie felt slightly uncomfortable at the way her aunt was behaving to her. She seemed to have had an injection of virulent good fellowship. None the less, Connie was on guard. She had always suspected Rachel was at her most dangerous in this kind of mood. There was no such thing as a playful python, only a python newly wakened from a sloughing sleep by the scent of inexperienced game. Connie lit the cigarette and inhaled the smoke deeply, affecting a spurious sophistication.

Beatrice stuttered in with the tea things on the heavy oak tray. Connie thought Beatrice had aged tremendously since she had been away from them. Getting up from the side of the couch where she had been perching, she took the tray from Beatrice's cold, flat fingers and laid it down on the table under the window. Beatrice sat down opposite Rachel and both the sisters scrutinised her. Connie thought they were rude but, in spite of her feelings, she did not say anything. Beatrice leant over sideways so as to get a better look either at Connie's legs or at the sort of shoes she was wearing, or possibly both. Connie poured out their tea and looked sidelong at Beatrice who was once more rising to the surface to sit straight on her big chair. The cigarette held clenched between her teeth threw up a plume of pale grey smoke that sat in the red hair like an ostrich feather before disintegrating.

'Want syrup in it, Auntie B?'

'No dear, not this time. I'm trying to cut down. I'm forty-six around the bum now, and rising I'm afraid.' All three of them laughed and Rachel took the silver-backed brush that she had hidden under the cushion behind her head and began to stroke it through her hair.

'I think I'd have to be shot if my hips reached a spread of

over thirty-seven. Poor old Beatrice, she doesn't deserve it, do you sweetheart?'

Beatrice's crazed cheeks flushed pink under the layer of pale powder, and she closed her violet eyes, making a determinedly tight mouth.

'Can't understand it, but Beatie's just like our Mum, she always did look like her even when she was a girl. I favoured Dad and was always the one to be referred to as "handsome". Well, with Beatrice the beautiful as your elder sister, what else could they say?' Rachel put away the brush and shook out another cigarette. 'Want a ciggy, Beatie?'

'No, thank you, dear, I've just put one out and I've got my tea now. Oh, by the way, dear, do you still want me to make those telephone calls before six or will they wait now? You gave me the numbers on a little piece of paper. It's just behind the clock somewhere.' Rising on her spindle-turned legs to investigate the area at the back of the clock, she poked about behind it with her fingers. Her wide body blocked out the fire, temporarily eclipsed by the great purple bouclé dress she wore.

'For God's sake, Beatrice, stop fussing. It doesn't matter about the telephone calls because I'll be seeing Frank later on in the week and he will see to things for me. I was just panicking, thinking I'd be in bed with this bloody sciatica until the weekend.' Rachel lay back on the couch in pretended exhaustion and closed her eyes. Her hands held the china cup and saucer on the green satin swell of the eiderdown that covered her stomach.

'Oh, very well, dear, if you think it will be all right. It's no trouble to me you know.'

'Just put the paper on the back of the fire, Beatrice, and pass me another cup of tea.' She ignored Beatrice's mumblings and opened her eyes.

'I've had bloody sciatica, Connie, imagine, me. I'm so healthy as a rule. Hardly a day's illness and here I am with bleeding, sodding sciatica.' Rachel emphasised each of her last three words with a slap of her open palm on the plump green taffeta quilt.

'Anyway, as they say in the trade, how about you, dear? I don't quite believe you've got no boyfriends.' She winked at Connie, her face averted from her sister who had dozed off in the big chair. The ash from her cigarette held between her bloodless fingers fell in a thick cylinder on to the carpet.

'Let's just say I haven't exactly put up a sign, Auntie. There was a boy, though. Well, the least said about him the better.' Connie poured out more tea for Rachel and passed it over the back of the couch.

'Wasn't he nice, love?' Rachel screwed up her face in a display of distaste, as she prepared to drink her second cup of tea.

'No, it wasn't like that. He was all right, really. It was me that didn't exactly come up to his expectations. We were just too different, and I think we'd better leave it at that if you don't mind, Auntie.'

'Sorry, darling, I didn't know it was still hurting, but you really shouldn't let men get to you like that you know. They're all the same.'

'That's O.K. but it seemed to be going great at one time, and then things began to crack wide open. Oh, it's difficult to describe unless you're there at the time.' Connie stirred her own cup of tea and sat down testing the heat of the cup with her lower lip before drinking.

'The doctor says I'll be all right to get up in a few days. Anyway, come Wednesday, ready or not I'm going to be up and about.' Rachel rested her head back on the cushions that seemed to have been deliberately chosen to contrast with the thick skein of her shiny, light hair.

Connie drank her tea, constantly and silently reminding herself that these two brittle women were the same people she had known all her life. There had been none of the vicious recriminations she had expected on her return to them. Although she was glad to find that they were now prepared to consider her grown up, she knew that Rachel, as the prime mover behind the change of attitude, would remain forever an enigma. Whatever the reason for their mood, she was glad to be back, at least for the present, with her aunts.

Connie tidied away the tea things into the kitchen and put more slack at the back of the fire, so that it formed a thin crust over the boiling red flames which shot through tiny fissures sporadically like miniature sun spots. The two aunts dozed gently. Beatrice, her two fingers clutched in a pincerlike position around the last of her cigarette, sat slumped in the big, green armchair looking like a Bacon painting of a pope. Connie watched the knotted veins running sluggishly underneath their covering of pale skin that was mottled with brown spots like a plaice.

After tea they all watched television for most of the evening. Connie reminded herself that in this house there was an inside lavatory and a bathroom. No more twice-weekly visits to the municipal baths, bringing back a soggy towel wrapped round a piece of macerated soap almost turned to jelly. Beatrice had dropped off to sleep again but Connie could see a row of little bubbles filled with her breath which appeared and disappeared between her closed lips.

'Can I go up and have a bath, Auntie? If I sit anymore I'll drop off too, like Auntie B's done.' Beatrice twitched in her sleep. Connie got up off the footstool where she had been sitting, and stretched.

'Of course, my love, you know you don't have to ask. Go to bed if you feel too tired to come down again. It's the same bedroom. Beatrice has been keeping herself busy putting clean sheets on every week and sliding hot water-bottles about in the bed, all through the winter as if she expected you to walk through the front door at any time. Poor Beatie, she got quite upset when we discovered you had gone. She's one of those unfortunate people who, when they get a bee in their bonnet about something or other, worry themselves sick with it all. Me now, I just forgot all about you after a few days. It's a knack I have.' Rachel laughed as if at herself. 'Tell you who was upset about it, Connie.' She turned to look at Connie over the shoulder of the couch.

'Who was that, Auntie?'

'Frank, dear. Two days after you had gone, he and I went with a couple of punters for a meal. Well, he surprised me, kid, I can tell you. Burst out in a fit of crying for no reason at all. At the time he said it was just a song on the juke box, but I know different. Frank's not the sentimental type, and in any case you just don't get great big fellahs like Frank keeling over to music. When I got hold of him he was only one stop away from mugging old ladies in lifts, so I knew it wasn't true in any case, silly sod. I think you really got to him, Connie.' Rachel laughed again but her eyes remained coolly level, which Connie understood to mean that there was no warmth or pleasure in the laugh, which died away quickly in a nicotine finish.

Rachel opened her handbag and took out a mirror. She looked into it hard and pulled a wry face, before returning it to her bag.

'Anyway, Connie, I might as well tell you straight, I don't want you getting mixed up romantically with the "help". It could make things difficult. Understand, love?'

Rachel's voice was considerably cooled and had assumed a tone that made Connie realise that not only did Rachel mean what she said, but that there could be unpleasant consequences for her if she demurred.

Connie was completely taken aback by her aunt's revelation. She had always suspected Frank had felt something for her, but now there was proof of it. While Connie recalled the pleasant feeling of mutual trust that had grown between herself and Frank, Rachel watched her, as she lit a cigarette.

'You do understand, don't you, Connie love?'

'Yes, Auntie, I get the picture, but right at this moment I'm more interested in what a bath will do for me and not particularly moved by what Frank may or may not be thinking about. Do you know, I don't even like him all that much, and he always scared the living daylights out of me when I was a kid?'

'Well, I thought I'd better get that point cleared up, Connie. I wouldn't like it, if you and Frank . . . Well, I don't suppose I have to draw any pictures, do I?'

'No danger, Auntie. See you in half an hour.'

Connie went up to the bedroom that had lain in wait for her all through the winter. Beatrice had preserved everything in the room just as it had always been, pale pink and dove grey. The few things she had left behind were hung in thin polythene inside the little wardrobe. They rattled, as she ran her fingers over them, like helpless caddisflies in uncompleted metamorphosis. She was glad to be upstairs and away from the penetrating, serpent-like gaze before which she had felt herself begin to crumble.

In the living-room the couch was empty of her aunt. The sage green cushions on it had been arranged one at either end and one stuck cheekily in the middle. The brass table had been cleaned, and the big clear glass ashtray, although clean of the evening's cigarette butts, had one of Aunt Beatrice's Balkan Sobranies burning slowly in it.

'Auntie B, is that you in the kitchen?' Connie pulled the hood of Rachel's bathrobe, which she had borrowed to save herself dressing, from off her head, and began to rub her hair with a towel.

'Yes dear, Auntie Rachel's gone off to bed, she doesn't complain much you know, but that sciatica really does hurt her. The doctor gave her a shot when she first went down with it. She was in agony, didn't know which way to turn, poor soul. Of course we've both known Dr Muldoon since we were girls, and it's not quite the same on the National Health, is it dear? He brought her round a beautiful bunch of flowers the very next day; but to tell you the truth I think he's still a bit sweet on her.' Picking up her cigarette she pouted her mouth and stuck in the oval cork tip as if it were a further extension of herself.

'I'm sorry she's not been well, but I'm glad it was nothing to do with me going off. I don't think I deserve to be looked after by anyone, I'm always such a bloody nuisance. I wonder why you bother, at all.'

'Now now, Connie dear, all that's gone by now, nobody's blaming you for anything. You're back and everything's going to be fine. After all, even though you haven't told us much about what happened to you, it can't have been all that wonderful for you, now can it?'

Beatrice's sympathy seeped through to her and it was not difficult to indulge in tears.

'Oh, Auntie,' Connie bit her bottom lip in an effort to stem the flow. 'Most of it's been bloody awful. The worst thing was not having anyone to talk to, you know, working all day with girls like zombies and then reading to the old man and going to bed miserable. I've never been so alone. I hated it!' She covered her head with the hood of the bath robe to hide the pain she felt.

Beatrice put her arm around Connie's shoulders.

'You'll be all right now, Connie love, now that you're back with us Rachel doesn't want you to go on working. I know she's got marvellous plans for you, dear, just you wait and see. Anyway, you must tell me all about the place you worked at. What sort of job was it? We've never really worked for anyone else. Oh yes, I tell a lie, just in the beginning after Father died, we were clerks for a while. But it was all very boring, and the girls we worked with weren't very nice either. But then, I've always had Rachel to look after me. Now, she'll look after you too, so don't go upsetting yourself.'

Connie sobbed away under the borrowed hood, carried on a flood of maudlin sentiment. She enjoyed the unusual sensation of having someone who would assume complete responsibility for her for a while.

'Come on, Connie,' her aunt said, steering her toward the couch and pushing her gently down into it. 'I've made you something to eat, lovey, and I want you to sit there and enjoy it. I'll get you the tray.' Beatrice moved into the kitchen with an unusual air of liveliness. Connie dried her eyes on the hood of the robe. Beatrice breezed in with the tray and placed it on Connie's knees.

Later, as Connie lay in her bed, she could not but help thinking of Frank and tried to conjure up pictures of him crying because he missed her.

After a week or two, Connie got used to the demands and eccentricities of her two aunts as if she had never been away from them. All the time she made up fantasies about Frank and what he might say to her when he saw her, but Frank never returned to the house. Now and again Beatrice would be sent out to make telephone calls to him but he never appeared.

Rachel stood in the doorway and tilted her head to make sure the new hat she had bought herself that afternoon would pass through undamaged. Connie backed away from the front door, overawed by her magnificence.

'Hi, kid, we're going out tonight!' She pointed to the black silk pill-box hat that rested just above her right eyebrow. 'This thing's cost a fortune, so we're going somewhere it'll be appreciated. What do you say, eh?' Rachel adjusted the spotted veil and turned to close the door behind her.

'I think it makes you look as though you invented style,

Auntie. I think you're great.' Connie threw her arms around the surprised Rachel.

'Hey, come on!' Rachel put an arm affectionately around her niece's shoulders. 'We'll have to get galvanised. Is Beatrice upstairs?'

'Yes, Auntie, she's just gone to take five. She said she had a headache. I was supposed to waken her for tea but I forgot all about her going to bed. There was something she wanted to watch on the telly.'

Rachel laughed and removed the hat carefully before the mirror just by the door, and smoothed her hair down again. 'You know, Connie, it will be nice for us to go out together. We should do it more often, well, at least until you get some friends of you own, don't you think?'

Connie, feeling flattered that her aunt should choose her as a companion for an evening out, sat down in the big, green armchair.

'We're going to Mr Bonnie's Club. He's a very nice bloke. I've told him a lot about you, Connie. I think you'll like him. Not only that he's stiff with cash. Makes my skin crawl just thinking about it.'

Connie smiled, pleased that Rachel was proud enough of her to show her round to her friends.

'Don't be put off by the way he looks either, kid. He reminds me of a friendly hippo that's won the pools, he's got so much collateral embedded in his gums.'

Connie laughed out loud this time. 'Doesn't Beatrice ever go out with you, Auntie?'

'No, lovey, Beatrice doesn't like going out, not even to the pub nowadays. Sometimes I can persuade her to go down to the local if it's somebody's birthday, but otherwise, no.'

'It's a shame, isn't it?'

'It's her choice, Connie. Perhaps if she hadn't let herself go to seed, she'd feel better about being seen around, but she really has done a demolition job on that arse of hers, it's a sight.'

Mr Bonnie's Club lay behind the closed doors of a large Victorian house in the suburbs. The taxi took Rachel and Connie through the white painted gate and round the curved drive to the front door, where it stopped and was paid off by Rachel.

Inside Bonnie's, the only light came from the candles in the centre of each alcove table. Rachel took Connie's arm and together they parted the waterfall of beaded curtain that cut off the cloakroom from the Club, and went inside, sitting down at one of the first tables they came to. An ill-looking waitress came and took an order for their drinks while they waited for a table for dinner.

'Excuse me, madam, but won't you leave your fur with the cloakroom attendant?' The sickly looking girl with lank curls hanging around her face smiled at Rachel as if she already had the tip in her pocket.

Rachel looked up, annoyed that her habit of keeping the silver fox fur draped around her arms should be the cause of any concern to this girl.

'I never give this in here, unless Bonnie's gone and changed the girl on the cloakroom?' She turned to Connie and, frowning, stroked the fox fur. 'Caught the little bitch trying it on one night. She was lucky she didn't get her arse kicked.'

The waitress appeared to receive some sudden insight into the situation and, after leaving the drinks, drifted away to the bar where she stood still and expressionless, illuminated by a pair of carriage lamps.

During the meal, Connie watched the shadowy dancers who got up to perform uninhibited undulations on the tiny arena of a dance floor.

'Hello, Frank, fancy seeing you here!'

Connie caught her breath. She could hear a note of amusement in her aunt's voice and thought that perhaps she was just pretending.

'Don't I know this lovely lady from some place?'

Connie recognised the voice. It was unmistakably Frank's. She looked up, right into his face. The scar she so feared seeing had healed into fine silver and pink lines that reminded her of an abstract painting she had seen somewhere. Frank's face was tightly composed. Connie's eyes wandered over the design of the scar which looped under his eye and then plunged down in a straight line to his jawline, where it was intersected by another which seemed to rise and fit neatly into the hollow of his cheek. The flesh had not drawn so tightly as she had imagined it doing, although it did make him look more sinister than he ever had before. He still wore the dark glasses, but this time they were perched in his thick black hair. Connie half rose from her seat.

'Come on, lady baby, come to Daddy!'

She pushed herself forward to meet his outstretched arms.

'Oh, Frank, I'm so glad to see you. I've missed everyone like hell.' She kissed him on the good side of his face, a chaste kiss that could not possibly annoy her Aunt Rachel who, she knew, was watching every move, her cigarette held in the corner of her mouth, its smoke drifting up towards the black hat and the high chignon of her hair at the crown of her head. Connie still held Frank's hand and sat down with him by Rachel on the long back seat of their alcove. Connie enjoyed herself just being by Frank.

'Tell that waitress, the one that looks as though she's about to go down with beriberi, that we need some service over here, Frank, will you?'

Frank patted Connie's hand and got up to go to the bar.

'He looks very well, doesn't he, Auntie?'

'He looks exactly like a bloody ringmaster in that poncy ruffled shirt. If you ask me, the trouble with Frankie is that he's got nigger taste in clothes. If it isn't purple and red and covered in lace, he doesn't like it.'

Connie was taken aback by her aunt's cold-blooded, racist analysis.

'I thought you liked Frank!'

'I do, but you just can't ignore things like that, Con. It's true. He's got the colour sense of a Cree Indian painting a war pony. They're all the same.'

Rachel screwed the butt of her cigarette into the metal ash tray until the paper seam split and the yellow tobacco spilt out.

'Hello, Rachel. How long has it been? Two months at the least!' The greeting came from a big, but benign-looking, black man who seated himself opposite Rachel.

'Why, if it isn't Mr Bonnie. Funny we were just talking about you.' Connie cringed and hoped the man had no idea of the conversation before he came to the table.

'Nice to see you, Julius,' her aunt went on. 'How was it in Barbados, you lucky man? If I were you I wouldn't have come back.'

Mr Julius Bonnie rolled back in his seat laughing. 'Well, Rachel, you people keep on telling us to go back where we come from. Well I do now and again, just to see that everyone's behavin' theirselves.' He winked at Frank who had returned carrying a bar tray with their drinks on it. 'Got to keep an eye on the help you know, or they get upitty, don't they, Rachel?' They laughed together.

Frank held up his hands as high as his shoulders. 'Don't look at me folks, I never step out of line.'

Connie knew that Frank had realised the pecking order. She had never seen Frank look even mildly put out before, and was upset by the way Rachel seemed to delight in putting him down. Mr Bonnie called the girl at the bar by raising a gigantic, ring-festooned hand in the air. Mr Bonnie's rings were all gold. Each one had diamonds set into it, so that his hand looked like a jeweller's display pad. He was a man who appeared to be in a perpetually good mood, at least with his customers.

'Rachel, have you and little Miss Pretty enjoyed your meal? I told them to give you the best we had.' He put a giant finger under Connie's chin and tilted her head upward so that he could see her better.

'What did you say this child's name was, Rachel?'

'I'm sorry, Julius, how rude of me. Her name's Connie, Connie Marlowe, and she's my sister's girl. Remember, I told you about her. She's a clever girl, Julius. She writes poems for a hobby, don't you, Connie, lovey?'

Connie nodded in answer, knowing that Mr Bonnie had her under close scrutiny, and she felt she had to make a good impression for her aunt's sake.

'Why now, Rachel, Connie here is so pretty, it couldn't matter a damn to me if she couldn't write her own name, but poems, eh, that's a neat little bonus. I'm glad you told me, Rachel, I'm sure Connie wouldn't have, would you honey?' He smiled indulgently at her, which made Connie feel relaxed and happy.

'Probably not, Mr Bonnie, I don't usually bother telling anyone, because they just joke about it and think you're a bit funny, you know?'

'Don't you worry, Connie, no one here is goin' to make jokes about your poems. Anyway I think it's nice for a lady to have a hobby like painting or poem-makin', you know. I only wish some of my girls here would take up poem-makin', it might give them some class.' He shook his head slowly and pouted as if he were disenchanted with life. 'Because they could sure use it.'

Rachel and Mr Bonnie spoke together for some time, but Connie, feeling the effects of the wine she had drunk during the meal, did not listen, but watched the dancers pass before her heavy-lidded eyes. She wondered why Frank remained, so far, silent by her side, and from time to time would look at him to try to spark off some conversation between them, but her efforts were wasted. He seemed different after their long separation. Although he was friendly enough outwardly, the warmth had all disappeared. She was disappointed in his lack of response, and hurt that she could not evoke any of the feeling he had in the past indicated he had for her.

Rachel let the silver fox fur drop on to the seat beside her and Mr Bonnie took a cigar out of an inside pocket. He was still chuckling over something that Rachel had said to him.

'Dance, Frank?' Rachel's words sounded like a royal command. Taking the cigarette that Frank had just lit, she crushed it in the ash tray.

Frank rose to his feet, leaving his overcoat behind. 'Sure, Rachel, didn't think you felt like it, sure!' The couple moved off into the dim of the dance area where they began swaying together amid the younger and more frenetic couples.

Julius Bonnie beamed hugely at Connie.

'Make a nice couple, don't they Connie? Rachel loves to dance. You should see her and Frank on New Year's or at my Midsummer party. She can really move when she's a mind!'

Connie looked at him incredulously: her aunt a middle-aged raver, never.

'Go on, Mr Bonnie, you're kidding me. Rachel dancing I can believe; but not with Frank; she usually keeps him well at arm's length. Sometimes she even tells him off in front of me.'

'Don't let appearances fool you, Connie baby. Frank and Rachel have been makin' it together for years. Only she likes to pretend it isn't happenin', and it suits Frank. Didn't they ever tell you, honey?' Julius Bonnie laughed quietly, his dark lips opening briefly to allow the semi-suppressed sound to escape in the form of a low interrupted hiss.

Connie felt his body judder on the seat beside her as he took her hand, pressing it uncomfortably before putting his arm around her shoulders. Connie was tense with embarrassment and incredulity. She had not prepared herself for this. She felt a sudden panic least Frank had noticed the lovesick way she had sat looking at him during the evening. She wished she were back in the pink and dove-grey room where she could pick out the broken pieces of herself and paste them together again so that the joining hardly showed.

Shaking out one of Rachel's cigarettes she picked it up from the cloth and placed it between dry lips. Mr Bonnie leaned toward her and lit the cigarette. Keeping the flame alight, he studied her face for a second and then extinguished the flame. She turned away from Mr Bonnie so that he should not see the tears that had sprung hotly into her eyes.

Mr Bonnie passed her a handkerchief out of an inside pocket of his grey suit. She blew her nose hard on the handkerchief and then rolled it up, squeezing it in the palm of her hand. Opening her handbag, she took out her mirror and with a tissue cleared up a run of mascara.

'That's great Con, hon! Now, if you'll listen to me. I personally think you should have a break from all this carry-on. I'm goin' to London to see somebody about business. It's not goin' to take all that long. Then I'm goin' to Amsterdam for a bit of a break myself. What do you think Connie? I'm not much but I'm all I got. Come on, what do you say?' Mr Bonnie looked at Connie with pretended sadness, and held her hand.

Connie heard a voice inside her urging her on to make her move to advance the game. Fate was nudging her firmly up onto the next invisible platform.

'Why not, Mr Bonnie? Why not?' Connie amazed herself with the amount of control she suddenly found herself capable of.

His dark eyes glittered with delight. He lifted both her hands and kissed them.

Frank and Rachel came back to the table. Rachel was

flushed and laughing.

'Something long and cool please, Frank. I just couldn't stand another sticky gin and orange.' Frank went to the bar and leaned on the padded blue velvet. Connie watched him, blaming him for her jumbled emotions.

'Have a good time, Auntie Rachel? I had no idea you could dance so well. Mr Bonnie and me have had a fine time over here in our little corner, haven't we, Mr Bonnie?' Putting her arm around his neck she glanced provocatively at Frank and at Rachel who was calmly lighting a cigarette.

'Rachel, you don't mind if I take care of Connie for a while do you? We're goin' to Amsterdam, and then on some if we don't feel like comin' back.'

Connie eyed Rachel insolently over the top of her raised glass.

'Well,' Rachel said composedly, 'it all depends on how Connie really feels. As far as I'm concerned it's O.K., Julius. I know you'd look after the girl.' She rested back in her seat and looked strangely remote. 'What do you say, Con? It's your life, girl, you're quite old enough to start making your own decisions now, you know.'

Julius Bonnie grinned, showing two of his gilded front teeth.

'Yes, Auntie, I am old enough to make my own decisions!' Connie fired a warning shot bravely over Rachel's bows but followed it with a mending smile. 'I can make my mind up quickly when I want to. Anyway, I've never been abroad before and Amsterdam sounds great! Yes, I like the idea, that's if Mr Bonnie still feels the same when he's sober.'

Everyone laughed except Frank. Connie thought she saw him flinch and looked at him arrogantly. She hoped that he would feel cheated and dismayed at her decision, but he said nothing and sat drinking morosely, his eyes hidden by the dark lenses.

Rachel leaned forward and placed her hand on the chequered cloth, palm uppermost. It was immediately covered by Mr Bonnie's hand in a sweeping gesture.

'Good to feel skin, Rachel,' said Mr Bonnie, hugging Connie in a friendly, avuncular fashion.

Rachel smiled at her and then sat back, watching everyone while she drank pineapple juice from a tall glass with a straw.

Connie could hear the car draw up to the pavement outside the house. She had been sitting in the wicker chair by the side of her bed, looking out of the corner of the window in her room in preference to going downstairs and making small-talk with her two aunts. Now she stood by the pink painted window and looked down on to a solid black car below. Its sheen was already dulled by a fine mist of rain. From across the street came a couple of curious little boys who tried the door handles and peered in, shading their eyes with fingers like thin sausages of grey putty. Shivering, she felt her arms raise a horde of prickly gooseflesh.

She stood by the table downstairs and watched Beatrice in the kitchen stuttering out tears into the blue, plastic bowl. Julius Bonnie had been sitting on the green couch but rose as soon as he noticed Connie's presence in the room. He held a small china cup and saucer in the palm of his hand.

'Good mornin', Connie, I hope you feel like I do, all bright-eyed and bushy-tailed, because as soon as you're ready, we're off.' Taking her hands he kissed them gently as he had done the night before.

Connie, smiling, looked over to where her Aunt Rachel stood and noticed that she had on one of Mr Bonnie's gold rings.

'Hello, Connie, lovey, have you got all the things you need?' She took Connie by the shoulders and clasped her in a final embrace. Connie felt the ring catch in her hair.

Connie wanted to take nothing her aunts had given her. She would keep only her papers and Post Office savings book wrapped in a piece of plastic and lying in her handbag. She left the house, and sat in the front passenger seat of the car. The two little boys who stood by the wall of the opposite house giggled and made rude gestures at her from a safe distance. She closed her eyes feeling the seat next to her occupied by Mr Bonnie. She held her bag containing the only truths about her on her lap, her only precious thing. Rachel spoke to her through the open window. She presumed it was a goodbye of sorts but did not really listen. Turning, she was just in time to see Mr Bonnie give Rachel his gold watch.

'Sorry, Rachel, it's only worth a couple of hundred, but I'll see you sometime and we'll sort it out. O.K.? I need all my cash to spend on Connie bun here.' He put out a hand and stroked Connie's hair lightly.

The car started and moved away smoothly. Connie turned to look at the last of her people. Rachel stood on the edge of the pavement, her hand held high, determined to be the last image of home on Connie's mind. Beatrice stood a little behind Rachel and held a linen tea cloth to a face made red with weeping.

She watched them wiped from her vision by the rain which was now falling heavily. Still looking out of the back window, she saw the almost intact wing of a bone-shattered bird rise from the tarmac of the road with a gust of wind, and wave like a crazy, transparent hand.